PRAISE FOR DEBBIE VIGUIÉ'S
KISS TRILOGY

KISS OF NIGHT

"The premise is provocative: can a vampire be redeemed? ... hordes of vampire fans who, after their introduction to the vampire Raphael, will clamor for book two and the movie adaptation that must star Johnny Depp."

—*Publishers Weekly*

"Breathless tension coats Raphael and Susan's interactions with a right-on-the-edge-of-passion thrill ... I am eerily hooked ... It's a thought-provoking read that, like Mary Shelley's *Frankenstein*, may cause readers to question their definition of a monster."

—*USA Today*

"By the end of the book, I realized that I had entered a series that was far more epic in scope than I'd anticipated, with the unfolding of the beginning of a classic good versus evil battle unto the end. I came to the end wondering how I'm going to be able to wait for the second installment! The writing is action-packed, the characters are intriguing, and the plot is exciting and superbly crafted."

—ChristianFictionAddiction.com

"KISS OF NIGHT is good supernatural Christian fiction, a genre that's relatively new to me but one that I absolutely love. Along with the idea that no one is beyond redemption, the story effortlessly weaves in themes of sacrifice, love and prayer that flows well and is never preachy ... I will definitely be reading upcoming books in this series."

—*Truly Bookish*

"KISS OF NIGHT ends with the reader hanging on a precipice and desperately grasping for the sequel. I can't wait to sink my teeth into the next one ..."

—*The Overweight Bookshelf*

KISS OF DEATH

"Both paranormal and inspy romance readers will be captured by the new twists in this exciting novel and will be looking forward to the final title ...."

—*USAToday.com*

"This compelling romantic adventure takes place across centuries and throughout Europe as humans and vampires work together believably, strengthening each other's faith as they struggle with questions of redemption and loyalty. The action is fast, furious and violent, interspersed with fascinating diary entries that are slowly revealed as the cousins translate pages, creating a rising excitement that doesn't stop when the book ends."

—*RT Book Reviews*

KISS OF
Night

KISS OF
Night

A Novel

DEBBIE VIGUIÉ

NEW YORK • BOSTON • NASHVILLE

Copyright © 2011 by Debbie Viguié
Excerpt from *Kiss of Death* © 2012 by Debbie Viguié
All rights reserved. In accordance with the U.S. Copyright Act of 1976, the scanning, uploading, and electronic sharing of any part of this book without the permission of the publisher is unlawful piracy and theft of the author's intellectual property. If you would like to use material from the book (other than for review purposes), prior written permission must be obtained by contacting the publisher at permissions@hbgusa.com. Thank you for your support of the author's rights.

The author is represented by Alive Communications, Inc., 7680 Goddard Street, Suite 200, Colorado Springs, Colorado 80920, www.alivecommunications.com.

FaithWords
Hachette Book Group
237 Park Avenue
New York, NY 10017
www.HachetteBookGroup.com

FaithWords is a division of Hachette Book Group, Inc.
The FaithWords name and logo are trademarks of Hachette Book Group, Inc.

The Hachette Speakers Bureau provides a wide range of authors for speaking events. To find out more, go to www.hachettespeakersbureau.com or call (866) 376-6591.

The publisher is not responsible for websites (or their content) that are not owned by the publisher.

Printed in the United States of America

Originally published in trade paperback by Hachette Book Group
First mass market edition: August 2013

10 9 8 7 6 5 4 3 2 1
OPM

To the two women who encouraged me to make sure my vampire saga always stayed at the front of my mind and never got put on the back burner:
Juanita Mayeaux and Chrissy Currant.

ACKNOWLEDGMENTS

To all of those people who believed in me and encouraged me in the writing of this book I'd like to extend my deepest gratitude. Thank you to Beth Jusino and Andrea Heinecke, who represented the work. Thank you to my fantastic editor, Christina Boys, for her enthusiasm for the subject and our wonderful discussions about vampire lore. Thank you to my first readers, Rick and Barbara Reynolds, who always tell me what they like about particular chapters. Thank you also to my husband, Scott, without whose support and love none of this would be possible.

KISS OF
Night

PROLOGUE

The young mother had been by her child's bed throughout the night. Her face was stained with tears too numerous to count. Someone, though, had carefully noted each one. Her knees were raw from the hours she had spent in prayer. Gently, she kissed her little boy's brow. His fever seemed to have increased even more. The darkness intensified, heralding the coming of the dawn. February 4 had arrived. Fresh tears had started in her eyes. They had made it through the night, but it hadn't been enough. Her son would die today, exactly one year after his father had been killed overseas.

David had been sick for days and the doctors had no answers. All they could tell her was there was some kind of infection raging in his blood that they couldn't fight. The only thing they knew was that it would kill him. Every day had seen him grow weaker and now she knew it was the end. She turned her face to heaven in a silent cry for mercy, for understanding.

Nothing. No images of hope. No claps of thunder. Had God forgotten the widow and the orphan? That went against all that she had been raised to believe. The woman who had had to be so very strong felt her spirit fall. Her body drooped, though she was scarcely aware of it. Was it over? She looked down and was surprised to see two small gray eyes open into hers. The breath caught in her throat in a half-strangled sob.

Mommy, a little mouth formed the word without being able to verbalize it. Her heart broke. Then with a great effort the little vocal cords forced the words into audibility. "Mommy, the angel told me to tell you it will be okay."

Then his eyelids slid shut again and he slept. She looked all around her. Was her baby hallucinating? She saw no angel, but did that mean one wasn't there? She shuddered again and turned back to him. For the first time in a long while he looked at peace. So beautiful, so still. Slowly the same sort of peace seemed to fill her, and moments later she yielded to sweet slumber.

Outside the building a woman stood, her hand touching the bricks and her head bent in prayer. Constance knew the child inside was dying and so she prayed for him, though she had never seen the child or his mother before. She had been sent with a special mission, her prayers were needed and she had come. At last she pulled her hand away. The child would live. Constance turned and melted back into the night. She knew she was not the only one keeping watch and the presence of the other made her cautious. The other did not move from his silent post, though, but stood cloaked in mist, staring up at the building. A new day was indeed dawning.

CHAPTER ONE

And almost all things are by the law purged with blood; and without shedding of blood is no remission.

—Hebrews 9:22

The blood. It's all about the blood. Susan Lambert sank to her knees with tears streaming down her cheeks. Her city map of Prague slipped from her fingers unnoticed. She clutched her grandmother's antique silver cross and her hand tingled where skin touched metal. The floor around her was a crimson pool of light that was streaming from one of the stained-glass panels high overhead.

The panel showed the crucifixion and the light seemed to come from it instead of through it. That light painted the floor and pillars with brilliant colors. Her eyes fell back down to the bloodred light shining on the stone floor around her. *The blood of Christ*, she thought in awe.

She had been a long time coming to this city. She wished she could have come before it was too late, but at least she had made it. She tried to pray but was too overwhelmed by the beauty that surrounded her and the loss that tore at her heart.

She had come to the cathedral desperately needing to connect with God, to find the strength to survive the next few days. She had hoped to sense a bit of her grandmother's presence there as well. Her grandmother had spoken of the beauty of the cathedral she had often visited as a child and Susan had hoped to feel a connection with her one last time before the funeral. Then it would be too late. The cold, harsh reality would be undeniable and she'd be left with only her memories and her grief.

It seemed like all those she loved were taken from her so quickly. God and death were the only two constants in life, both unwavering. In the cathedral, though, she could focus on God and for a few precious moments forget about death.

She closed her eyes and thought about the blood of Christ, her grandmother's laugh, and a thousand other things. There was power and peace in St. Vitus Cathedral and she let them wash over her.

When at last she stood the colored light had retreated and the cathedral was being plunged bit by bit into darkness. *It's as though all the light in the world is being extinguished*, she thought. For some reason it unnerved her, watching as the light faded from all the windows and the shadows gathered, thick and deep and menacing in the corners. With the loss of the light all warmth seemed to flee as well and she could feel a deep cold settling into her bones. *Like the grave*, she thought with a shiver. She was exhausted and her grief was playing on the darker parts of her imagination. It would do her no good to dwell on the darkness.

She wiped her tears and turned to go. Her steps echoed loud on the stone floors and the sound pierced the fog of her pain. The cathedral looked empty, but it didn't feel that way. She half expected to hear some tired voice call out to her that it was time to leave, they were locking up for the night. Did they lock the cathedral or was it always open for those who needed a place to think and pray? She would have to ask. After the funeral she was sure she'd need a quiet retreat to pray. She took another half-dozen steps before the hair on the back of her neck stood on end.

Something was watching her. She could feel it just as she had felt the overwhelming sense of peace before. Susan turned her head slowly, trying to pierce the gathering shadows, but could see nothing.

"Hello?" she called tentatively, suddenly afraid that someone might answer.

There was only silence. She took a deep breath, trying to steady her frayed nerves. She let it out slowly as she forced her tense muscles to relax. Nothing was going to hurt her. There was no one there but her.

You're not alone. The still, quiet voice deep inside had never lied and it had saved her life twice before. The familiar icy hand of fear coiled itself around her and she spun back to the front of the cathedral, terrified that something might be behind her.

There was no one there. Her eyes caught a splash of color, her forgotten city map on the ground. She quickly retrieved it. When she straightened up and turned back to the entrance she jerked to a halt with a startled gasp.

A man was standing there, in the exact spot she had been a moment before. He was tall. His hair was fair but in the light she couldn't determine the exact color. He wore a long black trench coat over black pants and shirt. If it weren't for his eyes she might have thought of him as just another of the shadows rapidly filling the room. His eyes were a brilliant blue that seemed to glow just as the stained-glass windows had. They looked at her, seemed to pierce her very soul.

He was standing between her and the exit. Her mind reeled, wondering why he was staring at her that way, and why the rest of his expression was impossible to read.

She blinked and he was gone. She turned in a quick circle but saw only shadows. Her left hand gripped her cross necklace, squeezing hard.

Susan realized she was taking shallow, rapid breaths and her heart began to pound even harder until she began to be light-headed.

You're bleeding. This time she couldn't tell if the voice was inside her head or outside. She glanced down and saw she had squeezed the cross so tightly that it had cut her skin. Drops of blood coated her grandmother's necklace and slowly dripped onto the floor. Where before there had been only colored light now there was actual blood.

She began to walk toward the exit, every step moving faster until she was running. She didn't care how foolish it might be, she just knew there was someone inside the cathedral with her and he terrified her more than she had ever dreamed possible.

Her boots made a hollow clopping sound against the stone. A dozen steps from the exit she could swear she felt a hand brush her shoulder. She screamed and, twisting, she shot through the open doorway and outside.

She came up short in the cold night air with a gasp. A couple walking nearby hurried past her, clearly thinking her crazy.

She paused a moment, two. No dark figure lunged out of the cathedral to grab her, and even as she tried to fix his face in her memory she could feel it slipping, as though it had been only a dream the dawn chased away.

It's just my imagination. Too much has happened in the last few days, she told herself. She walked a few steps away from the door, thought about hailing a taxi, and then decided against it. Her hotel wasn't that far away and the walk might help clear her head.

And if there had been a man and he meant her harm, hopefully she could lose him on the streets. If she hailed a taxi then he might somehow overhear the address and she didn't want to wait here alone trying to flag one down. She was being paranoid and she knew it, but all the brochures she had read before departing had been emphatic that young women traveling alone should use extreme caution. That, coupled with all her grandmother's stories about gypsies who stole children in the middle of the night, had served to make her a basket case.

She had taken a half-dozen self-defense courses in college. That was little comfort at the moment, though, since she'd never had to apply any of what she'd learned to the real world. Mentally she rehearsed a few moves just in case.

As she began to walk, though, her fear began to ebb. Maybe the man had been a dream, or a hallucination brought on by extreme jet lag and grief. She forced her thoughts outward and she really began looking around her as she walked.

The city glistened like a jewel beneath the full moon. Its beauty was haunting, and Susan struggled to make herself focus on it. It was real. All of it. She was finally in Prague. Even as she marveled at some of the ancient buildings, though, she turned to glance over her shoulder every few steps, unable to shake the feeling that someone or something had followed her from the cathedral.

Every time she looked, though, there was nothing out of the ordinary. The shadows stayed where they should and the only people she saw were those going about their own business. If anything, she must look odd to them. After a few minutes she admitted to herself that she kept expecting to turn around and see him again, a hairsbreadth away, and have no idea how he had moved so close without her noticing.

She shivered. She tried to tell herself it was because she was in a strange city, one that had been given life in her imagination by what her grandmother had told her about growing up in Prague.

Susan had listened for hours as her grandmother spun tales of romance and mystery, mysticism and terror. They had gotten into her head. That was all that had happened back at the church. Nothing strange had occurred. The truth was she had probably frightened the poor man off with her screaming. *If there even was a man.* She touched her grandmother's cross and grimaced as she felt the dried blood on it.

As hard as she tried, though, she couldn't shake the feeling that someone was watching her, and so it was with relief that she arrived back at the Grand Hotel Praha and ducked inside. She was meeting family in a half hour for dinner at U Zlaté konviceon, a Czech restaurant in the hotel's cellars. She hurried upstairs to the room she was going to be sharing with her cousin Wendy, when she arrived the next morning.

The room was nothing like she had expected, but given her grandmother's stories she shouldn't have been surprised. All the furniture was antique and beautiful. The ceiling was ornately carved. The bathroom was all marble and glistened beneath the lights. Out the window she had a view of Old Town Square including the Týn Church and the Astronomical Clock, Prague's most famous sight.

As though compelled, she moved again to the window and looked out on the city, now awash with lights beneath the night sky. Her grandmother had been right. It was a magical place. She could feel it deep inside, like a singing in her blood or a quickening in her soul.

"Anything can happen here," she whispered to herself.

She turned and moved to her suitcase, which she hadn't taken the time to unpack when she had gotten in. She had been too eager to see the cathedral her grandmother had always told her about. It had been her moment of solitude, peace, before everything that was coming.

She remembered what it had been like at her parents' funeral when she was twelve. There had been so many people and so much chaos and she had longed to be allowed to go to her room and find some quiet to try and pray and understand what had happened. Her family members had had other plans, though, and they made it their mission to keep her from being alone. Now she couldn't help but wonder what the next few days were going to bring, since her grandmother had raised her from that point forward.

She squared her shoulders. She was twenty-three now and she would just have to make her own needs clear.

And if people wouldn't listen, well, she was going home three days after everyone else.

It was plenty of time to see the things she wanted to and to pay homage to her grandmother and bid her farewell in her own way. She wanted to return to the cathedral before she left.

And as she thought of the cathedral, she couldn't help but think about him. Who had he been that he had appeared and disappeared so quickly, without saying a word? She shivered slightly. There was something dangerous about him; how she knew that was a mystery to her, but she just *knew*.

Susan changed quickly into a simple blue sweater and black slacks, wishing she had brought a different dress beyond the one she would wear at the funeral. Then she made her way downstairs to the restaurant.

The restaurant was underground with vaulted ceilings and arches. Its rough rock walls were decorated with weapons, coats of arms, and murals of beheaded Czech lords. Wooden tables with simple wooden chairs reminded her that she was in a fourteenth-century alehouse.

One long table had been reserved for her family and she discovered she was not the first to arrive as Aunt Jane and Uncle Bob waved her over. They exchanged brief hugs and then settled back into their chairs to wait for the others.

"How are you holding up?" Jane asked.

"I'm okay," Susan said. "And you?"

"I'm going to miss Mom terribly, but at least she's in a better place."

"Although I'm sure she would have liked to see us all here," Bob said gruffly. "She loved this city."

Susan nodded. "I was always surprised she didn't ever try to move back, or at least take an extended trip."

"She was too concerned with her responsibilities at home," Jane said.

Responsibilities. As in me. Susan shook her head, unwilling to believe that she had kept her grandmother from returning to the home she loved, especially since she had left for college at eighteen and had lived on her own since.

Before she could say anything, the others began to arrive and soon she was hugging friends and family, some of whom she hadn't seen since that last funeral.

Her grandmother had managed her own funeral arrangements so that not only could she be buried in Prague but also all those close to her would have airfare paid for. Prague had been important to her. Family had been even more important.

When everyone was settled Susan had a chance to look at the menu. She was surprised at the number of choices, running the gamut from roast duck to schnitzel. She finally settled on the sirloin in cream sauce with cranberries and dumplings.

"How would you like your sirloin?" the waitress asked.

Bloody.

"Bloody," she heard herself saying then stopped, blinking. Why had she said that? She liked her steaks medium. She picked up her water and took a long drink. She was definitely suffering from jet lag and it must be affecting her more than she suspected.

When she put her water glass down she glanced across the room and gasped. The man from earlier was standing in the doorway, watching her. She blinked and he vanished. She sat for a moment, stunned. Had she imagined it? She was filled with an overwhelming need to know who he was or if he was even real and not some figment of her imagination.

She bolted up from the table and ran to where he had been standing, then looked up and down the hallway but saw no sign of him. Frustration filled her, but also a trickling of relief. Maybe she was seeing things. She shook her head hard and turned away.

When she rejoined her family they were regarding her with open curiosity.

"Sorry," she muttered. "I thought I saw...never mind."

Her uncle patted her on the shoulder and then conversation around the table resumed. The food was delicious and she found that she actually liked the steak rare. As the meal went on, though, she struggled to focus on the people and conversations around her. She yawned all the way through dessert and by then had completely convinced herself that her overtired brain was indeed playing tricks on her.

After they toasted Grandma Constance at the end, no one seemed inclined to leave, and everyone lingered around the table telling stories about Constance and sharing tears.

"I have to get some sleep," Susan said, finally standing up.

"I'll walk with you," her great-uncle Clarence said.

Susan tried to protest, but he held up a hand. Clarence was her grandmother's youngest brother and had just turned sixty three months before. His birthday was the last time the family had been together, to celebrate. Now they were gathered to mourn.

As soon as they left the restaurant he turned to her. "You mustn't let them bother you, my dear. She was a great spirit, and she will be missed, but especially by those of us who knew her well."

"Yes, she will."

"Most didn't understand her. She'd drive a hundred miles if she thought a stranger needed her prayers. She'd look at things completely different than other people and sometimes when the whole world, when every logical thought said to turn right she'd turn left."

"I remember. It always ended up being the best thing."

"I think you're a lot like her in that regard," he said, looking shrewdly at her. "I remember that day when, for no apparent reason, you refused to leave Constance's house. Your parents let you spend the night..."

He didn't have to continue. They both knew very well what had happened. Her parents had been killed in a car crash on the way home. She had spent untold sleepless nights wishing she could have gotten them to stay with her that night. But they had left and she was alive because they had let her stay.

Susan nodded, not sure what to say. They arrived at her room and she hugged him good night. He put a hand on her shoulder and looked her in the eyes. "She did come back here. I'm the only one who knows, but she did come back to Prague, twice."

Startled, she looked at him. "When? Why didn't she tell people?"

He smiled at her. "Those are stories for another time. For tonight, sleep well."

He turned and walked away, leaving her with burning questions and a deep sense of relief that her grandmother had been able to see the city she loved before she died.

She entered her room, locking the door behind her. When she turned around, she started as her eyes fell on the bed. In the middle of her pillow was a single red rose.

CHAPTER TWO

But if the watchman see the sword come, and blow not the trumpet, and the people be not warned; if the sword come, and take any person from among them, he is taken away in his iniquity; but his blood will I require at the watchman's hand.

—Ezekiel 33:6

David Trent sat in the first-class lounge at Heathrow, waiting for his next flight and trying to find a calm place inside himself. He was embarking on a new adventure, one he had volunteered for. But now that he had stepped foot on the path a great uncertainty seemed to weigh him down. When he'd left Boston the night before he couldn't shake the feeling that his life was about to change. He only wished he knew whether it was for the better or the worse.

He had no idea what waited for him in Prague and even though he had bought and read three different guidebooks, he still felt like he didn't have a grasp of the place. *You'll just have to figure it all out as you go*, he told himself.

He glanced around at the other passengers in an attempt to play his favorite kill-time game, *Who are you?* He looked at each of them in turn and asked the question and then tried to answer it based on what he observed. He had been a fan of Sherlock Holmes since he was a little boy, but unlike the fictional detective he had never dared to posit his guesses out loud.

There was a gentleman in his fifties with well-defined muscles and an equally well-defined air of boredom. David guessed him to be a business owner, one to whom money was no new thing. The young woman sitting next to him wearing the micro minidress and strappy heels who was trying but failing to reflect his boredom would be his newest trophy wife.

Across the room another man sat incredibly still, spine rigid, eyes closed. David decided after watching the unchanging nature of the man's posture for a minute that he was either terrified of planes or dead.

A third man posed no challenge as his collar declared him a priest. David turned his attention to the last two but was again denied his opportunity to guess who they were as soon as he realized they were discussing a series of lectures and astronomy conferences they were attending that would culminate with a group viewing of the coming solar eclipse in a couple of weeks. Apparently, for both, the highlight of the event was going to be getting a look at Prague's famed Astronomical Clock, built in 1410. The clock was on David's list of sights to see when he wasn't busy working.

He sighed and closed his eyes, wondering what the other passengers saw when they looked at him. Six feet tall with blond hair and hazel eyes, average build, twenty-six, briefcase. They probably saw a businessman, which was close enough to the truth. Then again, he'd never been very good at fooling people into believing that he was more than he was.

A minute later he opened his eyes again and noticed that two new passengers had entered the lounge—a man and a young woman, who were clearly not together. The man was tall, with slicked back hair and a cheesy smile. His suit was expensive and he was quick to shake hands with the older man and his trophy wife.

Politician. Has to be. David continued to stare. The man had incredibly pale skin in sharp contrast to his dark hair. *Politician or vampire, either way a bloodsucker*, he joked with himself.

He turned his eyes to the young woman, who sat down next to him and busied herself in digging through her purse. Tears were sparkling in her eyes.

She probably just wants to be left alone, he thought. *Just give her space.*

He tried to look away, but he couldn't. She was clearly in pain. "I'm sorry, but are you okay?" he asked.

She turned to look at him and the tears that had been threatening began to streak down her face. "No, I'm not," she squeaked. "My boyfriend has been cheating on me."

As she poured her heart out to him he listened patiently, offered comfort or advice where he could, and then realized if she was seated next to him, it was going to be a long flight.

When it was time to board, David led the way out of the lounge, the other passengers following behind him. Another first-class passenger was already ahead of them, though, at the gate. The man was slightly shorter than David with dark red hair cropped close to his head. He turned and regarded the rest of them with a look of such amused superiority David was floored. Even more surprising, the politician, who had been standing next to him, seemed to shrink back. *Guess he found the one person on the plane he doesn't want to schmooze.*

The newcomer turned and boarded the plane. David tried to take a step forward, but his feet refused to obey him.

"What's wrong?" he heard one of the scientists ask him.

"I'm afraid," he whispered.

"Me, too," he heard a shaky voice say. That would be the man who had been sitting so rigidly in the lounge.

"It's okay, planes are perfectly safe," someone else tried to reassure them.

David finally was able to make himself move forward. *What's wrong with me?* he wondered as he walked down the ramp. *Am I really that freaked out about this move? It's only temporary. A few months and I'll be back.*

The redheaded man was already seated in the first row when David entered the plane. He faltered and then forced himself to hurry past as he realized he wasn't terrified of the move. He was terrified of the man.

Wendy's plane arrived in the morning and Susan was up and ready to greet her cousin. When Wendy finally made it to the room she gave Susan a quick hug and then sprawled on the bed. "Mom and Dad wouldn't stop asking me questions about school the entire way from the airport," Wendy moaned.

Susan bit her lip. She guessed that those questions had revolved around asking her why she had changed her major yet again. It had been a topic discussed at length at the dinner table the night before. With her white blond hair the girl looked more like her father than the rest of the family, but she hadn't inherited his sense of discipline.

"I'm sorry," Susan said out loud.

Wendy burst into tears and Susan moved quickly to sit beside her.

"Are you okay?"

"No! I'm tired and I'm hungry and I can't believe Grandma's gone and all they could do is ride me for switching from political science to theater studies."

Susan rubbed Wendy's back while she cried. "I think they're just not ready to deal with the fact that she's gone, so they're focusing on anything else that they can."

Wendy rolled onto her back and stared up at her with her amber eyes awash with tears. "Why do they have to pick on me? Why can't they start in on when are you going to find a husband?"

"Don't you dare bring that up in front of them," Susan warned. "I don't want to deal with that this week."

"When are you going to find a guy?" Wendy asked, her words somewhat slurred.

"When I find a man who I'd want to be my husband," Susan said.

"It's that stupid list of yours. You have to throw it away," Wendy said with a yawn. "No guy is going to fit all those criteria. Not in this world."

Susan stood up abruptly, but Wendy grabbed at her hand. "I'm sorry. I'm just tired and sad. Why aren't you crying about Grandma?"

"Because I'm not ready to."

Wendy yawned again and her eyes drifted shut. "I think that's why you haven't found a guy."

Susan bit back a harsh retort, realizing that Wendy was

practically asleep. She stayed silent for about a minute and her cousin was out cold. Being able to fall asleep quickly had been one of Wendy's traits she'd always admired and been irritated by at the same time.

Susan sighed and covered her with an extra blanket. She then walked into the bathroom and splashed some cold water on her face. She pulled her long, chestnut hair into a ponytail and tried not to let what Wendy had said bother her. Too many women she knew had settled or were about to settle for guys who would ultimately make them miserable. That was because they were never clear in defining what it was they wanted in a man.

Susan had actually written down the things she was looking for the summer before she started college. She'd made the mistake of sharing it with Wendy who enjoyed mocking her over it. She put on some lipstick to add color to her face. It looked pale and strained to her critical eye. From the other room she could hear Wendy snoring. She was going to be out for a while. Susan wasn't in the mood to spend time with family and with Wendy asleep it freed her up to do some more sightseeing.

She walked back into the bedroom and her eyes fell on the rose in a water glass on the table next to her guide map. Her first crazy thought the night before had been that it had been the mystery man who left it, but she had soon dismissed that as ridiculous. More likely it was part of the hotel's welcome or turn-down service. Either way her instinct had been to throw it out, but for some reason she couldn't bring herself to do it. It was the first time someone had ever given her a rose, no matter who or what the reason. She smiled. Maybe she could keep Wendy guessing about it later, at least for a little while.

There was no formal dinner scheduled for that evening, so she theorized she could do as she pleased. She scrawled a hasty note to Wendy and left it on the bathroom counter where her cousin would be sure to see it. Then she grabbed the guide map and her purse and headed out the door.

As magical as the city had been the evening before it was no less breathtaking in the cold light of day. The blend of ancient and modern, coming together in a kaleidoscope of architectural styles, was enchanting. The Astronomical Clock, with its history and beauty, was stunning. And at the heart of everything was Prague Castle, the largest castle in the world. It had seen so much history that, as she made her way through it, she could close her eyes and practically feel it. As she explored the castle she soon found herself completely lost in the massive complex that was made up of several cathedrals, palaces, museums, and gardens.

After a while she found herself in a long corridor lined with closed doors. She drifted down it and a sense of cold began to pierce her bones. She had read of some of the terrible events that had occurred in the castle including fires and looting by enemy armies. During World War II the Nazi occupiers had used it as a headquarters. She glanced at the doors as she passed them and couldn't help but wonder what secrets were behind them.

As warm and welcoming as the cathedral had been the night before, this part of the castle felt cold and hostile. *I shouldn't be here*, she thought. It made sense. She had gotten herself thoroughly lost and she knew parts of the castle were off-limits for various reasons. Some were still in need of repair and others were being used by the current government. She must have wandered into one of those sections. It would explain all the closed doors.

While drawing abreast of a dark red door she made her decision, turned, and retraced her steps out of the hallway. A few minutes later she found herself back out in the gardens and she breathed a sigh of relief. Her stomach growled and she relaxed as she went in search of someone who could direct her to a place to eat.

After lunch she continued to explore the city. With the help of half a dozen friendly locals she managed to find the house her grandmother had been born in. She stood and took in the beauty and the age of the building with its heavily ornamented windows and crumbling façade. It had such an ancient, romantic feel to it. It helped explain why her grandmother, so quick to believe in the whimsical and the mysterious, had been so out of place in her adopted California, where most buildings were austere and only a few decades old.

"Grandma, I wish I could have come here with you, seen this place through your eyes," she whispered.

Finally, she forced herself to leave before anyone decided to interrupt her private moment by asking her what she was doing standing on the sidewalk ogling somebody's home. As she walked through the city, taking it all in, she let her mind drift.

It seemed too terrible to contemplate that they were actually burying her in the morning. Trying to fight back the pain, Susan's thoughts turned to what Clarence had told her the night before.

When had her grandmother come back to Prague? What had she done? What had she seen? She began to make a game of it, wondering if she was walking on stones her grandmother had walked upon. As she encountered each new sight she tried to remember what her grandmother had said about it, if anything, and tried to hear her speaking in her memory.

There were a couple of moments where it was almost like her grandmother was there with her. The sunset was a blaze of colors and it filled her with awe. She snapped a few pictures with her phone, wishing she hadn't forgotten her camera at home. When the last color faded from the sky she turned her steps back toward the hotel, planning to stop and eat along the way. It was then that she began to feel like someone was walking in *her* footsteps, watching her.

David woke up as the taxi driver screeched to a halt in front of his hotel. He glanced at his watch and yawned. It was a little after eight at night Prague time but the jet lag made it feel like four in the morning. He paid the driver, collected his luggage, and staggered into the hotel where he was going to be spending his first few nights in the city.

He walked up to the front desk and a young woman cheerfully accepted his printed-out hotel confirmation.

"Are you in Prague on business or pleasure?" she asked.

"Business."

"And you will be staying for three nights?"

"Three months," he answered.

Her eyes widened and she looked at the piece of paper. He grimaced. "No, sorry. I'll be here for three nights; I'll be in the city for three months. My company rented me an apartment, but it won't be ready until Friday." He hid a yawn behind his hand.

"Oh, I see. You will be in room twelve," she said, handing him his key. "Breakfast is served every morning in the café, you will find the information here as well as a city map," she said, handing him a neat packet of documents.

"Thank you."

She hailed a porter who hurried over and took charge of David's bags.

The room was nice, with a large bed, writing area, and a view of the Astronomical Clock out his window that he was sure would make the scientists on his plane jealous. As soon as the porter moved his luggage into the room and left, David locked the door, shuffled over to the bed, and fell full-length on it. He was asleep in moments.

Susan breathed a sigh of relief when she entered the lobby of the hotel. She hadn't been able to shake the feeling that something was following her. In the lobby she waved to her cousin Wendy, who was stepping out of the elevator in a short black dress. She looked refreshed and wide awake, a stark contrast to her earlier exhaustion.

Wendy made a beeline for her, eyes wide in excitement, and she grabbed her hands. "Susan, a friend is taking me out dancing, isn't that awesome? Would you like to come?" Wendy asked.

Susan shook her head. Only Wendy would go out dancing the night before their grandmother's funeral. Since they were children Wendy had been terrified of death and went to extraordinary lengths not to think about it, even when it was right in front of her. "No, thank you."

"Please, please, please. It will be a lot of fun, just like when we were kids."

When they were kids they had often pretended that they lived in Neverland. Instead of being Wendy, though, her cousin had always opted to be the more capricious Tinker Bell. Susan had always ended up as Peter himself, a role she had never been entirely sure suited her since as a child she had been so very eager to grow up.

"Sorry, Wendy," Susan said. "I didn't know you had any friends in the city," she added.

"I just met him at dinner tonight."

Susan rolled her eyes. She should have known. Wendy was pretty and flirtatious and more than capable of deciding that a guy she had met five minutes earlier was the greatest guy ever.

Suddenly Wendy lit up and waved. "He's here," she said.

Susan turned as a man with dark hair and eyes, dressed in a red silk shirt and black pants, came striding up. "You look beautiful," he said to Wendy who blushed as if on cue.

There was something smarmy about him, overly suave and slippery, just Wendy's type. There was something more, though, something...wrong. When he turned to look at her Susan's first instinct was to stab at his eyes with the key in her hand. She shuddered and moved away, horrified at her response. She grabbed Wendy's arm and tried to pull her with her toward the elevators.

"Wendy, we really need to get some sleep. The funeral's very early in the morning and—"

"It will be fine. We're college girls, pulling an all-nighter is no big deal."

Susan didn't bother to remind her cousin that she had just graduated the month before. It didn't matter. What did matter was getting her away from the guy who was staring at them both as though they were fresh meat.

"But Wendy, I really need to talk to you about Grandma, I just need to be able to open up to somebody and let it all out. We'll cry, order room service. I think they have ice cream."

Wendy shook off her hand. "That's what tomorrow is for. I say live life today. Besides, Garridan is a gypsy, he's promised to tell me my future."

"I can do that right now and I promise you won't like it," Susan said through gritted teeth, grabbing Wendy's arm again.

"One second," Wendy said to Garridan before moving away a few feet.

"What are you doing?" Wendy hissed. "I met a guy and you're acting like a psychopath. I know that you're all freaked out about Grandma and you don't share my taste in men, but come on. If you don't want to go that's fine, but I am going."

"Wendy, I've got a bad feeling about this. There's just something really creepy about the guy. Please, please don't go. If you just stay here tonight I promise I'll go clubbing with you the day after tomorrow."

"Tempting, but I've got a bird in the hand already," Wendy said. "Don't wait up."

Susan wanted to scream. For one moment she thought about grabbing Wendy by her hair and dragging her back upstairs, but knew her cousin well enough to realize that would only delay her date by an hour at the most. Susan was exhausted and wanted nothing more than to go upstairs and pass out on her bed.

"Wendy, you win. I'll go with you."

Wendy smiled triumphantly. "Go change, we'll wait five minutes."

Susan ran up the stairs and a minute later was in her room changing into a black turtleneck. She decided her jeans and black boots were just fine and headed back downstairs. When she hit the lobby it was empty.

She ran out to the sidewalk and looked up and down the street but saw no sign of her cousin. She whipped her cell phone out of her pocket and dialed Wendy's phone but it went straight to voice mail.

Wendy had ditched her. Garridan must have convinced her that three was a crowd and now she was who knew where with him. "Not good," Susan muttered under her breath.

She turned to walk back into the hotel when the same feeling she had had in the cathedral swept over her.

"You should not let her go off with him," a voice purred in her ear.

Susan jerked around and found herself face-to-face with the man from the cathedral. He was there, standing a breath away from her, real, and more frightening than she had first thought. She wanted to run, but his eyes were almost hypnotic and she found herself staring into them the way she had seen birds do with snakes right before they were killed.

"It's you," she breathed, heart beginning to pound.

He nodded.

"Who are you?" she asked.

"Someone who is deeply concerned with your welfare, and that of your cousin. I can help you find her."

And some part of her believed him. The rest of her, though, stiffened in fear. She ran back inside the hotel lobby, grateful for the brightness of the lights, and grabbed the back of a chair while she tried to calm herself. She took several deep breaths and turned anxiously to make sure he hadn't followed her inside. He hadn't.

It's okay. You just have to be firm with him. You've heard that European men can be aggressive and persistent, she reminded herself. Like Wendy's date. Her mind back on her cousin, Susan went up to the woman behind the desk.

"Can I help you?"

"My cousin was here in a black dress with a man wearing red and black. Did you see them?"

"Yes."

"Did you hear them say anything, where they were going?"

"I'm sorry. I just heard him say 'let's go' and then they left."

"That's it?" Susan asked. That wasn't much in the way of persuasion. Surely it would have taken more than that to get Wendy to leave her. A cold, sick sensation settled in the pit of her stomach and it reminded her of the way she had felt before her parents were killed.

"They were supposed to be going dancing. Do you have any idea where they might have gone?"

"There are several clubs. I can give you a list if you like."

Susan bit her lip. She could hear the clock on the wall above the counter ticking out the seconds. "Yes, please."

The woman pulled out a copy of the area map and began marking things with a yellow highlighter. She marked three of them with *X*s. "If he's local, he would be more likely to take her to one of these three unless…"

"Unless what?"

"Unless he took her to one of the clubs off the beaten path."

"Thank you," Susan said, grabbing the map and heading for the door.

She stepped outside and glanced down at the map, her eyes seeking out the closest *X*. Nebe Kremencova Cocktail and Music Bar. It was just one of sixteen places that were marked. The overwhelming nature of her task took full hold when she noticed that *he* was still there, watching her.

"You'll never find her in one of those," he said. "I can help you. I know where he took her."

"Tell me the name of the place," she said, hating that she could hear her voice shaking.

He shook his head. "It has no name. It is very private, exclusive. It caters only to those few who know it. But I will take you there."

Susan took a step back. There was no way she was going anywhere with him. She stared at him and was about to tell him to stay away from her and her cousin.

His lips moved and suddenly she wanted to kiss them, even though he was a stranger, even though he terrified her, even though there was a darkness coming from him that was unlike anything she had ever felt before. As though sensing her desire he bent close and brushed her lips with his.

When he touched her all she wanted was him. Thoughts of her cousin, the funeral, everything seemed to disappear. She slid her arms around his neck, pressing closer to him as one in a dream.

"I'm not this girl," she whispered against his lips. He

had to know, this wasn't her. She didn't kiss strange men. She didn't feel this deep hunger inside.

"I know you're not," he said. "But I am this man."

And suddenly, he was standing ten feet away, his hands in the pockets of his trench coat instead of on her waist. She jerked and nearly fell. She caught herself on the wall behind her.

"What happened?" she asked in bewilderment.

"A suggestion," he said with a shrug.

"I didn't hear you suggest anything," she said.

"Ah, but I did. I told you that you wanted me."

Her head was spinning and the fear was returning. "If that's true, why?"

"To show you that you should not blame your cousin for leaving you. You see, the man that she is with made certain she wanted nothing more than to go with him."

"He told her he was a gypsy."

"He's not. He's something much different and not half as friendly."

"Are you a gypsy? A magician?" she asked. It sounded stupid, but how else could he have hypnotized her?

Susan shook her head to clear it of the dark thoughts colliding within her. She pushed off from the wall, relieved to see that she had regained her footing. "I have to find her," she said.

"I will help you."

"Why would you do that?"

"Because Susan of Bryas, I need *your* help."

He knew her first name. That realization hit her but was quickly overshadowed by what he had said. She flushed, imagination running wild with what kind of help he could be alluding to. She couldn't risk a repeat of whatever he had done to her. She hadn't been herself and that frightened her even more than he did.

"I'm not going to—" she began hotly.

He held up a hand. "Don't worry. Next time you kiss me it will be because you want to."

She was astounded by his arrogance, and anger flooded her. "Trust me, that's not going to happen."

He smiled. "I know the women of your family, their spirit, their passion."

She had a thousand questions for this stranger who terrified her, who knew her name and had taken her breath away. They could all wait, though, because the clock was still ticking and the fear inside her was growing with every passing second. "Where is my cousin?" she demanded. That was the only question that mattered at the moment.

"Not far, but we must go quickly," he said, turning to walk.

She hurried to catch up with him. Being near him she still felt the fear but the desire was gone and she was grateful for that.

This is crazy, she told herself, but she still continued to walk. She believed him when he said he knew where Wendy was. What awaited her at their destination she didn't know, but she couldn't leave her cousin alone. She wished she had the pepper spray she usually carried with her. She hadn't been able to take it on the plane, though, so it sat on her dresser at home.

They turned immediately off the main street and she dutifully followed as the man beside her led her through several streets. They twisted and turned enough that she began to worry about finding her way back. More than once she thought about stopping. She had heard all the nightmare stories about young female travelers kidnapped in foreign cities and she prayed fervently that she wasn't going to be one of them.

She kept going, though. He had been able to hypnotize her, persuade her to kiss him. Garridan must have done something similar to convince Wendy to leave without her. What might he do to Wendy once he had her alone? Like it or not, the man beside Susan was her only chance at finding her cousin quickly. Wendy was flaky and self-centered, but she wouldn't have ditched Susan without a compelling reason. And if Garridan could be half as compelling as the man beside her, then Wendy was in serious trouble.

At last they turned down a narrow alleyway and stopped before a black door that bore no signs of any kind. The light was dim and she knew instinctively that this was a part of the city that was not on the maps they handed out to tourists.

She turned and her escort was looking at her, his blue eyes blazing. She took a deep breath, praying for strength and guidance.

"Your cross," he said.

"Yes?" she asked, hand flying to it. It was still covered in dried blood; she kept forgetting to clean it.

"Hide it."

Susan wanted to argue with him, but she had a feeling it was an argument she would lose. She tucked the necklace inside her turtleneck. She could feel the cool of the metal against her skin and she drew comfort from it.

"What now?" she asked as he seemed to hesitate.

"Susan of Bryas, I am about to take you into a dark world. One you won't want any part of. But your cousin needs your help and frankly so do I."

"Why do you keep calling me that?" she asked.

"Bryas is where your family was from when I knew them."

"I don't understand."

"I know. I should have taken the time to explain to you, but as it turns out time is the one thing we don't have."

"Then what are we waiting for?" she asked, trying to keep her voice from quavering.

"While we are inside, do as I say and do not leave my side, no matter what happens."

"What's in there?" she asked, staring hard at the door.

"Death. You can turn back now if you wish."

"What will happen to Wendy if I do?" she asked.

"She will die."

"Then I should call the police."

"They cannot help you. Only I can and perhaps your God."

She took a deep breath. She had come this far with him, and she wasn't ready to turn back yet. Not if what he said about Wendy being in danger could even possibly be true. "Let's go."

"Do not touch any others. If any approach you, say my name. By exchanging a kiss my scent is upon you. I have marked you as mine, so to speak."

"What is your name?" she asked.

"Raphael."

He pushed open the door of the club and a wave of nausea drove her to her knees.

CHAPTER THREE

What profit is there in my blood, when I go down to the pit?

—Psalm 30:9

Susan staggered to her feet, helped by Raphael, and stared into the darkness beyond the door. She could hear music coming from the club. The darkness was nearly absolute, but she could see the top of a staircase that led downward. There was a feeling of evil so intense, so overpowering, that for a moment she didn't think she could go inside even if Wendy was in danger.

"It can be a bit overwhelming," Raphael said. "Especially if you are sensitive to such things as you so clearly are."

He grabbed her arm and helped guide her down the stairs. The light was so dim that she would have fallen off the last stair had he not caught her and set her on her feet.

"Thank you."

"Do not thank me," he said darkly.

He took her hand—his felt odd to the touch—and pulled her toward what looked like a tunnel. The walls were covered with some sort of residue and she yanked her hand away after touching one briefly.

"What is this place?" she asked.

"An old sewer. It will take us to where we are going."

"And where is that?"

"An underground club. Literally. Those who wish to...indulge...in private come here."

Twice she tripped over unseen debris on the floor of the tunnel. The slow, pulsing beat of the music grew louder until it seemed to merge with her own heartbeat.

She glanced sideways at Raphael. His features were obscured by darkness. *This is crazy. Wendy's probably a block away from the hotel in some upscale club doing Jell-O shots and being told a lot of nonsense by a fake gypsy while I'm letting a man who terrifies me lead me through the sewers under the city. I think I'm the one that's in trouble,* she thought. *Maybe I'm still hypnotized. But, if I were hypnotized would I even be able to ask that question?* When she had been under his spell she hadn't fought him, hadn't wanted to. Wasn't that proof that she was acting of her own free will now?

The end of the tunnel came into sight and a minute later they stepped out onto the edge of a dance floor. The lights were incredibly low in the club as well and the music wasn't what she would have expected from such a place. It was slow, moody, seductive. Couples swayed on the dance floor to it, like shadows moving in a darkened room. The light was so dim that she couldn't make out their faces. How would she find Wendy if she was there?

Raphael pulled her toward the bar and from there they surveyed the room.

"Do you see her?" Susan asked, desperation filling her.

She wanted to leave, wanted it more than anything in the world. She needed to find Wendy and drag her out as fast as she could.

Next to her at the bar a couple was making out. Susan looked away, trying not to think about Raphael's hand wrapped around hers or about the kiss they had shared.

What was happening to her? The magic of Prague, that's what her grandmother would have said. Whatever it was, she didn't like it. She started giving serious thought to heading straight for the airport once she found Wendy, without collecting their things at the hotel or attending the funeral in the morning.

"There she is," Raphael said suddenly, nodding to the middle of the dance floor.

"How can you tell?" Susan asked, squinting to make out features in the darkness.

"Come with me," he said, not answering her question. He led her to the dance floor and once there pulled her into his arms.

She tried to push away from him, but he gripped her tighter. "Do as I say," he whispered in her ear. "There is an easy way to do this. You don't want to see the hard way."

Reluctantly she put her arms around his neck and they moved slowly through the other dancers. She turned her head and finally caught a glimpse of Wendy. She was dancing with Garridan and they were kissing.

"It's her," Susan said as she tried to avoid colliding with a couple next to her.

"Try to get her to go with you, say whatever you need to," Raphael whispered softly.

They moved until they bumped into the other couple. Wendy looked at Susan with wide eyes, her pupils dilated more than they should have been even in the dim light. Susan grabbed her hand. "Wendy, I met the most amazing guy. I have to use the restroom, come with me and I'll tell you all about it," she said, putting as much excitement into her voice as possible.

Wendy stared at her as though she didn't even recognize her.

"Wendy, hello, let's go," Susan said, tugging on her.

"I don't think the lady wants to go right now," Garridan said, his voice menacing.

Susan looked at him. The mask was off and Garridan was showing his true colors. There was lust in his eyes and a cruel look on his face.

"Wendy!" Susan said.

"She's coming with us," Raphael said, his voice so low it seemed to vibrate the air around them.

Susan glanced up at Raphael. His eyes were glowing even more brightly and he parted his lips to reveal long, wicked fangs where his incisors should have been.

Susan gasped and jerked away from him, jostling into Garridan. He let go of Wendy, grabbed Susan around the waist, and twisted her head to the side. Susan squealed in fear and tried to fight free, kicking at him with her legs and pounding with her fists but his strength was incredible and he didn't even flinch under her onslaught.

"Hey, if you wanted to swap, all you had to do was ask," Garridan said.

She twisted her head to look at his face and saw that he, too, had fangs.

Around them other dancers came to a halt and the

music died. "Help me!" she screamed at the top of her lungs.

Nobody moved.

She reached her hand into her shirt and yanked out her cross. Around her several observers shrunk back a step or two. She shoved the cross backward and heard a scream before she was thrown onto the floor. She jumped to her feet just in time to see Garridan clawing at his face. It was on fire. He crashed to the ground, his whole body going up in flames, and the dancers scattered in all directions.

An arm grabbed her hard around the waist and she felt herself being picked up.

She turned, cross in hand.

"Put it away," Raphael roared as he scooped Wendy up with his other arm.

She did as he said and a moment later they were racing down the tunnel they had entered through so fast that the wind stung her eyes. "Put me down!" she shouted over and over to no avail.

Then they were at the stairs, which Raphael seemed to leap up before kicking open the door to the outside world.

The night air washed over her, cold and clean, but she still felt the stench of evil clinging to her.

After running for a couple of blocks, Raphael came to a stop and set her on her feet.

"You're a vampire!" she screamed.

He raised an eyebrow. "I never said I wasn't."

"But you never said you were. How can you even exist?"

He laughed, a cold, hard sound. "A discussion for another time. First we have to get the two of you back to your hotel."

"What's wrong with Wendy?" she asked as she looked at her cousin's slack face.

"I think she's still under his spell."

"Didn't he die? Wasn't that what just happened?"

"Yes."

"Then how can she be under his spell?" she shouted.

"It takes more than that to break the spell," he said. "Now do you want to talk or do you want to help her?" he asked, his voice deepening.

She could feel the fight going out of her body. "I want to help her," Susan admitted.

"Good, then let's go."

Susan walked beside Raphael, struggling to keep up with his long strides as he carried Wendy. No one they passed by even gave them a second look. What kind of insane city had she come to?

"People often see only what they want to see," Raphael said suddenly. "That's how vampires can walk among humans undetected. All these people passing by, they make the assumptions that work for them, that fit their worldview. To them, I'm carrying home a drunk friend who partied too much."

"Way too much," Susan said.

Her mind was churning and she felt like she was going crazy. There were no such things as vampires. How could this be happening? Maybe the grief over her grandmother's passing had addled her brain. *Addled*, that was a good word, one her grandmother had loved. That was it; she was definitely addled.

They arrived back at the hotel faster than she had expected. She fully believed that they would be questioned as they walked through the lobby, but no one even gave them a second glance. Reluctantly she led Raphael upstairs. She opened the hotel room and stepped across the threshold. She turned and stared hard at Raphael.

"Do I have to invite you in?" she asked, wincing at how ludicrous it sounded.

"It's the polite thing to do," he said.

"Anything special I have to say?"

"'Come in' will work just fine."

"Okay, come in."

Raphael stepped across the threshold. Suddenly Wendy, who had been out of it since they took her from the club, seemed to come alive. She screamed and began to thrash in Raphael's arms.

"Put her on the bed!" Susan said, kicking the door.

Raphael set her down as Susan flicked on the lights. Wendy slammed her hand into the wall behind the headboard and whimpered. Susan ran over and saw blood on Wendy's throat.

Raphael bent over her and Susan hit him in the face as hard as she could. He jerked up with a roar, eyes blazing and teeth bared. Her blow had split his lip but otherwise she seemed to have done more damage to her hand than to him.

"Help me," he hissed.

"What do you want me to do?" she asked, realizing it hadn't been him that had bitten Wendy.

"Hold her down. Now!"

David woke up to someone banging on the wall behind his bed. He struggled to roll over and sit up, rubbing his eyes. Shouts and screams of fear drove him to his feet.

Whatever was happening over there it didn't sound good. He should call someone. He reached for the phone and lifted the receiver. Nothing. Frowning, he pushed the button for the front desk. Still nothing.

He headed for the door and in the hall debated whether to go all the way down to the front desk or to confront the problem directly. With a sigh he headed for the elevator. He had no desire to go downstairs but he didn't cherish the thought of getting involved in something that was none of his business. Then he heard a woman whimper, "Please don't hurt me!"

Something in her voice stopped him. As terrible thoughts swarmed his mind he turned and strode for the door of the room next to his. It was slightly ajar and when he knocked it swung open. A blond woman with the face of an angel was lying on the bed, whimpering, while another woman was pinning her down as a man stared at her intently.

"She's been bitten," the man was saying. "And he is still controlling her even though he's dead. Hold her tighter."

"I'm trying!"

"What is going on?" David demanded.

The man looked up at him and David saw that his teeth were dripping blood.

With a shout David jumped backward into the hall and turned to run. Something grabbed him, though, and picked him up. The next thing he knew he was flying backward through the air. His body twisted and he stared down at the floor as it rushed toward his head. He slammed down on it and everything went black.

* * *

Raphael was furious. With all the noise they were going to have the entire hotel breathing down their necks soon and he didn't have time to mesmerize or incapacitate all of them.

The girl on the bed was screaming again and thrashing uncontrollably, her mind still trapped by the will of the dead vampire. He had seen it before, humans who were under active control by a vampire at the moment of the vampire's death. It almost always destroyed the mind of the human completely. He couldn't let that happen to Susan's cousin, not if he expected her to help him.

Susan was struggling to pin her cousin's shoulders to the mattress, but strong as she was she was no match for the hysterical girl who was lashing out blindly, incapable of telling friend from foe.

He cast one final glance at the man crumpled unconscious on the floor then turned back to Susan. "Lock the door and don't let anyone in."

She hesitated and he growled. Instinctively she moved toward the door. He knew it wasn't because she wanted to follow his directions but because she wanted to get away from him. Regardless of the motive she did as she was told.

With one hand he caught both of Wendy's wrists and squeezed them together. He put a knee on her stomach and applied enough pressure to immobilize her without crushing anything.

"Look at me," he said, dropping his voice and allowing its hypnotic effect to wash over her.

She twisted her head away. The hold Garridan still had on her was strong, magnified by the attraction she had felt for him that had been entirely of her own making. It would be easier to sever a link that had not been reinforced by positive feelings on her part.

He clamped his free hand down on her forehead, forcing her face back toward him. She screamed, but he ignored it. She squeezed her eyes shut but he reached down and using his thumb and index finger pulled up her eyelids as gently as he could. She whimpered and writhed as her eyes met his.

"Wendy," he said, knowing that the sound of her name would penetrate her fog as nothing else would. "Wendy, you have to listen to me. You're having a nightmare. Do you understand?"

Slowly he could see thought entering her eyes. She did hear him. "You will listen only to me," he said, pushing, supplanting Garridan's will with his own.

She gasped and convulsed as Garridan's control of her began to slip away and Raphael instead took over. Garridan was a weaker vampire, younger, and so it was possible for Raphael to break the hold he'd had over Wendy. It would have been nearly impossible had the other vampire still been alive, but death had weakened the connection even though it had not severed it.

"You will forget that other man. There is no other man. There is only me."

"What are you doing?" he heard Susan demand.

He ignored her and continued to work. "You will listen only to me, do you understand?"

"Yes," Wendy whispered after a pause.

"Who am I?" he asked.

"Everything."

"Good. Now do as I say. Go to sleep and forget everything that has happened this evening. You will not remember meeting any man but me and you will remember me only as the man Susan introduced you to. Do you understand?"

"I understand," she said, her voice stronger.

"Good. Sleep."

Her body went completely slack and he let her eyelids fall shut. He continued to hold her down for a moment before releasing her. He straightened, preparing to deal with the intruder who was still unconscious on the floor. He turned and jumped backward as he saw Susan's hand inches from him brandishing her cross necklace at him. She had removed it from around her throat so she could put more distance between them when she held it.

"Who are you and what did you do to her?" she hissed.

He could feel the power coming from the cross and it confirmed his earlier suspicions about her and it.

"I saved her life and her sanity." He hit her hand, sending the necklace skidding under the chest of drawers, and spun her around until he was standing behind her, arms wrapped around her, pinning hers to her body. She struggled and fought, first trying to punch him with an elbow then trying to slam her feet down on his.

He bent his lips to her ear and whispered. "As for who I am, I will tell you, Susan of Bryas, but you have to stop fighting me."

"Don't try to hypnotize me!" Susan shrieked, fear pounding through her as Raphael held her, helpless in his arms.

"It's called mesmerism and the fact that you can even say that should prove to you that I'm not, and I will not as long as you calm down and listen to me."

His lips were so close to her ear as he spoke that she could feel them brushing against her skin. It startled her, frightened her, and yet she couldn't deny the feelings that stirred inside her.

He has to be doing this to me, like with the kiss, she told herself.

"I am doing nothing to you."

Fresh panic flooded her. *Can he read my mind?*

She stopped struggling for a moment and he released her. She turned to face him and there was weariness in his eyes, but no amusement, no cruelty. And when he spoke again his voice sounded normal, not like the deep one he had used on Wendy.

"Why don't you have a seat?"

"I don't want to sit down," she said.

He shrugged. It was such a simple gesture, so human. It gave her pause. The choice to sit down or not was clearly hers and it was probably a good idea. She took a deep breath and realized that she was trembling and exhausted.

She moved to the table, careful to step around the man lying on the floor, and pulled out a chair. She sat down and stared at Raphael, her mind a jumble of thoughts.

Vampires! How can there actually be vampires? Maybe I'm the one having a nightmare.

No, the glowing eyes, the fangs, they all had to be a trick of the light. They couldn't be real. But how come Garridan burst into flames when she touched him with her cross? She glanced toward the chest and thought of the cross that was beneath it.

There was a knock on the door and she stiffened. How could she explain this to anyone? What could she say that wouldn't make her sound crazy? She glanced at the man on the floor. Was he hurt, dead?

She looked back up and Raphael was opening the door. She blinked. How had he moved that fast? She hadn't seen or heard him move. She blinked again as she realized he was shirtless. His shirt and trench coat lay in a pile just inside the front door, easily viewable to whoever was outside.

She heard him and a man outside muttering and then he was closing the door, a satisfied look on his face.

Susan sucked in her breath as she looked at him. He was incredibly well muscled, far more than she would have ever guessed seeing him in his shirt and trench coat. He looked like a bodybuilder except for the fact that his skin was bone white.

"We keep the body we had when we were cursed," he said. "Except, of course, for skin color," he added with a smirk.

She blushed and turned away as he put his shirt back on.

"Did you mesmerize whoever that was?"

"No need. I simply allowed the manager to make his own assumptions," Raphael said.

"Which were?" she asked.

"What do you think?" His voice was practically a purr.

She thought of him standing half dressed in the doorway. There weren't that many rooms in the hotel, the manager would know that it was registered to her and not to him, so the only reason for him to be there looking like that was— "Oh no!" she burst out as realization hit her. "They think that we . . . No! What will my family think?"

"If your family knows you at all, they'll think that

you're not that girl. They might have their doubts about your cousin."

"This is terrible!"

"It's okay. He will be very discreet."

Susan pressed her face into her hands.

"And that's what it takes to overwhelm you," he said, and she didn't have to look to know he was smirking again.

"It's just too much," she said, struggling to hold back tears of fear and exhaustion.

He pulled her hands away from her face and looked deep into her eyes. He was crouching in front of her, head tilted to the side, as though he were studying her, reading her very soul.

"Your hands aren't cold," she said. "They were colder at the club, but now... They're not warm, they're just... not there."

"You expect them to be cold because that's the legend you have heard. But have you not met people with cold hands?"

She nodded.

"And were they like me?"

"No one is like you," she whispered.

"I am a dead thing, as devoid of what you would call life as that desk. Therefore, my skin reflects the temperature of my surroundings. Cold when it is cold, hot when it is hot. I don't feel it, but the touch of one of my kind can be very unnerving because it can feel like touching air."

She shuddered and her eyes swept past him to the man lying still unconscious on the ground. "I can't—" she said, struggling to articulate what it was she was feeling.

"You can. I know that you're strong enough to handle this. This and much more."

"I don't want there to be more."

"Dear Susan," Raphael said with a shake of his head. "There is always more."

CHAPTER FOUR

*Then washed I thee with water; yea, I thoroughly
washed away thy blood from thee, and I anointed thee
with oil.*

—Ezekiel 16:9

Raphael stood quickly. He had knelt before kings and
before God and resented it in his heart. That much
had never changed. It was a subservient position and he
hated it with a passion.

He glanced at Susan. She was coping remarkably well
with the fact that she had killed a vampire. Maybe the
realization hadn't hit her yet. He had seen men fierce as
lions on the battlefield crying in their tents long after the
fighting was over about what they had seen and done.

He wondered if that was going to be her. Better she
collapse under the strain after the danger was over than
during. Now he just had to figure out how to tell her that
the danger had only just begun.

When he had seen her praying there in the cathedral
he knew that it was a sign and that she would help him
in his quest. But he had not had time to approach her as
he wished, to introduce her gently to his world and let her
adjust before thrusting her into the heart of battle.

Instead, Garridan had to cast his eye on Susan's cousin and by the time Raphael knew it was too late to do any different. He closed his eyes briefly. Garridan had been one of his grandchildren. Not of his flesh, but certainly of his blood. The scent of his sire had been strong upon him. Raphael had hoped to accomplish two purposes that night: to rescue Susan's cousin and so engender her trust, and to torture out of Garridan the location of his master. The one who had cursed Garridan had himself been cursed by Raphael years before. *My greatest failure*, he thought bitterly.

But Susan's actions had denied him that opportunity. There were other vampires walking the streets of Prague, but he had not been able to detect such a close connection with the one he sought and those others.

So, now Susan knew what he was, if not who he was. And Garridan would be missed and it would throw him and his revolution into the harsh light of day. *And burn us both.*

On the floor the man who had thought to be a hero groaned and Raphael really looked at him for the first time. He was young, wearing a suit that looked like it had been slept in.

"What are you going to do to him?" Susan asked, her voice shaking ever so subtly.

"Mesmerize him for his own good."

"Is he hurt? Do we need to call an ambulance?"

Raphael glanced up at her. "If he was that injured I'd be killing him instead of mesmerizing him."

"Don't, please," she begged, panic in her voice.

Raphael winced inwardly. *Remember to keep those kinds of thoughts to yourself.* He turned away from her without answering and watched as the man rolled onto his side and then slowly began to sit up, rubbing his head. "What happened?" he asked. He looked up and saw them and his eyes opened wide in fear. "What are you?" he asked Raphael.

Raphael crouched down directly in front of the man. "Nothing. Who are you?"

"David," the man stuttered.

"David, listen very carefully," Raphael said, allowing his voice to drop down. He focused on David and watched as David's eyes locked on to his and slowly began to dilate. Raphael pushed more of himself, more of his will, into the words. "You were in a car accident on your way to the hotel."

David shook his head. "No, I wasn't. You, you threw me—"

He was resisting, and he was stronger than most, especially given that he was injured. Raphael allowed himself to start breathing, slow, powerful breaths like a predator. *Just like my sire showed me.* "David," he said, dropping his voice even lower and slowly punctuating each word. "You were in a car accident."

"No."

His own frustration built at that single word. Next to him he could smell the fear on Susan as she became more convinced that something bad was going to happen to her white knight.

David was fighting him, struggling not to succumb to the mesmerism. Finally Raphael pinched the artery in David's throat with his fingers and after a momentary struggle David collapsed.

"You killed him!" Susan shrieked.

Raphael cursed under his breath. "No, I did not kill him," he snapped. "I just knocked him out for a while."

"Why didn't you do to him what you did to her?"

"I will. It's just going to take a lot more effort. One in ten thousand humans can resist mesmerism and he is one of those. I'll do what I can, but it's going to take a long time and I can't be certain how long it will last or what will cause him to remember the truth."

He looked up at her and then back at David. "Your questions will have to wait until tomorrow night. I can't be sure how long this will take and there must be no distractions."

He stood and picked David up, tossing him easily over his shoulder.

"Where are you taking him?"

"His room."

"What am I supposed to do?"

"I'd advise you to get some sleep. I'll see you again tomorrow night."

And as he turned and left Raphael knew that she was hoping it was all a nightmare and that she would never see him again.

Neither of us is that lucky, he thought.

David had his room key in his pocket and moments later Raphael was pushing open the door and walking inside. He dumped David on the bed before turning back to close the door.

Nobody in modern society had any clue how to keep a vampire out of their home. Susan, like so many others, had bought into the lie of the invitation. But soon she would have to know what was true and what was merely myth if she was going to survive the coming war.

* * *

Susan ran to the door and locked it as soon as Raphael and David had left. She slid down the door into a sitting position, shaking and trying to pray as she took in what had happened.

"It can't be real, it can't!" she said as she rocked herself. Because if it was real then the world was full of monsters and a much more frightening place than she had ever guessed. And if it was real then she had killed one of them. How had she done that? All the stories she'd heard said that crosses burned vampires, but they didn't incinerate them.

But that's exactly what had happened. She had seen it with her own eyes.

If her eyes could be believed anymore.

Maybe it really was just exhaustion and stress and grief. Maybe she was so tired she was hallucinating. Maybe it all was a nightmare and she'd wake up and Grandma Constance would still be alive and wearing the cross instead of her.

The cross.

She slid across the floor and reached under the chest, fingers flailing for the necklace, but all she seized was air. She looked at the chest. It was large and heavy looking, but she should be able to move it just enough to reach the necklace.

She glanced over at Wendy who had begun to snore softly. Of course, if she made that much noise she risked waking her up. Or worse. Someone could complain again and send the manager back. The thought was humiliating.

No, she'd just have to wait and get it in the morning. She dragged herself to her bed and thought about taking a long, hot shower. It sounded heavenly but by the time she got undressed she was swaying on her feet. She quickly put on her pajamas and got into bed. *Tomorrow. Everything will have to wait for tomorrow.*

It was still dark in the room when she awoke and stretched. The horrors of the night before had faded away. *It was just a terrible dream*, she thought, savoring that belief. She flipped on her back and opened her eyes. She could see Wendy inside the bathroom, brushing her hair. She was singing to herself very softly and Susan wondered if that was what had woken her.

She stood up and made her way over to the bathroom. "Good morning."

"Good morning," Wendy said brightly. "How are you?"

"Tired, and you?"

"I slept like a rock. It felt great."

"I'm glad," Susan said, struggling to keep the relief out of her voice.

"I have to say, though, that these mosquito bites really itch."

Horror stole over her as Susan turned to her cousin and saw the two bite marks on Wendy's neck. The other girl was checking them out in the mirror.

"Yeah, but you really shouldn't scratch mosquito bites," Susan said, her breath catching in her throat.

"I guess you're right. Well, I'm ready to go, the bathroom is all yours."

Susan stared as Wendy bounced into the other room. She seemed...fine...which was just so weird because things couldn't have been further from fine.

* * *

David woke up slowly, his body throbbing with pain. He groaned and opened his eyes to see a coffered ceiling above him. He stared at it for a moment in confusion. Then he remembered. He was in a hotel somewhere. Where was it? He winced as he tried to sit up. Prague, that was it. He breathed out slowly, struggling to understand why he felt so terrible.

He staggered into the bathroom and flipped on the switch then stared at himself in the mirror in surprise. Exactly what he'd done to get a black eye escaped him. His jaw also seemed swollen to him.

"There was a car accident," he said, testing the words. They came from deep inside him but they didn't feel right, like they weren't his. "There was a car accident on the way from the airport," he said more forcefully.

But he didn't believe it. "There was no car accident," he whispered and something told him that was the truth. So, where had the lie come from?

Jet lag must be hitting me worse than I thought. He gingerly touched his injuries, wishing he could remember how he had gotten them. The last thing he knew he had fallen asleep on the bed with his clothes on. He was still wearing his clothes and nothing in his room seemed to have been disturbed when he poked his head back into the bedroom.

He took off his shirt and noticed a bruise on his chest as well as several on his arms. One in particular on his left forearm was a nasty, deep purple tinged with green.

He moved back to the bedroom and picked up the telephone. There was no dial tone. It should have surprised him, but somehow it didn't. Like he had tried using it before, but when? He checked the back of the phone and noticed that the cable was loose. He jiggled it and tried again. It worked and he called down to the front desk. The woman on duty said she'd been downstairs for the past two hours and hadn't seen him go out or come in. She promised to check with the night clerk as well and barely managed to restrain the curiosity in her voice.

David hung up and felt himself getting nervous. He'd heard all sorts of horror stories about the things that could befall foreigners living and traveling abroad, but since nothing seemed disturbed in his room he couldn't fathom what might have happened.

He showered and changed clothes quickly and when he exited the bathroom he saw the message light on his phone blinking. He listened grimly as the woman explained that she had called the night clerk at home and while she had been able to confirm that David had checked in the night before, there was no evidence that he had left the hotel the entire night.

He hung up slowly. That meant whatever had happened had to have happened in his room. *Or at least in the hotel.*

He got some ice and began applying it to his swollen eye and jaw while he searched through his bags to double-check everything.

Nothing was missing. Belatedly he thought to check the door. It was bolted from the inside just as it had been when he'd gone to sleep. He glanced around the room. The only other way in or out was through the window. He moved to check it and discovered it was closed, but unlocked.

He poked his head out, looking to see if an intruder could have entered or exited that way. It seemed unlikely, as there were no obvious foot- or handholds to aid in ascent or descent or even to getting to the room next door.

The room next door.

He straightened suddenly enough that he slammed the back of his head on the window with a grunt. "And that's probably how you injured yourself. Probably fell right off the bed, and climbed right back on without waking up," he chided himself.

With no evidence to the contrary it was the only reasonable explanation. He closed and latched the window and considered ordering room service. He finally rejected the notion, realizing that even though he looked terrible that was no reason to lock himself in his room. He made his way downstairs to the café, which he'd been told specialized in pastries of all sorts.

It was still dark outside and there were only a few other early risers in the café. He was relieved that the other patrons didn't give him more than a single glance. He in turn studied all of them, wondering who they were as he chewed away.

He glanced up as a couple of women were being escorted to a table. The taller of the two had chestnut hair and walked with a tired step. *Who are you?* he thought out of habit.

There was something oddly familiar about her and he couldn't shake the feeling that he should know who she was. No name sprang to mind, though, no matter how hard he tried to place her.

Frustrated, he turned his attention to the blond woman beside her and a jolt of recognition went through him, driving him to his feet. She turned and glanced at him, smiling sweetly.

But in his mind he could hear her screaming, crying, begging for his help. Pain exploded in his brain and he collapsed back into his chair with a gasp. Waves of nausea rolled through him, leaving him weak and shaken.

He could still hear her screaming in his mind even though she seemed calm enough as she sat down at a table across the room. His head pounded, the pain so bad his vision began to blur. For a moment he thought he was going to black out and he struggled to maintain consciousness. Sweat dripped out of every pore and rolled down his forehead to sting his already failing eyes.

I have to help her! he thought.

No! Leave her alone, another voice seemed to hiss at him.

She needs me.

You endanger her.

I have to save her.

You will kill her.

I think I...

Don't think. Just run. Run far and don't look back.

He staggered to his feet and made it back to his room before collapsing on his knees in the bathroom and throwing up.

What's wrong with me?

Susan's heart had raced when she had walked into the café and her eyes had met David's. For a split second she had thought he recognized her. Then he had averted his eyes and she had breathed easier as she hurried Wendy over to the table where the other girl's parents were waiting. A few moments later David had left and she had slumped in relief.

It had taken her ten minutes to position a black silk scarf just right so that no one would see the bite marks on Wendy's throat. She still thought they were bug bites and seemed to have no memory of the night before.

It looked like the vampire's mesmerism of David was holding as well, despite his misgivings.

Thank heavens Raphael didn't kill him, she thought as she took her seat.

"Did you sleep okay?" her uncle asked.

"Like a baby," Wendy said with a wide grin. "It was amazing. I think that's the softest mattress I've ever felt."

Susan marveled at the effects of the mesmerism and the deep sleep Wendy had experienced because of it. She herself had barely slept at all and struggled not to yawn as she ordered her food.

Breakfast was over too soon. Finally it was time to head to the cemetery and Susan found herself reluctantly climbing into the back of the rental car her uncle had brought around the front of the hotel to collect them in. As they drove through the darkness Susan couldn't help but stare out at it, wondering what manner of creatures were watching them.

Her grandmother had chosen the cemetery and a sunrise funeral for herself. Given all that had happened Susan wished they could have stayed safe in their hotel until the sun was fully up.

As soon as they stepped foot into the cemetery the first rays of the morning sun lit the sky and Wendy and her parents started crying. Despite her relief to see the sun, Susan felt an aching loss that made her wonder if she'd ever be happy again. She knew from experience that it would pass with time. She took a steadying breath and distracted herself by looking around.

Olšany Cemetery was the final resting place of many famous Czechs, including artists, writers, and politicians. Somehow it seemed strange that it would be Susan's grandmother's final resting place as well. She had lived the vast majority of her life in America and had loved her adopted country. Why then had she chosen to be buried so far from friends and family?

Susan couldn't shake the feeling that it was to ensure her granddaughter made it to Prague.

But why? she silently asked her grandmother as she stared at the coffin.

The cemetery itself was beautiful. Plots were marked with raised stone borders and soaring headstones. Many graves were covered with little potted flowers, sometimes as many as a dozen. She had seen monuments to victims of both world wars and a cross and large, rough stones marked "POA," which stood for members of Vlasov's army who freed Prague in May 1945. There were art nouveau monuments scattered about. And everywhere she looked she saw crosses carved into stone. In this city even the cemeteries were tourist attractions.

As her eyes roved over the seemingly endless graves a new thought occurred to her. *How many of them are empty?* She shivered and wrapped her arms tightly across her chest. Her uncle, misunderstanding the cause, put his arm around her and squeezed her shoulder. She could feel the grief coming off him and it was her grief, shared for a moment. But where he was crying freely, tears wetting his cheeks, she could not. Would not. Not until she was ready.

She glanced at Wendy and saw that her cousin looked slightly dazed. Whether it was from the sorrow of the moment or the lingering effects of the mesmerism Susan didn't know.

She just hoped Raphael kept his word and released Wendy from his control. She shivered as she remembered her cousin's face when she had first seen her in the club, under the other vampire's influence.

They were the last to arrive at the graveside and they took their seats on folding chairs up front. Sunrise had always been her grandmother's favorite time of day. She said every sunrise was a promise that God would always free His children from bondage, that good would triumph over evil, that no matter how dark the night, the rays of hope burned bright.

Almost two dozen friends and relatives were present to bid her farewell.

And at least one who was neither.

Susan felt her eyes widen in shock as she saw him in a copse of trees a hundred feet away. She blinked, but her eyes weren't deceiving her. It was Raphael. He stood, cloaked in the shadow of the trees, and watched.

She still had so many questions that he needed to answer. She glanced at Wendy. If she weren't under his spell still, Susan would refuse to see him again, choosing instead to go home and leave him and his secrets far behind. But she couldn't leave her cousin vulnerable to him, controlled by him. Not even death or distance seemed to dull the control of the vampire from the club.

Her mouth was dry and she wasn't listening to the words that the minister spoke. She shifted in surprise as her uncle stood up from his seat and began to give a brief eulogy. When she turned her eyes back to Raphael she discovered that he was no longer looking at her. Instead his eyes were focused to the right of their little cluster.

She discreetly tried to turn her head, wanting to see what he was staring at. There, half hidden by one of the taller grave markers was a man. The hair rose on the back of her neck. Someone else was spying on her? But why?

She grabbed Wendy's hand and squeezed it in a protective gesture. The girl squeezed back and glanced up at her with a tear-streaked face.

Why can't they just leave us alone? she thought.

She glanced again at the newcomer. She couldn't see his face, but he couldn't be a vampire because he was standing in the sun.

Or is that just a myth? she thought, panic beginning to set in as she glanced back at Raphael. Did he have to stand in the shade or could he, too, come forward into the light?

I don't know anything about them!

"Are you okay?" Wendy leaned over and whispered in her ear. "Your breathing sounds strange."

Susan realized she was taking short, shallow, quick breaths and that she was on the verge of hyperventilating. She forced herself to slow down and nodded at her cousin to indicate she was fine.

Wendy looked doubtful but she returned her attention to the service. Susan tried to force herself to as well, but her skin crawled and she couldn't focus knowing that she was being watched.

CHAPTER FIVE

When he maketh inquisition for blood, he remembereth them: he forgetteth not the cry of the humble.

—Psalm 9:12

David stood behind the stone monument, an angel holding a cross, and watched the funeral that was in progress. He felt uncomfortable. He had never gatecrashed an event before and it felt morbid and intrusive. Still, he had to know what it was about the two women that was so familiar. He knew he knew them, but could feel the memory slip out of his grasp every time he reached for it. So, he watched and waited and tried to let his mind relax, knowing it would eventually find the answer on its own.

The darker haired girl glanced over at him, but if she recognized him she gave no indication. From what he could hear of the service he guessed it was her grandmother they were burying.

His eyes glanced from time to time toward the other who was also watching. He couldn't quite see him and every time he tried to force a clear image of the man in the trees he found his mind suddenly drifting elsewhere. He didn't like it.

I'm not this man, he thought in frustration. *I don't crash funerals and stalk women. I don't meddle in the affairs of others. And I don't feel this overwhelming sense of fear when I try to make out the face of a stranger.*

Maybe it had been a mistake to come to Prague. Already things had happened to him that he couldn't explain. He touched his face briefly, wincing at the pressure. *God, what has happened to me?*

The funeral ended and the mourners moved off to their cars. He watched as the two girls were spirited away and he turned to look for the other, but he was gone as well.

After a minute David was left standing alone in a cemetery and wondering what exactly he was doing there.

Contrary to what Susan probably believed, Raphael had not been at the funeral because of her. He had been there to pay his final respects to Constance. He owed her that much. She had been a beautiful, proud woman, much more so than any of those gathered to mourn realized.

Only Constance's granddaughter and brother realized there was an extra mourner among them. But he wasn't the only outsider. He watched as David studied Susan and Wendy. He saw him struggling to remember. The mesmerism was breaking apart far sooner than he'd hoped. He'd spent hours working on the young man the night before and it was all going to be for naught shortly.

At least one part held. David was unable to look at him directly even though he was aware of his presence. Aversion and fear were two of the easiest things to implant in a human mind. That was why people closed their eyes at night, terrified to see what lurked in the dark. He had played on those primitive emotions, ensuring that no matter how much David's conscious mind wanted to see him, his subconscious would never allow it. *Because deep down he knows I'm a monster, he doesn't have to see it to prove it to himself.*

As the mourners left, so did Raphael. He yawned as he picked his way swiftly through the trees. He had carefully scouted his path so that he could remain cloaked in shadow as he journeyed back to his temporary home. He ran, fighting the pull of sleep that was nearly overwhelming. Most vampires were unconscious within seconds of sunrise. He had spent centuries learning to fight the pull one second at a time. It hurt greatly and staying up so late he ran the risk of succumbing and losing consciousness somewhere along his way.

That would be fatal and he kept that thought foremost in his mind as he pushed through the exhaustion. At last he reached a small house on the outskirts of the city. Inside all the windows had blackout curtains, but he still took the precaution of making his way down to the basement where he had his bedroom.

He was halfway down the stairs when he realized someone else was waiting for him. He yawned again and fell as his knees buckled. He'd only be able to fight the sleep a few seconds longer. He landed on the floor of the basement and pulled his head up just far enough to see that a man, a monk by his dress, was asleep in his bed.

Raphael cursed him soundly but the other figure lay still as Raphael passed out on the stone floor.

* * *

The reception afterward was at a small building adjacent to the cemetery. Susan milled around with the others and got tired of having people shove food into her hands. She wasn't hungry. Finally the food was cleared away, but the discussion continued. She remembered her parents' funeral. People had eventually begun leaving that one until, by the end of the evening, only a handful remained. Here, though, the mourners had no home to go back to, no other friends, family, or commitments. If they left it would be for their hotel rooms and silence most of them weren't ready to handle. As the day wore on they began to discuss dinner. Arrangements were made at a restaurant near her hotel. They loaded up in cars and headed there.

By the time Susan stepped out of her uncle's car onto the sidewalk in front of the restaurant she needed just a few minutes of peace from the incessant talking and crying. The air had turned cool and rain clouds threatened overhead. Susan wanted a bit of space to breathe before joining the others inside.

"What is it?" Wendy asked.

"I'm just going to run back to the hotel for my sweater. Tell everyone I'll be along in a few minutes," Susan said.

"Do you want me to go with you?"

"No, I won't be long."

She waited until her cousin went inside with the others then she breathed a sigh of relief. She closed her eyes for a moment, wishing it would rain and that the water would wash away the sorrow and the confusion she was feeling.

She began to walk, savoring the cool of the late afternoon and the sensation of finally being alone. People and cars passed by but it was the first time she had felt truly alone since arriving in the city.

Maybe that means no one is watching me, she realized.

The hotel was only two blocks away but she walked slowly, intent on stretching the minutes as long as she could. She finally arrived at the hotel and stepped inside.

I wonder where she stayed when she came here? Did she stay at this hotel?

She dashed away a few tears. *Not yet, soon*, she promised herself. Crying in the middle of the hotel lobby was not exactly her idea of comforting.

Just ten minutes alone would go a long way to helping her regain her composure. She crossed to the elevators and was brought up short by the sound of her name.

"Susan Lambert?"

She turned, startled. The speaker was a man in his forties wearing a dark suit and sunglasses. With his short cropped hair, muscular build, and confident stance he looked like some sort of bodyguard, like she would have expected a member of the secret service to look.

"Yes, what is it?" she asked.

"A gentleman wishes to see you."

"Who?" she asked, a chill racing through her.

"Pierre de Chauvere, he's an attorney."

"Oh," she said, moving from suspicion to confusion. "What is it regarding?"

"The estate of your late grandmother. That is all that he told me. I was sent to bring you to his offices."

"Let me just run upstairs and get my sweater," she said. She'd had enough with going with strangers to last her a lifetime.

"As you wish. I will wait here," he said.

She nodded and then made her way hastily to her room. Once there she locked the door and called down to the front desk. "Yes, hi, this is Susan Lambert. I was wondering if you could tell me whether there was a lawyer who practices in the city by the name of Pierre de Chauvere?"

"There is," the clerk on the other end assured her.

"That was fast. You didn't have to look him up in a phone directory or on the Internet or anything?"

"No, miss," the clerk said. "Pierre de Chauvere is one of the most famous lawyers in the Czech Republic and one of the wealthiest citizens of Prague."

"Thank you," she said, biting her lip as she hung up. If his name was that well known then it didn't help her any. The guy downstairs could be some sort of thug who just used that name as a convenient one, knowing it would be simple for her to verify his existence.

She scrawled a hasty note to Wendy, telling her where she was going and asking her to call the police if she wasn't back by eight.

The note was going to garner her some uncomfortable questions when she returned, but if she didn't return it might be the only thing that saved her life. Finished, she grabbed her sweater and headed back down to the lobby.

Her escort led her to a black limousine waiting outside and despite her misgivings, she felt a thrill of excitement as she slid into the backseat. He joined her in the back and moments later they were pulling away from the curb.

"Would you care for something to drink?" he asked, waving his hand at a bar set up near him.

"No, thank you," she said, determined not to accept any drink proffered until she was satisfied that it was safe.

"I didn't think my grandmother had any property or anything in this country," she ventured.

"I don't know the details of her estate," he said.

Susan turned and stared out the window. It was clear she wasn't going to get any more information from him so she could at least try and remember her way back.

Grandmother, why have you brought me here? What have you gotten me into?

The car soon arrived at its destination and Susan got out and was quickly escorted into a large building, as ancient looking as many in the city. She looked in vain for some sort of sign out front proclaiming it to be an attorney's office, but saw no such evidence.

As she was ushered into a foyer with marble floors and a winding staircase disappearing upward into darkness, her fears increased. It looked more like a mansion than an office building. She turned and glanced at her companion who hadn't said a word since their arrival. He bypassed the stairs and she followed him toward the back of the house and into a room with floor-to-ceiling curtains, antique furniture, and an elaborate gold claw-footed desk, behind which a man roughly her age sat studying her.

He waved his hand and her escort departed, closing the door behind him. The man stood and walked around the desk, extending his hand. "I am Pierre de Chauvere, but you may call me Pierre. You, of course, are Susan Lambert," he said, eyes quickening with thought as he took her in.

"Why 'of course'?"

"Because my assistant wouldn't have brought anyone other than Susan Lambert."

She felt like an idiot as he waved her to a seat in front of his desk. "And besides, you look just like her," he said, gesturing to the wall on her left.

She turned and there, in a gilded frame, was a picture of her grandmother when she must have been Susan's age. She started, never guessing in a million years that the man would have such a picture hanging on his wall. Had it been taken on one of her mystery trips to Prague that only her uncle seemed to know about?

She looked young, wistful, and there was something more. Susan stared hard at the portrait until she realized what it was. *She looks like she's in love.*

Her grandmother had looked like that in the pictures she had showed Susan of her wedding day. Light seemed to sparkle in her eyes and there was the ghost of a smile curling the corners of her mouth up. A light blush graced her cheeks. And around her neck was the very cross that she had given to Susan.

Susan reached for the cross, but it was still under the chest in the hotel room. She had forgotten to retrieve it that morning.

"I believe she meant to give you that necklace," Pierre said.

"She did give it to me," Susan said.

"Ah. And where is it now?" he asked, leaning forward.

"It's—" Something made her hesitate and before she could stop herself she said, "At home. I didn't want to risk losing it."

"I see," he said, clearly disappointed.

The hair on the back of her neck lifted and she was grateful for whatever notion had prompted her to lie about its whereabouts.

"The cross is an heirloom. It's been in the family for a long time," she added.

"It has indeed."

"What do you know of it?" she asked.

"It was forged during the time of the Crusades and it belonged to one of your ancestors who wore it into battle and then brought it safely home. Our firm... acquired the necklace for your grandmother more than thirty years ago. My father, Pierre Senior, handled the transaction."

"I thought it had been in my family for generations," Susan said, surprised at the news.

"It had been. But then it was lost, here in Prague, during the Renaissance. Your grandmother knew of it through stories, letters, portraits. She wanted it found and after much searching, it was."

Its history was longer than Susan had suspected.

"What else can you tell me about my grandmother?"

He shrugged. "She had a great many admirers, a very few close friends, and a couple of powerful enemies. Much more than that, I do not know. These were things she or my father spoke of, guardedly, to me."

Enemies.

"Who were these enemies?" she asked, licking her lips.

"Why? Has someone been bothering you?"

She hesitated and then decided to share her concerns. "There's a man, his name is Raphael."

Pierre's face hardened when she said the name. He leaned across the desk, his eyes intent. "I was afraid of that. You must stay away from him. He is a beast."

Susan blinked. "Beast" was a rather strong word to attribute to any man. She thought of her encounters with Raphael and wondered if it could be true. Dangerous, yes. Dark and frightening and powerful? Yes. But a beast?

Then again, he was a vampire, which didn't exactly make him human.

"I don't know what to think," she confessed.

"Then don't think, trust. Trust me, trust my word. My family has looked out for yours for... a while. We have a history together and I will not steer you wrong. This Raphael is more dangerous than you can possibly know."

"Because he's a vampire?" she asked, surprising herself.

Pierre smiled and leaned back in his chair. "Among other things."

"You know."

"Yes. As I said, my family has been watching out for yours for some time and trying to solve the riddle of what attraction you pose for these creatures."

"You mean, I'm not the first member of my family that has met a vampire?" she said, stunned. What was it Raphael had said to her? Something about knowing the women of her family? She had thought he was just being brash at the time, but could it be true?

"Unfortunately, no, you are not the first. There is a long and dark history with contact between your family and the undead. It rarely ends well."

"Why is this the first I've heard of it?" she breathed.

"Who would want to admit such a thing, particularly in this day and age? Had your grandmother sat you down as a child and discussed vampires with you, your relatives would have had her committed. Had she told you when you were an adult, you would have had her committed."

"And how come no one has had you committed?" she asked bluntly.

"I know how to be discreet. And my dear lady, this is

not America. There are still mysteries here, things that are unexplained, magic and devilish things. That is understood by the people who live here."

"Grandmother always spoke of the magic," she admitted.

"Doubtless. I know that she missed that sense of wonder, the unexpected, deeply."

"Perhaps then, you knew her better than I did."

"I very much doubt it."

"Why am I here?" she said abruptly, changing subjects because she didn't want to deal with regretting the things she had not known.

Pierre inclined his head. "Your grandmother left certain things for you in our possession, to be delivered to you and you alone upon her death."

"Why would she leave them here?"

"She knew she was going to be buried in the city and I suspect she wanted you to have them as quickly as possible, and for our firm to be available to you while you were here."

"Then why didn't you send for me two days ago?"

"My apologies. I was away on business until this morning and did not hear of her passing until then. I am, by the way, deeply sorry for your loss."

"Thank you," she said the words by rote, an autonomic response it was beginning to seem.

Pierre stood and walked to a large antique safe that stood in the corner behind his desk. Despite its antiquity it seemed out of place among the room's delicate furnishings. He spun the dial and a moment later the safe was creaking open.

He pulled something in a purple velvet pouch free before closing the door again. He returned to the desk and laid the pouch down in front of her. Susan glanced up at him questioningly and he nodded encouragement.

Carefully she picked it up, feeling a long, hard rectangular shape beneath its folds. She untied the rope that bound it and then folded the velvet layers back to reveal a small black box with a mother-of-pearl scene carved on the top.

She stared at it, an echo of memory stirring. She had seen the box before, as a small child. She had found it at her grandmother's when she had been in her bedroom playing dress up. Her grandmother had been angry, almost frightened, when she came in and saw Susan holding it. As Susan touched the box now the memories came back, bringing a fresh wave of tears. That day had been the only one where her grandmother had yelled at her and it had hurt and scared her deeply.

"What's in it?" she whispered, not daring to open the lid herself.

Pierre shook his head. She couldn't tell if that meant he didn't know or that he wasn't going to share.

She took a deep breath and lifted the lid. It swung open silently, revealing a folded piece of paper, yellowed with age. She pulled it out and looked at it. It looked like a legal document of some sort, but it was in French.

She handed it to Pierre who took it and studied it for a moment. "It's a deed, to properties in Bryas, which is in France."

A jolt went through her body and she gasped.

"What is it?" he asked swiftly.

"Bryas?" she questioned.

"Yes, why?"

"He called me Susan of Bryas."

"Who?"

"Raphael. How did he know?"

Pierre hesitated and she looked him in the eyes. "I cannot say, mademoiselle," he said.

It was a lie. She could tell by the way he looked at her, the way he hesitated. She could feel herself beginning to panic. "What aren't you telling me?" she demanded.

"I do not know what to say," he said, lifting his hands and shrugging. "But it appears that there is something else in your box."

She looked down and saw that he was right. There was a purple velvet bag at the bottom and she picked it up and slid out a gold key.

"What does this go to?"

"I very much wish I knew," he said.

And that, she could tell, was the truth.

CHAPTER SIX

Only be sure that thou eat not the blood: for the blood is the life.

—Deuteronomy 12:23

Susan perched on the edge of her seat across the desk from Pierre and put the key and the deed back into the box, wondering what she should do with them. He was watching her in a way that made her deeply uneasy. She was also disturbed that he had lied to her about not knowing how Raphael had correctly identified her family's ancestral home. And why was he so disappointed when she told him she didn't have the cross with her?

"Is there anything else I should know about my grandmother?" she asked.

"Probably, but those discoveries must be your own."

It was such an irritating answer Susan had a desire to throw something at him. Why did people keep tantalizing her with half answers? First her uncle, then Raphael, and now Pierre. Her patience was wearing thin.

"However, if there's anything more I can do for you, please do not hesitate to contact me," Pierre said, handing her a card.

She stared at it as she took it. "How did a French family wind up in Prague?" she asked without thinking.

He shrugged. "How does anyone end up anywhere? My grandfather moved here as a young man, looking for opportunities, chasing a girl, and voilà! the French invasion of Prague."

She smiled and couldn't help but wonder if a man would ever be willing to leave his country for her.

"Thank you," she said, standing. "If there's anything more I'll let you know."

"My assistant will escort you back to your hotel," Pierre said, walking her to the door of his office. He opened it and the man who had brought her rose from his seat just outside the door, locking eyes with his boss. Susan had the unnerving feeling that he had remained where he was, not waiting to be summoned, but guarding against something.

The moment passed and she followed him out to the car and climbed into the back. As soon as the car began moving she thought of her family waiting at the restaurant and felt a twinge of guilt. She should have called someone to let them know she was going to be late, but then she'd have had to explain her appointment and she wasn't sure she could even if she wanted to.

She looked down at the box that she was gripping tightly. More mysteries, more secrets. She sighed and slid down in her seat, wishing she could just rest.

They arrived back at the hotel and she hurried upstairs, where she buried her treasure in her suitcase underneath some of her clothes and tossed the note she had left for Wendy in the wastebasket. She should have asked Pierre more about the property. There would be taxes and she had no clue what the inheritance laws of France or the Czech Republic were or even which might apply since her grandmother had been an American citizen.

She was going to have to hire an attorney as soon as she got home to straighten it all out for her. She just prayed it wouldn't cause problems with other family members when they found out about the whole thing.

She headed back out the door, hoping that people hadn't noticed her absence too much at the restaurant. As soon as she reached her destination she was relieved to discover she needn't have worried.

Food was set up on a buffet table and people were milling about talking to one another. Wendy waved when she saw her and Susan hurried over. "Did you tell people where I was?"

Wendy shrugged. "No one asked."

Susan blinked, grateful that nothing terrible had happened since clearly no one would have noticed her absence quickly enough to do anything about it. She grabbed a plate of food and steeled herself to talk with the others.

She joined the people standing with her oldest cousin, Tyler. He was recounting a story about medical school. "So, my roommate was alone in the building and it was late. He leaned over the cadaver and accidentally pressed down on its chest. All the air escaped from its lungs and it made this moaning sound. He ran out of the building as fast as he could and didn't go back for his books until morning!"

Maybe it was a vampire coming back from the dead, Susan thought as others chuckled at the story. She moved quickly away, not ready to hear more about medical school and cadavers. She walked by a group of her older relatives who were crying openly.

"If I could just talk to her one more time I'd tell her that I wished we had seen each other more often," one of them said.

You could talk to her again if she came back as a vampire.

Susan kept moving, growing increasingly agitated at the talk of death that was surrounding her. She paused near Wendy's parents who were with one of her grandmother's oldest friends. The lady was shaking her head. "Did you see how pale she looked? It was quite a shock. I knew she was dead. She was never that pale when she was alive."

Susan couldn't help but think about Raphael, the bone white of his chest and the paleness of his cheeks. *Maybe she's a vampire.*

"Stop it!" Susan told herself, loudly enough to draw the attention of those around her.

"Susan? Are you all right?" her aunt asked, turning toward her.

She had to say something, quick, before they thought she was yelling at any of them. She opened her mouth but couldn't think of anything to say. She felt tears stinging the back of her eyes. She was tired, so very tired and scared, and her grandmother was very, very dead. And not a vampire.

"I don't want to cry," she whimpered.

Then she collapsed onto a chair sobbing.

Susan couldn't remember ever being so humiliated in her life. Following her complete breakdown in the restaurant her family had taken turns shoving food and drink down her before helping her back to her hotel room and putting her in bed.

She shivered under the covers, not because it was cold, but because she was, inside and out. Her heart ached with grief that had been pent up for too long and fear over everything she had witnessed in the last two days. Her grandmother dying, the attack on Wendy, the vampires, the secret box with its deed and key, the summons to the lawyer's home office, the funeral. All of it was more than she could take.

Wendy stayed with her, crying on and off herself. When Susan rolled on her side to look out the window all she could see was darkness. She wondered what Wendy would think if she begged her to get some garlic to hang on the windows and door.

She burst into a fresh round of tears when she realized she had no idea if it would even work.

Finally she got herself under control long enough to send Wendy back to be with the rest of the family. Alone again she found it easier to think, to breathe, and slowly she came out of the nightmare fog she felt like she had been under. She got up, scrubbed her face, and then she sat at the table and waited for him to appear.

David paced his room, pausing only long enough to take more headache medication even though he was convinced what was wrong with him couldn't be fixed by painkillers. He had realized after the funeral that his room was next door to that of the two women he had been watching. A couple hours earlier the one with the darker hair had gone inside, exiting a minute later with a sweater.

He had stared hard at her door after she left until he had a memory of pushing it open the night before. The pain that had exploded in his brain when he finally remembered that had driven him to his knees.

He had managed to crawl into his room before collapsing onto the floor, praying and crying and holding his head and wishing he could die, it hurt so badly.

God, what's happened to me? he prayed for the thousandth time. He didn't know what to do. He had thought about and ultimately dismissed the idea of trying to find a doctor or a psychiatrist to help. What kind of doctor did one go to for losing a memory of an event? He needed to remember fast and he couldn't shake the feeling that his problem wasn't entirely a natural one.

What does that even mean? Every cheesy television program he had seen about mind control and hypnosis had come to him while he struggled to make sense out of everything.

But even if it was possible and his memories had been intentionally stolen from him, had they also been stolen from the two women? Why didn't they acknowledge him?

He had nearly worked himself into confronting the women when he saw them again, but had changed his mind when the one with chestnut hair had been brought back to the room sobbing uncontrollably.

He had been able to hear the noise through his door and he had felt only a tiny bit ashamed as he eavesdropped. For a moment he thought that she was suffering the same debilitating headache until he heard her talking about her grandmother and realized that she was grief stricken instead.

His heart bled for them both. The blond woman had tried to calm her, but she had been crying, too. The last thing they needed was some crazy stalkerlike guy bursting in on them and demanding to know how it was they knew him.

The blond woman had finally left and it had been over twenty minutes and she hadn't returned. *She's probably at dinner, but what of the other one? Is she okay? She should be alone. I could try to talk to her now.* Somehow he felt that she would be more receptive to his delusions than the other one.

He walked to his door and stood, leaning against it. He closed his eyes and prayed, not knowing what he should do. It was craziness, all of it, and the sensible part of his nature wanted to forget the job and fly home, leaving the mystery a mystery. He could be okay with that.

But then he thought of the blond. She had looked about four years younger than him, vibrant, beautiful, and somehow very vulnerable. What would become of her if he left?

The turn of his thoughts puzzled him. Why should she seem more helpless than the one who was crying so hard? It made no sense.

And then, a scream ripped through his memory, and he saw himself pushing open the door to their room. She was on the bed and she was screaming. He pushed but the image went black, leaving him with an overwhelming sense of terror.

She needs me. I can't leave her or she'll die.

He had no idea how he knew that, but he was willing to bet his own life that it was true. He took a deep breath, left his room, took two steps down the hall and knocked on their door.

It took Raphael a full minute to come awake. In that minute his mind was alert, his senses active, but his body was frozen. He always hated that minute, dreaded it. This time was infinitely worse, though, because this time he was not alone and he could tell that the other vampire was already awake and moving around.

The waking paralysis affected all vampires to a greater or lesser degree though none seemed to know why. His sire, Gabriel, used to be functional within five seconds. The longest he had heard of was three minutes, which must always feel like a lifetime to the vampire trapped by it.

At last, with a wrench, his muscles lost their rigor and were his to command again. He jumped to his feet and spun to face the intruder in his home.

The monk raised an eyebrow and did his best not to smile.

"Paul, what are you doing here?" Raphael asked, both relieved and concerned as he recognized his grandsire.

The older vampire shrugged. "Rumor has it that the apocalypse is coming. I just wanted to see it for myself."

Raphael sat down on the bed. "You scared me."

"Good to know I still scare someone," Paul said with a flash of fangs.

Raphael stared hard at him. "You know you scare everyone."

"Ignorance breeds fear."

"One of these days you have to tell me how you manage to hide in a monastery, wear crosses, the works."

"As I told Gabriel many times, the light of God only burns those who struggle against it."

Raphael snorted disbelievingly. The older vampire was an anomaly, doing what others did not dare and escaping unscathed.

"So, tell me about the apocalypse," Paul said, as casually as if he were asking about the weather or a nice place to go sightseeing.

"Haven't you had visions about it?"

Paul's eyes narrowed, the only sign of irritation he ever gave. Raphael had not met Paul many times, but he had seen the look often when he did.

"You have mistaken me for someone else."

Raphael studied the other. His old self wouldn't have backed down, would have spoiled for a fight even against incredible odds. He was older, wiser, though, than when they had last met. "My apologies," he said, though he gritted his teeth as he said it.

Paul nodded to himself, looking supremely satisfied.

"What?"

"I thought you might be finally worth knowing," he said.

"I appreciate the vote of confidence," Raphael replied sarcastically.

Paul shrugged. "It wasn't confidence. I was simply playing the odds."

"That wasn't intended to make me feel better."

"It should. It means things are progressing normally for you. I know you have your doubts."

"More than my share."

"We all have them."

"Not you," Raphael said.

Paul shrugged. "Lack of faith has never been my short-coming."

"I've always had my suspicions about you, about who you really are...were."

Paul smiled. "You're free to have them. You won't be the first, nor I dare think will you be the last."

"You won't tell me, will you?"

Paul shook his head.

"Fine, old man, keep your secrets. But tell me why you're really here."

"I've come to offer my services, such as they are. I've never been a fighter, but the millennia have taught me a few things."

"You want to see the shard, don't you?"

"It would mean a great deal to me," Paul admitted, voice lowering reverently.

"Help me survive this and I'll make sure it comes to you," Raphael said. "I've been either guarding it or chasing it for too long."

"I find it curious that you would have allowed yourself to be so burdened by it, so chained to it, given your own doubts."

"You weren't there when it was entrusted to me," Raphael muttered. He shook his head slowly. It had been given into his keeping, yet someone had taken it from him.

"Do not be troubled. You will find it," Paul said.

"Armand is here. He's gathering an army, creating new vampires as inhuman, as monstrous, as devoid of conscience as he is," Raphael whispered.

"I know."

"I don't know how many."

"A great number, from what I've heard. Most of them, of course, are young, freshly turned. They don't know any better and they're willing to follow anyone who promises them unlimited freedom to indulge their own base natures."

"I haven't yet run across any more than half a century old."

"That's to be expected," Paul said. "However, I do know that there is one vampire here who is older. One whom I believe you have had dealings with before."

"Who?" Raphael asked suspiciously.

"The one who has taken science as his god."

"Michael? Here?" Raphael hissed.

"Rumor has it he has joined with Armand."

Raphael closed his eyes. He had last met Michael four hundred years before in Florence during the Renaissance. The memories still haunted him.

FLORENCE, 1618

Florence had been drawing people from all over the world who wanted to participate in the worship of learning, to embrace science, art, and humanism. It had attracted architects, musicians, and its share of vampires. Raphael, too, walked its streets.

But unlike the others he wasn't there to participate. He was there to kill one of his own kind. He had heard that a young vampire was running wild, indulging his particular vice. It was something that happened to all vampires when they were young. But this one had an obsession that was manifesting in dangerous, unexpected ways.

His particular obsession was for science, most especially biology, and his experiments in life had been at the very best cruel and at the worst monstrous. Once he had been turned, he had focused that obsession on understanding vampirism, what it was, how it was transmitted, everything.

Which meant he had to study it.

So he was trapping and dissecting vampires while they were still alive.

It couldn't be allowed to continue. Not only did he risk exposing them to the world, but it was also intolerable that he was preying on his own kind. Raphael wasn't the only vampire in the city seeking him, but he was determined to be the first to find him.

He had been trying to swear off killing people. But Michael wasn't a person. He was a monster who needed to be put down. The thought gave Raphael such pleasure that he stalked the streets for six nights from dusk until dawn searching, hoping for a sign of the elusive scientist.

Every time he thought he had found him he would arrive too late. The grisly handiwork was the only sign of his having passed. Bloody surgical instruments, foul-smelling fluids, and the occasional severed limb.

And then one morning, as the light of dawn touched the sky and Raphael went to sleep, he knew that the coming night would be different. He knew for a fact Michael would be at an abandoned building less than a quarter of a mile away. He could cover that distance in no time as soon as he awoke.

As his eyes began to close he thought for a moment

that something moved in the corner of his vision. There was nothing he could do because the sun rose and he was asleep...

Raphael woke with a start. He waited for the temporary paralysis to pass, and as soon as it did, he realized that something was terribly, terribly wrong. His arms and legs wouldn't respond to him. He couldn't even lift his head up.

He growled low in his throat, fear washing over him. He could smell death and blood all around him. And then he realized, in horror, the blood he was smelling was his.

A figure loomed over him, the candles in the room throwing shadows over red hair and a face that was already demonic with its glowing eyes and fangs half exposed by a twisted smile.

"You must be Raphael. I understand you've been looking for me. Congratulations, you have found me. I am Michael," the figure said. "One of my servants was good enough to bring you here. Actually, that was yesterday. He drugged you and you missed all the fun I had last night. No matter, the drug wore off hours ago, and you haven't missed the best part."

"If that's true, then what have you done to me?" Raphael asked, his words slow and slurred to his ear.

"Why can't you move? I'll tell you. I have taken from you what you take from others. I have drained your blood to the point where you would be dead, if you were still alive."

"Why?"

"To see what would happen, of course. Why else would anyone do anything? It's the pursuit of knowledge, understanding. Lady science is quite demanding."

"You have to stop."

"I really can't see why. Cheer up. You've donated your body to the quest for truth and there is no higher calling than that. You will live on through my research. Maybe one day I'll even be able to publish a book with my findings. Wouldn't that be amazing? You think you're immortal now, I have clearly proven you wrong. But I shall restore that immortality to you through the knowledge we will give to the world."

He was completely insane and even more dangerous than Raphael could have guessed.

Raphael struggled to make his body respond. He knew that starvation could weaken a vampire, but he had never heard of massive bloodletting before. He couldn't die like this, not on a table like an animal being cut into. He had to die on the battlefield, as was his right, his destiny. That was his higher calling. He had come to slaughter a mad sheep and instead found himself the one on the altar.

He racked his brain, trying to think of a way out. There had to be something he could do, something he could say that would buy him a little extra time. There was nothing he could offer Michael in exchange for his life. After having stalked him for days Raphael knew that the only thing Michael cared about was the experiments he performed in his quest for understanding.

Raphael saw the glint of metal, a knife, hovering in the air. He felt the pain as it sliced his skin, over and over. His body kept healing the wounds but the process was more painful than he had ever known and with each new slice it took longer to heal.

He screamed out in agony. And then, finally, the cutting stopped. His vision cleared and he saw the stake in the other vampire's hand.

It was the end of the experiment and so the end of him. And that certain knowledge was just what he needed.

"Don't you want to see how long it takes me to die from the blood loss or even if it will be fatal at all?" he whispered, his vocal cords feeling as if they were scraping together in the effort.

There was a pause and the stake hovered hypnotically in the air above him. He watched it carefully to see if it was going up or down. Up or down. Life or death.

It went up and disappeared from his sight.

"Yes, I would like to see. That is an interesting experiment indeed."

"I thought so." Raphael had to struggle to hear himself.

"I'll be back after I attend to a few things. I'm wagering you'll last at least another four hours. You will try to wait until I return? There's a good boy."

And then a door slammed and Raphael was alone.

Well, almost alone.

Around him in the dark he could hear scurrying and scratching as rats explored the room for morsels of food. There were at least a dozen of them by the sound of the paws on the floor and inside the walls.

He tried again to lift his arms or move his head but with no luck. He knew he wasn't strapped down. He could feel no such pressure against his skin.

And so in the dark he waited, cold, motionless. He could only hope that the vampire wouldn't return before he could gather his strength. He waited, straining his ears to stay focused on the scratch of the tiny claws. And then, finally, he could tell one was climbing the leg of the table on which he was laid out.

He tried to push a little air out of his body, hoping the

rat would smell the blood on his breath. He felt the furry body scrambling over his ankles, its body so very warm. He could feel its heart beating against his skin.

It bit him experimentally but apparently didn't like the taste. He breathed out again and this time seemingly got the rat's attention. It made its way slowly up his body, scrabbling over his legs and up his stomach. It paused on his chest, and frustration nearly overwhelmed him.

Very quietly, very gently he exhaled once more with the last of the air that had been in his lungs. The rat shifted slightly on his chest, tiny little razorlike claws digging into his skin. Then it took a step forward, and then another. It crawled up over his throat and he tried to remain calm.

Slowly, cautiously, it made its way up onto his face, its filthy, scratchy fur scraping against him. And when it was close enough, he bit it.

Its blood seeped down into his throat, rejuvenating him until he could move his head slowly to the side, enough to spit the body onto the floor. The sound and the smell of the fresh blood got the attention of the other rats. That was good, because he was going to need them all.

PRAGUE, PRESENT DAY

"I thought Michael was dead. That someone had succeeded where I failed," Raphael said, snapping back to the present and turning his eyes on Paul.

The older vampire shrugged. "He went underground for a very long time. I'd heard rumors that he resurfaced during World War II."

"Helping the Nazis, no doubt."

"I do not know. I had hoped, believed, he might be changed by now, that he had matured."

"One can only hope."

"Or pray," Paul said pointedly.

"You could not have brought worse news with you, old man. I don't know what to do," Raphael admitted.

"You're doing it," Paul assured him.

"Then why—"

And then he felt overwhelming fear. He lurched to his feet.

"What is it?"

"Someone is attacking one under my sway."

CHAPTER SEVEN

And there are three that bear witness in earth, the Spirit, and the water, and the blood: and these three agree in one.

—I John 5:8

Susan rose and walked to the door with her heart in her throat. It had to be Raphael. Wendy would have just used her key.

"Come in," she said as she opened the door.

It wasn't Raphael but David.

"Thanks," he said, pushing past her into the room. She shut the door but didn't lock it.

"What are you doing here?" she gasped.

A look of triumph passed over his face. "If I was a stranger to you, your first question would have been 'Who are you?' I take it you know who I am since you're more concerned with why I'm here."

She stood, stunned, not sure how to respond. She didn't want to break the mesmerism. She was afraid of what would happen to him if she did.

"Who—who are you?" she stammered. "Get out of my room or I'll call the front desk."

"I don't think you will," he said.

"Why?"

"Something happened last night. It happened here, and someone doesn't want me to remember what it was. That means they probably don't want me talking about it."

He was too clever and she was afraid it was going to get him killed. She struggled, needing to stall for time. Where was Raphael? The sun had been down a long time and he should have arrived. Unless he had tracked Wendy to the restaurant and was trying to release her from his mesmerism like he had promised.

Or he could be luring her away.

"You have to get out of here," she said, trying to make her voice forceful. "It's not safe."

"For who?" David asked.

"You."

Before he could respond there was another knock on the door. "Come in!" she shouted, praying it was Raphael.

The door slammed open so hard the room shook and a short, ugly man with a bulbous nose and skin even paler than Raphael's strode into the room.

"Don't mind if I do," he sneered as he slammed the door behind him.

"Get out!" she hissed, realizing her mistake and moving away from him.

He made a tsking sound. "It doesn't work that way. No take-backs, you know?"

"Who are you?" David asked, moving to block the newcomer's way.

And as terrified as she was Susan couldn't help but note that David had actually asked *Who?* first. Of course it didn't matter that she hadn't lied to him well, because they were both about to die anyway.

"David, get away from him!" she warned.

The use of his name seemed to bring him up short and he turned with wide eyes. "You do know me."

"Yes, I do. Now get over here!"

He hesitated for only a moment and then moved to stand beside her. "What's wrong with that guy? He looks like a—"

David groaned and fell, collapsing half on the chair and sliding to the floor clutching his head.

"Are you all right?" she asked.

"What's the matter?" the intruder asked as he sauntered closer. "Cat got your tongue?"

"He's a, a, a—"

"Can't say the word?" the vampire sneered. "Not part of your reality?"

Thanks to whatever Raphael had done it didn't seem to be.

"What about the lady? It looks like it's part of her reality."

"Stay away from us!" she shouted.

"Unlikely," the vampire chuckled.

She grabbed for her cross necklace but it was still under the chest. She couldn't get to it before the vampire reached her.

She thought of the club. Had he been there? Had he seen? Had he followed them to avenge the other vampire or maybe just because he could? She remembered what Raphael had said, about the kiss putting his scent on her.

"Raphael!" she burst out. He had told her to say it

in the club if any approached her. She just prayed it worked.

"What about him?" he asked, voice and face suddenly inscrutable.

"I'm-I'm with him," she stammered.

There was a pause and then he smiled, slowly, wickedly. "Yes, I know. His scent is all over this room, all over you."

"So, you should go now," she said, trying to force confidence into her voice.

"I don't think so. See, it's because of Raphael that I'm here. My master wishes to speak with him, and what better way to get his attention than by going after his woman?"

"I'm not his woman!" she flashed angrily, before she could stop herself.

The vampire cocked his head to the side and studied her for a moment. "You really believe that? Because I think you are his woman. Even if you don't know it yet."

She dropped to her knees, thrusting her hand underneath the chest, fingers groping for the cross.

She felt a rush of wind and smelled decaying blood as a hard hand seized her shoulder. He twisted her head around and she was staring into the monster's leering eyes. Her fingers brushed the chain of the necklace and she stretched, trying to hook a fingernail at least around it.

"You smell familiar to me. Have we met before?"

"No!"

"Hmmm…must be someone else I was thinking of. A relative perhaps, an ancestor? It really doesn't matter I suppose. Whoever you are, you're going to die now."

David, who had steadied himself in the chair, kicked out and connected with the vampire's jaw hard enough to make him release his hold on Susan's shoulder. She lunged sideways, grasped the cross, and pulled it free, holding it up in front of her.

The vampire hissed and took a step back.

And suddenly the window exploded inward in a shower of glass. A dark figure hurtled through it, landing in a crouch in the middle of the floor. Susan screamed as bits of flying glass hit her, stinging where they connected with skin. The figure rose with a roar and she could see Raphael, fangs bared, eyes blazing, gloved hands smoking slightly, each holding a wooden cross.

He swung the left one toward the other vampire who dodged it easily. He, like Susan, couldn't see the second one, though, as Raphael's right arm blurred. The cross connected with the vampire's cheek and the smell of seared flesh filled the air as the creature jumped backward, clutching at his charred face.

Raphael leaped after him, still swinging while Susan blinked in shock. He hadn't burned up! The vampire in the club had caught on fire when she hit him in the face with her cross. Why hadn't this one?

Next to her David gave a great gasp and then staggered to his feet. "Vampires, they're both vampires!"

"Yes," she said. "But the new one is on our side...I think." She continued to clutch the cross necklace even though she was beginning to wonder if it was as effective a weapon as she had believed.

David grabbed the chair he had been slumped against and smashed it against the floor twice. Susan heard the cracking sound of wood and she stepped back as David stomped three times on one leg of the chair until he was able to wrench it free. The jagged piece of wood he held in his hands was nearly a foot long and he spun toward the battling vampires.

"What are you doing?" she demanded.

He didn't say anything but instead leaped forward. A moment later he was flying through the air as one of the vampires, she couldn't tell which one, knocked him back with a swing of an arm.

"Stay down!" Raphael roared and she guessed it was him who had thrown David clear.

The remains of the chair leg fell at her feet as David hit the ground with a thud. She snatched it up and brandished it in front of herself, holding it in her right hand and the cross in her left. The smell of the charred flesh was turning her stomach as she strained her eyes, trying to track the movements of the two vampires.

I'm going to die.

David felt like his chest was going to explode as the wind was knocked out of him. *God, protect us*, he prayed, as he lay, unable to move, blinking rapidly and struggling to retain consciousness. He included the woman in his prayer though he didn't know what her role in everything was.

When the second vampire had arrived something had seemed to unlock in David's mind. He remembered everything from the night before, including hours the vampire had spent trying to erase those memories. He was the one that had been attacking the blond woman, but now he had seemingly come to the other one's rescue. Or was he just protecting his territory? Susan had told the other she was with him—Raphael, she'd called him.

David struggled to flip onto his side so he could see what was happening. He managed it and bit back a cry as pain knifed through his ribs. He could see the woman holding the improvised stake in front of herself defensively.

From the way she was holding it she didn't have a prayer of using it successfully. His college roommate had been captain of the fencing team and David had picked up a lot just by listening and watching. Of course, he should have known better than to leap blindly into the fray without first observing and understanding his opponents—their speed, their strengths.

He sat up, ignoring the searing pain. He had no idea how badly he was injured or whether he would make it worse by getting up. He knew, though, that if he stayed on the floor he was dead. He scrambled slowly to his feet.

"Give me the stake," he told the woman.

Reluctantly she handed it to him and he turned to watch the battle happening on the other side of the room.

The two vampires were still locked together, each seeking the upper hand. When Raphael spun the other so that his back was to David and Susan, David took several quick steps and slammed the stake as hard as he could into the vampire's back, hoping he would reach its heart.

"Deeper," Raphael grunted, grabbing the other vampire and preventing him from turning on David.

David grasped the stake and shoved with all his might. Suddenly there was an agonized shriek and the vampire slumped to the ground, landing on a pile of luggage. He lay still for a moment before his body dissolved, turning to ash.

The woman ran forward, stepping in the ash in her

haste. Her hands plunged into one of the suitcases and grasped something. David turned his attention back to Raphael. The vampire was intent on Susan, staring at whatever it was she had.

David dove for the chair and snapped off a second leg. He spun to face Raphael. The vampire was still distracted and he rushed at him, plunging the stake into his breast.

Raphael roared in pain as the stake rammed into his chest, stopping as it struck bone. He yanked it out and dropped it to the ground. The wound instantly began to seal over and he gritted his teeth as the flesh burned and tingled and itched.

Susan was staring at the box in her hands, seemingly oblivious to what had just happened. He turned and glared at David and wrapped his left hand around the human's throat as rage filled him.

David began to choke, nails ineffectually clawing at Raphael's hand. *I could kill him. All I'd have to do is squeeze.* His fingers twitched slightly and he cut off the man's air completely.

The mesmerism had failed, as he knew it would, and now there was no chance of convincing David of anything other than the truth. He couldn't take that risk, and with the human intent on murdering him, there really seemed only one choice. He wouldn't crush his windpipe. He would drain him dry instead.

He pulled David closer, regretting only that Susan would see. But it was best this way. She needed to know what she was up against and whom she was helping.

He twisted David's head as easily as that of a rag doll and prepared to sink his fangs into his throat, unwilling to waste the food when he needed it so badly. There was something familiar about the scent of his skin and he hesitated for a moment, sifting through his memories.

"Stop!" Susan screamed.

Raphael turned to look at her. She was pale and shaking, but her eyes were smoldering at him in a way that let him know she was deadly serious. In her left hand she still clutched the small box that she had rescued from her suitcase. In her right hand, though, she held the cross.

A wave of fear swept over him at the sight of the tiny silver symbol. Whatever happened, he couldn't let her touch him with it.

"I cannot mesmerize him again," he said, fangs still extended.

"That doesn't mean you get to kill him," she said, voice firm, gaze steady. She would make a formidable opponent and, in time, a skilled warrior.

"Then what do you suggest? He knows about my kind and I refuse to let him go free so that he might stake me someday."

"You said you needed help."

"I do," he growled.

"Well, then you're going to need *his* help. I can't help you."

"Why?" he demanded, dropping David onto the floor for the moment. The man began to cough violently as air suddenly rushed back into his lungs.

"In three days I go home. And it may end up being even sooner than that. I'm going back to California where the sun shines and there are no nightmares lurking in the shadows."

He smiled. "There are more than just vampires who lurk in the shadows there," he said.

She shook her head. "I don't care. I'm not staying. If you need a human to help you, truly, then you might as well pick him. I mean, he actually staked one of you."

"It's you I need," Raphael said, taking a step toward her.

She shrunk away, but kept the cross extended before her. "You can't have me, so adapt."

"You don't understand, this war is as much yours as it is mine."

"I'm sorry, but I can't be a part of this—whatever this is. I want you to release my cousin and then we're going back to California where we're going to do our best to forget that any of this ever happened."

"You won't be able to," he said, stepping closer, debating whether he should chance doing a light mesmerism on her.

"Watch me. I just want to live a boring, quiet life."

And that was the lie. He could read it in her eyes, smell it in the change in her body chemistry. She didn't want boring and quiet. She wanted exciting and extraordinary. She was just afraid to admit it, afraid of what it would mean and what it would change.

"Help me and I can show you things you never imagined," he pressed.

"I'm not a warrior. I'm just a girl."

"An extraordinary girl who has held her own against monsters."

"Like you?"

"Like me."

And there, a spark of curiosity flashing in her eyes.

More than she craved excitement, Susan craved knowledge. It was her weakness, but he could teach her to make it her greatest strength.

"I can tell you everything you want to know. I can unlock the secrets of this world for you."

"Why?"

"Because, as I said before, I need you. I can't win this war without you."

She stood there, and he could read the thoughts that flashed across her face. She was conflicted and with just the right amount of nudging he believed he could get her onto his side. He held out his hand to her. As she stared at it, the silence stretched between them. The hand holding the cross slowly began to lower.

And then, from the floor, David croaked, "What war?"

They both turned to look at him as he rose slowly to his feet. There were red marks on his throat where Raphael had been choking him.

"Excuse me?" Susan said.

"What war?" David demanded.

There was a sudden pounding on the door and Susan stiffened glancing from them to it and then around the room. "I think we're in trouble," she muttered. The room looked like a hurricane had gone through it.

"Follow my lead," Raphael said.

He suddenly grabbed the front of her dress and she heard a ripping sound. She looked down and saw that he had torn it half off her body. With a gasp she dropped the box and did her best to cover herself.

"What's he going to do?" David asked as Raphael moved toward the door.

"What he's been doing to people nonstop it seems," she hissed, flushing as she tried to cover her bra.

Raphael opened the door and a hotel security guard entered the room, eyes warily taking everything in. Raphael said in a deep, slow voice. "A stranger entered this room and attacked this woman. The gentleman here heard her cries and came to her rescue. Her attacker ran off. Do you understand?"

The man nodded briefly and Raphael slipped out of the room.

He's gone! He just left, again, without explaining anything. How could he do that? Susan stared after him, still clutching the remains of her tattered dress, the only one she had brought to Prague with her. The chain on her cross was wound around her fingertips tightly and they began to throb. She stared down at them and could feel her own pulse, the ebb and flow of her blood. It frightened her and made her feel dizzy, like she was standing on the edge of a cliff and staring down into the void.

There were voices around her. David was talking and so was the security officer. After a minute she realized he was talking to her.

"Did he hurt you, ma'am?" the guard asked.

She glanced down and noticed the tiny cuts from the glass that covered her skin. "He broke the window and the glass cut me," she said. "And he tore my dress. I think otherwise I'm okay."

But she wasn't okay. She felt numb all over except for her face, which prickled. That and the throbbing of her fingertips was all she could feel. The tiny cuts were there, but she couldn't feel them.

"She's lucky you arrived in time," the man said, turning to David.

She could see David struggling to keep up. "I'm just glad I could help," he said finally. He turned and she saw him wince in pain and noticed he was holding his side. It shook her. He was hurt and he had come very close to dying. *He might still.*

"I think he's hurt," she said. "Please, please help him."

"Sir, are you okay?"

David shook his head. "He knocked me down pretty hard. I think I broke a rib."

"I'll call for paramedics."

"Thank you," Susan said. She looked down at her ruin of a dress. "I want to change."

The guard winced. "I understand, but I would ask you to wait until the police arrive. I want them to see... to see for themselves what happened to you."

"Okay," she said.

He used his phone to call for the police and the paramedics and then turned his attention back to them. He asked for a description of her attacker. They were both able to give him a detailed description of the vampire, minus the fangs and yellow eyes, and Susan couldn't help but think of the irony given that they would never be able to find him. Several times the guard walked right across the monster's ashes, spreading them further around the carpet.

The paramedics arrived and began to examine them both. Susan winced as they dabbed antiseptic on her cuts and removed glass with a set of tweezers from several of them.

She glanced over and saw that David had his shirt off

and a wicked bruise was already forming on the right side of his chest. Fingerprint bruises were also visible around his throat and she realized that compared to him she had gotten off easy.

Police had also arrived and were checking the room over. Fortunately they didn't ask either of them any questions they couldn't answer. They were just finishing up and the paramedics were making noise about the hospital when she heard a gasp from the doorway.

She turned to see Wendy and her parents standing there, stunned looks on their faces. She tugged again self-consciously at her dress, not wanting them to see what had happened to it. She didn't want them to worry about her, but there was nothing she could do about it.

"What happened?" Wendy burst out.

"Ma'am, I'm going to have to ask you to leave," the security guard who had been the first to arrive told her.

"No, this is my room, and that's my cousin. What's happened?"

The security guard glanced at Susan and she nodded. It would be easier if he explained, hopefully it would save her from having to go into too much detail. She turned to glance at David. He was ashen-faced and staring at Wendy as though he had seen a ghost.

David couldn't help but stare at Susan's cousin. He thought he had heard Susan call her Wendy. It suited her. She was beautiful and with the worry in her eyes she seemed so vulnerable. *Who are you?* he wondered silently.

"I'm afraid your cousin was attacked. She's fine, thanks to the efforts of this young man. They're both going to be okay, but they're going to have to go to the hospital for some tests. Don't worry, we have a full description of her attacker and we will find him. Staff downstairs saw him enter the lobby earlier and know to be on the lookout for him."

At least they were able to confirm their description with staff witnesses. David figured that had to go in their favor. Of course, he doubted that any of those witnesses had identified him as a vampire.

He shook his head. It seemed too incredible to believe, but there on the floor, being spread further around and ground into the fibers of the carpet was a pile of ash that proved otherwise. He had never thought that something like that could exist. What was it Christ had told Thomas? *Blessed are they who have not seen and yet have believed.*

It hardly applied here, though. He couldn't imagine that anyone who knew the truth about these creatures was blessed.

"Susan, are you hurt?" Wendy asked in an agonized voice.

"Not really. Just a few cuts from some broken glass."

Wendy turned and stared at him with enormous eyes. "You're a hero," she said.

He didn't know why, but hearing her say so made him feel proud and embarrassed all at the same time.

"Not really," he said.

"Yes, really," Susan said emphatically.

He inclined his head toward her.

"We're finished," one of the police officers told a medic.

"Sir, we will get a stretcher for you to take you to the ambulance," the man told David.

"That's not necessary. I can walk."

"I'm afraid I will have to insist otherwise."

David glanced over at Susan and she shrugged.

"Please, let them take care of you," Wendy begged, stepping into the room and walking over to put a hand on his arm.

His skin tingled where she was touching it and his heart began to race. *Do not fall for her!* he lectured himself.

"I will," he assured her.

"We'll follow you over to the hospital," Wendy told Susan, her hand still on his arm.

"Okay," Susan said.

He studied Wendy quietly, the way she looked at him, the despair in her eyes when she looked around the room, and the fear when she looked at Susan. He finally concluded that she had no memory of meeting him earlier or of what had happened to her the night before.

Raphael must have mesmerized her, too. In her case, maybe it was for the best. He wasn't sure she could have handled the truth of everything that was transpiring.

But the question that haunted him was, what exactly had he walked in on? He was no longer sure that it had been what it seemed. He could see bite marks on Wendy's throat where a carefully placed scarf was slipping. He glanced over at Susan, finding it hard to believe she would have just stood by and let Raphael bite her cousin.

During the fight Susan had said she thought Raphael was on their side. Was it possible she was under his spell as well? Or did all of this have something to do with the war they had been talking about?

He grimaced. All he had were questions with no answers in sight. It would be hours before he had a chance to get Susan alone again, maybe longer. Maybe never if she left for home immediately like she seemed to want to do.

The paramedics brought the stretcher up and he submitted to their care.

CHAPTER EIGHT

And now art thou cursed from the earth, which hath opened her mouth to receive thy brother's blood from thy hand.

—Genesis 4:11

Raphael hated hospitals. It was more than the sterile white, the overly bright lights that left no shadows to hide in, and the omnipresent smell of antiseptic. The smell of blood and death was nearly overpowering to him. All vampires that he knew of hated hospitals for those and numerous other reasons. For him, though, it was deeply personal. Hospitals reminded him of the closest he had come to dying permanently four hundred years earlier on Michael's operating table.

Raphael shuddered at the memory. It had been the lowest point in his entire life. It had also given him an aversion to rats. As he moved through the hospital he was at least grateful that the only creatures he had to be concerned about at present walked on two legs and wore scrubs.

He had gathered enough strength by feeding on the rats all those years before that he was able to move, barely, and to escape before Michael could return to finish his experiments. He had killed three humans that night while in a state he could only equate to being like insanity. The pain and the thirst had been unbearable and when both had finally eased he had been appalled at what he had done.

And Michael had left Florence far behind. For years Raphael had searched halfheartedly for him, afraid of being captured again, but still convinced that the vampire needed to be destroyed. Eventually he'd come to hope that someone else had succeeded in killing him where he'd failed.

If Michael was alive and in the city he had to find him and kill him before there was any chance of a repeat performance. He would have to keep an eye out for the scientist's human minions as well. But that was okay, this time he would have some of his own.

If he could convince them to trust him.

If he could convince them to stay in the city.

If he didn't kill them himself through accident or rage.

It had been fifty years since he had killed an innocent person. A lifetime for most and yet such a short time from his perspective. He worried that it would happen again. He thought of his sire, Gabriel. He had successfully stopped killing humans altogether by the time they met. *Of course, he made an exception in my case*, Raphael thought ruefully.

He found Susan and managed to observe her with her family while remaining unseen. He looked at her face and saw the faces of so many others he had known in his lifetime. They had all been strong, fiercely independent. He had managed not to entangle his life with any of theirs. That was all about to change, though. Not ready to meet her family, he turned away and went in search of David.

After taking X-rays, the doctor determined that David had a broken rib. The news didn't surprise him, but he didn't look forward to the weeks of recovery. *Still*, he reasoned, *it could have been a lot worse.*

They wrapped his torso tightly in bandages and then insisted they were going to keep him until the morning. Frustrated, he finally lay down, wishing he knew where Susan was. The knowledge that they were probably going to release her before him just made it worse.

He fell quickly asleep after he was left alone in the room. Nightmarish figures haunted his dreams, though, and a little after four in the morning he found himself jolted awake.

He lay, gasping, drenched in sweat, and fought to calm down. A flicker of movement in the corner of his eye caught his attention and he turned.

Standing near his bed, silent and menacing, was Raphael.

"Give me one reason why I shouldn't kill you," the vampire said.

David's heart began to pound but he forced himself to meet the other's gaze. "Tell me about the war."

Raphael stared hard at David, but the other didn't look away. He thought of the battle in the hotel room with the other vampire. He felt cornered and he didn't like it. There was no doubt in his mind that Armand had been the one who had sent the vampire to kill Susan. He had not expected Armand to know of Susan so quickly, or to move against her without warning. Raphael shouldn't have been surprised, though.

When he was human Armand had an impressive network of men willing to kill and die for him. It looked like he had brought his networking skills with him into the twenty-first century. Susan wasn't safe. Armand had missed killing her, but he would try again.

And once again, David had attempted to intervene. He stared at the human lying on the hospital bed with his ribs bandaged. The man was staring back at him, face brave and heart racing like a frightened rabbit. And he wanted to know about the war.

"You meddle," Raphael accused.

"Excuse me?" David asked.

"Meddle. Go looking for trouble. Stick your nose where it doesn't belong. Take your pick. Twice now you've come riding to the rescue to save a damsel from a vampire. At least tonight the damsel was actually in danger from the vampire you attacked. Well, one of them at least."

"Both times it was an accident. I didn't even know vampires existed until tonight. Wait, I guess I knew last night before you tried to block my memories, but either way I haven't had a whole lot of time to process this. Tonight I just wanted to talk to Susan, find out what it was I couldn't remember about her. The vampire attacked after I went over there. And the night before I heard Wendy screaming and it woke me up."

"A sensible person would have just called the front desk or ignored it."

"I was going to call the front desk, but the phone wasn't working. And then...it wasn't right to let something happen to her when all I thought I had to do was intervene."

"The world needs more people who think as you do," he admitted grudgingly. To himself he pondered the non-working phone. Could it be truly coincidence? It seemed strange, especially for a hotel with as impeccable standards as that one. It would have been too soon for it to be some kind of interference from his enemies. What did that leave? Divine intervention?

He shook his head, not sure he wanted to believe that. Maybe Susan was right, though. Maybe he did need David for the war.

"Does that mean you're not going to kill me, then?"

Raphael wanted to kill him. Wanted to sink his teeth into his throat and taste the blood as it pumped out of him. He shook himself, hard, wondering if the cravings ever went away. It was something he'd have to remember to ask Paul.

"How did you know to stake him in the back?" Raphael asked, deliberately not answering the question. "That's not exactly how it's shown in modern entertainment."

David shook his head. "It was the target I had available to me."

"I'm glad. It's a much better one, you know. It's practically impossible to stake a vampire the way they show it on television."

"Why?" David asked. There was open curiosity in his eyes. It was a mixture of a desire for the information and puzzlement over why Raphael was explaining it all to him.

Pay attention, kid, I'm about to tell you how to kill me. And if you ever try it again, you won't live to regret it.

"If you try to drive the stake straight or at a downward angle, the odds are incredibly high that you're going to hit a rib instead. Now you can keep applying pressure until the rib breaks or moves, but that requires more strength than most people are capable of, and in the time it takes to do that, he'll likely kill you by biting you or ripping your head off. Understand?"

David nodded.

"To kill a vampire with a stake from the front, you need to go in low, under the rib cage, and angle upward to hit the heart. It's easier to stake them from behind, though."

"No fangs or hands to worry about?"

"That's just part of it. The ribs are spread out over a greater distance in the back and you have a much better shot at putting a stake between them, like you did."

"It took a lot of force."

"You still had to punch through all that muscle. It's like trying to punch through a steak with a toothpick."

David grimaced and for a moment Raphael thought he was going to be sick. The human quickly regained his composure though. "How else do I kill a vampire?"

Raphael almost smiled. It was more than an academic question. David hadn't asked how *someone* could kill a vampire, but how he personally could.

"Sorry. That's on a need-to-know basis and I'm not sure yet if you're going to live long enough to need to know."

"In that case can you at least tell me what was going on with Wendy last night?"

He flushed slightly when he said her name. It would have been imperceptible to a human, but Raphael saw it.

"A very bad vampire had mesmerized her. Susan killed him, but it takes more than that to break the hold a vampire has. I was attempting to do so when you stumbled in."

"Why did my mesmerism wear off?"

"You're a resister. There's only a handful of your kind on the planet."

"Nice to be special."

Raphael smiled despite himself. "It would have been a lot easier on all of us if you weren't."

"What about decapitation? Does that kill a vampire?" David asked, switching back to the earlier topic.

"To the best of my knowledge decapitation kills *anything*."

"What about sunlight?"

"That's a bit trickier. Yes, sunlight kills us. However, how quickly it will do so varies from vampire to vampire. If a vampire hasn't fed recently, the death is almost instantaneous. For a vampire who has recently fed, though, there can be a lag time. Some vampires work very hard to build up an immunity to sunlight, allowing them to be out in it for a short period of time without combusting."

"How long?"

"Again, it varies. For vampires who have always played it safe, even a few seconds in the sun, regardless of whether they've fed, will kill them. Myself, I can withstand direct sunlight for almost five minutes. My sire could handle it for almost thirty. Of course, what's harder to deal with is the coma-like state induced by the sun. Again, some have more success in fighting it than others. My sire is the only vampire I've ever heard of that could actually bring himself out of it during daylight hours."

It was a terrifying trait and just one of the things that made him such a formidable opponent. He was rendered unconscious at daybreak along with the rest of them, but he could free himself from sleep when necessary. More than once it had saved his life.

"Sire?" David asked. "Would that be the vampire who...what do you call it, turned you? Brought you across?"

"Cursed me. That's what I call it. And yes, my sire is the one who cursed me."

David's fear was being eaten away by his curiosity. He struggled to sit up a bit. "Cursed you? Does that mean you don't like being a vampire? You didn't choose to be a vampire?"

Raphael laughed, startling both of them with the sound. "Choose this? Are you kidding? Not in a thousand years would I choose this. No one in their right mind would choose this. I would have rather died that day and been buried for all time than become this."

"I don't understand."

"Of course you don't," Raphael growled. "Because the movies you see, the books you read, they all get it wrong. They make it seem so glamorous. They showcase vampires as these romantic leads, all noble and tortured, and good deep inside. It's a lie."

"Then what's the truth?" Susan whispered behind him.

Raphael spun, cursing himself for allowing her to sneak up on him. He should have heard her, should have smelled her. It was a bad sign that he had not.

She stood, pale and weak-looking in the doorway. The bandages on her arms marked the places where she had been cut by flying glass from the window he had smashed through. Even trying to save her he had managed to hurt her.

"Vampires are the most evil of all creatures. Not because we are vampires, but because when we were alive, we were the worst of the worst, so terrible in fact, that death was too good for us. In your world you execute your worst criminals. In mine, we sentence them to death without the possibility of parole. When you meet a vampire, you're staring at someone who was so consumed, so evil as a human that a vampire felt compelled to curse him, to damn him to this existence for all time."

"What were you in life?" David asked.

"I was a knight. I fought during the Second Crusade. And I was evil."

DAMASCUS, 1148

"There is no God," Raphael whispered fiercely. There was only him and the battlefield on which he stood.

Someone moved behind him and he turned in one swift motion, beheading another knight whom he had fought beside for three days. He laughed as the man's head rolled away and came to rest beside a Muslim corpse.

The crusaders were losing the battle for Damascus. He could see it in the pained faces of his comrades, feel it in the surge of intensity from the infidels. It was no matter. Raphael cared nothing for holy wars and popes. He fought for himself, for the opportunity to better his station in life by winning glory and placing himself within the eyes of King Louis.

"You killed Peter!" another man shouted at him, pointing to the headless body.

Raphael pulled his knife from his belt and hurled it. It lodged in the man's chest and he fell. Raphael was on him in an instant. "God forgive me," the dying man gasped.

Raphael leaned down, twisted his knife in the man's chest and snarled. "Better you should have prayed to me."

He pulled his knife free before sticking it in his belt. He stood and quickly glanced around in case any others wished to challenge his actions. The king loved champions, but even he might not approve of Raphael slaying his men. He'd be far less pleased if he knew that Raphael was responsible for the death of a dozen of his knights. With his sword in his hand Raphael felt at peace. Slaughtering men was no harder than slaughtering pigs, easier because they were not so hard to catch. With his sword swinging and blood spraying from slashed throats he felt truly alive and it didn't matter who he had to kill to keep feeling that way. Sometimes he had to remind himself that he was actually on a side and not just fighting the entire world himself.

He glanced to where one of the lords was, a proud figure astride a magnificent stallion. He was always carefully guarded and surrounded by his most trusted advisers. A man, shrouded in a cloak, seemed to have his ear. Raphael always tried to position himself within view of the lord, knowing that the best way to get close to a king was to gain the trust of one already at his side.

Carefully Raphael maneuvered his way toward the edge of the battlefield closest to where the lord stood watch. The fighting was thick there and he had to focus all his attention on the battle to keep from joining the ranks of the fallen. He also took care to only strike at the enemy whilst the lord might be watching. The last rays of the setting sun lit the sky when he looked up again.

There was a messenger with the lord. Raphael turned and thrust his blade through a child's stomach. The boy couldn't have been more than ten. It was his own fault for thinking he could fight beside men. He glanced back to see what was happening. Messengers came and went carrying word between the king and the lords who oversaw the battle. It shouldn't have been of import, but Raphael found himself doubling his efforts, his sword flashing silver and crimson in his sight.

"Raphael!" a knight nearby shouted to him.

"Yes?"

"The lord commands you to his side!"

"Then that is where I must go," Raphael said, drawing his sword across another throat.

He picked his way quickly through the field and then ran up the hill to the lord. He reached him and dropped to one knee obediently.

"I am Raphael of Decazeville, milord. You sent for me?"

"Rise, Raphael."

He did as he was ordered.

"The king has sent word that he needs the service of the bravest and fiercest of his warriors."

Raphael's pulse quickened. This was his moment. Still, he knew that the game was only just beginning.

"I can recommend one or two quite highly, if that is your wish," he said, feigning naïveté.

"If you do not know that you are the fiercest fighter on this field then know it now."

"I'm humbled by your consideration."

"Save your flattery for the king. You might be the fiercest fighter, but you are also one of the most reckless. Your actions often endanger your comrades needlessly. The field is better off without you. The messenger here will take you to His Majesty."

Raphael toyed with killing the man as he sat so pious on his horse. He knew better, though, than to kill a nobleman in cold blood while others could see him. He marked the man's face well in his memory. There would be nothing to keep him from finding the lord some dark night and slitting his throat while he slept.

Raphael turned aside and the messenger handed him the reins of a gray horse. He mounted with ease and was soon galloping behind the man who was taking him to see the king.

As the king's encampment came into sight Raphael smiled in triumph. This was where he belonged and it had come to pass. He expected to be made to wait and had willed himself to be calm. The king was busy with many things and it was the duty of his subjects to await his wishes. Finally, he was escorted into the king's tent.

"Sire, this is the knight you sent for. He is Raphael of Decazeville," the man said in introduction.

Raphael knelt as the king looked down on him. He was magnificent in his robes, and jewels flashed as he moved. Raphael regretted his own filthy, unkempt appearance and wished he'd had a chance to wash. His fair hair was dark from smoke and grime and gore. His long fingers were stained in blood. He had had no chance to change. His father had often told him that if he wanted to be a pig herder then it did not matter how he appeared but if he wished to make his way into the king's court then he should dress as though he belonged there.

But I am in the king's court, he thought triumphantly. He had slain dozens of enemies upon the field of battle and it had not gone unnoticed by his lord. Although, thankfully, his lord had not bothered to count the number of crusaders also dead by his hand. Some of the blood on his clothes and crusted under his fingernails was theirs.

"Arise, Raphael," the king ordered.

Raphael stood up and dared to meet the king's eyes. He realized then that the king didn't care how he looked because the king wasn't really seeing him. He seemed to be staring through him at something on the other side of the tent.

"I have need of your good sword arm, your cunning, and your loyalty."

"All that I have, all that I am, is yours to command." He didn't mind killing for the king or in the name of God. Men could do whatever they wished so long as they could attribute their deeds to one of the two.

PRAGUE, PRESENT DAY

As always, Raphael's memory was vivid, as if he was living it again for the first time. If those who forgot the past were doomed to repeat it, then vampires should be the last to ever repeat a mistake. Perfect memory of events was in itself a curse. There was no hiding the truth in the mists of time as humans so often did. "In my own mind, and in my actions I was a god. I rained death and destruction down on whom I chose, regardless if they were friend or foe."

Susan shied away from him and David renewed his efforts to sit up, despite the obvious pain it was causing him.

"That's right, boys and girls. I was a monster long before I got these," he said, exposing his fangs.

"Then, if that's true, who are you going to war against that you would expect us to help you?" David asked.

"Someone just as evil, but out of control. Someone whose soul is broken, if it was ever there at all. His name is Armand. But you will know him by a different name."

"What name?" Susan asked.

Bohemian kings and Roman emperors had called the Prague Castle home. The original castle covered eighteen acres by itself. With its labyrinth of palaces, museums, and churches there were thousands of rooms, half-forgotten spaces, and a number of secret passageways. It was the perfect place to hide, or to launch an attack.

Armand Jean du Plessis de Richelieu, once known as Cardinal-Duc de Richelieu, needed it for both purposes. It had been centuries since he had served as one of the most powerful and feared men in France, but though he had been out of the public eye for a very long time he had not forgotten how to manipulate things behind the scenes.

After faking his own death, a necessary inconvenience, he had waited and worked for this place, this time in history. The world hadn't been ready for a vampire ruler before, but times had changed.

The secularization of the modern world had left a gaping hole in the psyche of mankind. To fill it, man preoccupied his time with consideration of the supernatural—ghosts, vampires, psychics. Man was designed with a need for the spiritual, a sense of the miraculous, in life. When it became unpopular to believe in God, or to talk about angels and demons, humans found another outlet.

And as a real vampire, one who had lived for centuries, witnessing history, when he revealed himself to them, he would be worshipped as a god. It was only natural. To mere mortals his powers and abilities, his knowledge and experience, would seem godlike. They needed someone to worship.

He needed to save the world.

It worked out well.

As he thought, he stroked the bejeweled box that he held absently.

He heard the door open and he glanced up, irritated at being disturbed. The vampire standing there was one of his personal guards, dressed in crimson as was tradition, and Richelieu sighed. The man would not be disturbing him if it wasn't important.

"Your Eminence," the guard said, bowing deeply.

"What is it?"

"The girl escaped, and Raphael with her."

Rage flooded him. "Then bring me the one who failed."

The guard hesitated a moment. "He's already ashes, Eminence."

Richelieu sat back in his chair and closed his eyes. Retribution would not be his. At least, not against that one. "Bring me the Raiders," he said.

"At once."

When the guard had left Richelieu sighed and leaned his head back against his throne.

"Raphael, you know you cannot win. Why do you try?"

He moved his eyes to the box he held. He would never forget the moment he realized he was different from other vampires. It was the day Raphael had realized it, too. Richelieu had known his sire was going to kill him, in his mind he had to.

And so he had fled, taking his sire's most prized possession with him. It was only right that he should. After all, it hadn't really been Raphael's, either. It had come to him during the Crusades and he had guarded it fiercely and jealously since then.

But it belonged with someone like him. Someone who respected its power and wasn't afraid to use it. Because power was not for hiding away. Power was to be used for the good of mankind, the glory of one's country.

And who better than he, the greatest protector France had ever known, to use this awesome power? But Raphael would not give up. He had chased him for two hundred years and now at last they were both in the same city. And only one of them could survive the coming days. But while Raphael had continued his solitary existence, Richelieu had been planning, building his network of spies and allies. Raphael had taught him that the first duty of the vampire was to hide his existence from the world. That isolation and centuries of hiding would in the end be his sire's undoing.

He flipped open the box and marveled at what he saw inside.

CHAPTER NINE

Whatsoever soul it be that eateth any manner of blood,
even that soul shall be cut off from his people.

—Leviticus 7:27

From the first, Susan had sensed darkness about Raphael and a kind of evil, but not to the extent that he had told them about. There had to be more to the story than he was sharing. Otherwise why would evil fight evil? When accused of exorcising demons by the power of Satan, Christ had answered that if Satan cast out Satan then he would be divided against himself and his kingdom would fall.

No, she was prepared to believe that Raphael had been evil, but she wasn't convinced that was still true. Still, she stayed near David while a doctor examined his chart and she kept a close eye on Raphael.

She kept expecting the vampire to slip away, as he always did, when others were present, but he surprised her by staying. He had his arms folded across his chest and he was leaning against the wall, looking so casual that it seemed absurd to her who knew the truth.

The doctor finally turned and glanced at her and Raphael. "Are you family?" he asked.

"No," Susan said.

"Yes," Raphael responded at the same time.

"Visiting hours are over for all but immediate family. I'm afraid you'll have to go," he said to Susan.

"She's a patient, too," Raphael said.

"We're friends," David piped up.

The doctor nodded. "In that case you may stay a little longer, but get back to your own room and get some rest."

Susan nodded and he left.

"Which room are you in?" David asked.

Susan shook her head. "They're releasing me. I just told my family I needed a few minutes alone with my rescuer."

"You should go before they come looking for you."

Susan glanced back at David, not wanting to leave the two of them alone together.

"I promise not to kill him tonight," Raphael said.

Tonight. What about tomorrow?

She turned to look at David who nodded slowly. "And I promise not to give him a reason to want to... tonight."

She bit her lip to keep from saying something. Telling the two of them to play nice with each other would just be absurd.

"I want to know more. You've only hinted at wars and monsters, but you haven't told me much at all yet."

Raphael looked at her, eyes cold and glittering.

"You've already declared your intention to leave."

"But I want to know."

"Why?" David asked. "So you can end up even more injured, or worse, dead?"

Susan looked from Raphael to David in frustration. She heard footsteps coming down the hallway, but all she could think about was what she had just heard.

"Dead?"

"Who's dead?" Aunt Jane asked as she walked into the room.

Susan blinked at her in surprise. "No, no one. Thankfully."

"There's the hero of the day!" Jane said, moving over to David. "How do you feel?"

"Uh, okay, I guess. I've got a broken rib, but it could be worse."

"Who are you?" Uncle Bob asked Raphael unceremoniously. He wasn't usually quite so blunt but it was the middle of the night in a hospital, Susan reflected.

Before Raphael could answer Wendy walked into the room. "Oh, he's Susan's boyfriend," she said distractedly.

Boyfriend!

"What?" Jane asked, eyes wide.

Susan opened her mouth to tell her it wasn't true, that Wendy was mistaken, but she heard Raphael say, "It's true. My name is Raphael." When he spoke he used a thick accent, which made him sound more like the locals. It made him that much more attractive and she felt a catch in her throat even as she stared at him in horrified disbelief.

He was smiling broadly, though somehow managing to hide his fangs while he did so. He shot her a glance out of his eyes; it was dark and smoldering, as though defying her to say otherwise.

"Oh!" Jane said, clearly at a loss.

Bob continued to eye him uneasily but extended his

hand, which Raphael shook. "Nice to meet you, young man."

It was all Susan could do not to snort. Raphael, though, said, "A pleasure to meet you as well," without breaking stride.

It makes sense. He has to be used to people assuming that he's in his early twenties.

But he wasn't, and she had to remind herself of that as she watched the two men interact. She thought of Raphael's kiss and blushed furiously at the memory.

Wendy smiled at her. "I'm so happy you finally found someone," she said. "Just think, the two of you might be the real deal."

Susan couldn't believe it. She had never heard Raphael suggest anything to Wendy that would make her assume he was with Susan. Still, she didn't understand exactly how the mesmerism thing worked. She glared at Raphael, though he gave no indication of seeing it. He had better break his hold over Wendy like he had promised, and soon.

Or what? she asked herself sarcastically. *You can't kill him, and even if you managed it, that wouldn't help poor Wendy out.* She had to face the fact that there was nothing she could hold over his head to get him to do what she needed.

"Come on, Susan, time to get you back to the hotel," Bob said at last.

Susan glanced uneasily at Raphael. She still didn't want to leave him alone with David. She turned to David and realized that he had fallen asleep, despite the number of people present.

"He's had a hard day," she said quietly.

"Rest is the best thing for him," Jane insisted.

"You're right, of course," Raphael told her.

"Raphael, can we give you a lift somewhere?" Bob asked.

"Yes, please. I will accompany Susan back to the hotel just to make sure that she is safe."

"I see," Bob said with a slight frown. "Well, then let's get going everyone who's going."

Susan began to protest but Raphael turned and looked at her and let just the slightest hint of fang show. She shivered, knowing it was a threat. But which of them he was threatening, she wasn't entirely sure.

Ten minutes later Susan found herself in the backseat squeezed between Raphael and Wendy and feeling frightened and miserable. With every moment that passed she was painfully aware that Raphael could kill them all and she still wasn't sure why he wouldn't.

They turned down a narrow street three blocks from the hotel. Suddenly she heard her uncle shout. A man and a dog were standing in the middle of the road. Her uncle spun the steering wheel as he hit the brakes. The car began to slide and she realized that Raphael had thrown open his door and leaped out.

The car slammed into a building and the airbags deployed. Susan sat for a moment, stunned. In the middle of the backseat there was no airbag. Susan looked to her cousin, who seemed to have been knocked unconscious. So were her aunt and uncle, she quickly realized. Susan's first panicked thought was to get out and find help. She managed to slide over to where Raphael had been sitting. The door was still open and she saw Raphael fighting the man who had caused the accident. She quickly realized it was another vampire. She started to take a step outside when Raphael shouted a warning. The dog was racing toward her, growling. She grabbed the door and slammed it shut just as the animal threw itself against the glass. She jerked back in terror. It was a rottweiler, but something about it didn't look right. Its teeth were long and curved, saliva dripping from them. With a gasp she saw that its eyes were glowing just like a vampire's.

She held up her cross, pressing it to the glass in front of the dog's face. It whined and backed up. It turned its head, looking to its master for instruction, but when none came it sat down and stared at her, teeth still bared.

Behind her, Wendy groaned, and a wave of relief passed through Susan as she turned to see her cousin's eyes were open.

"I'm okay," she assured her parents, who had also come to and turned to look over the back of the front seat. They had barely noticed the dog; it had all happened so fast. As her family took stock of injuries, Susan could see glimpses of the vampires as Raphael fought for his life and theirs. Suddenly the two figures collapsed onto the ground and one turned to ash beneath a streetlight. She held her breath, fear tearing at her. Slowly, the survivor staggered to his feet and turned to look at her.

She sobbed in relief when she recognized Raphael. He took three quick strides forward and lifted the dog into the air before slamming it onto the ground on its back. He straddled it and she could hear him speaking to it, but couldn't make out the words.

The dog was barking and snarling but the sounds slowly turned into a high-pitched whine. Then Raphael got up. The dog jumped to its feet and raced off into the darkness.

Susan leaped from the car and flew to him. "What?"

"He was one of the Raiders. Time to get out of here."

"But the dog, he was a vampire."

"I noticed. It's forbidden... cursing animals. He got what he deserved."

"What did you do to the dog?"

"I freed him from his old master and sent him into the forest."

"But... he's a vampire. You should have—"

"I don't kill dogs," he snarled.

"But—"

"I don't care what he was. I've never hurt a dog and I'm not going to start regardless of the reason."

The fury in his voice was overwhelming and she took a step back.

"Susan," he said, grabbing her shoulders and giving her a shake. "We have to go now."

"To the hotel?"

"You can't go back to the hotel. You need to come away with me right now."

"I'm not going to abandon my family," she protested. "Besides, the sun's almost up."

Raphael growled low in his throat. "If one Raider found you the rest can't be far behind. They already know you're staying at the hotel. And they've already put your family at risk."

She bit her lip. "I'll move before sunset."

"Where will you go?"

"I don't know, maybe home," she snapped. "Then, at least, I'll be safe."

He looked away.

"What?" she pressed.

"If they've marked you, it doesn't matter where you go. They won't stop hunting you until you're dead."

"What are you saying?"

"I'm saying you're not safe until they're dead. Your best chance of surviving is to stick close to me."

Which was exactly what she didn't want to do. He frightened her. He also intrigued her, which frightened her even more.

"Susan?" she heard Wendy call weakly.

"Are you going to mesmerize them?" she asked.

"No. They swerved to avoid a man and a dog. It's perfect, no mess. They didn't see what happened afterward."

She nodded and turned back to the car. "Is everyone okay?" she called out.

She heard some groaning, followed by a yes from each person. The airbags had deflated and all three carefully got out of the car, shaky on their feet. "We need to call the police and report this," Bob said.

"Susan, are you okay?" Wendy asked.

She nodded, but realized that every moment that passed was bringing another vampire closer to all of them. She had to get some distance and fast. "I'll walk to the hotel and send back help," she volunteered.

"It's not safe to go alone," Bob said. "Crazies on the street this time of night."

"I'll go with her," Raphael and Wendy said simultaneously.

"I'll escort the young ladies," Raphael continued, his voice deepening slightly.

"Good idea," Jane said. "We'll wait here."

They turned and swiftly made their way toward the hotel. Susan jumped at every shadow that presented itself and even screamed when a cat climbed down a stairwell nearby. Wendy grabbed her hand and she could tell the other girl shared her terror even though she probably had no idea why she felt as she did.

They arrived back at the hotel and made their way to the front desk. The clerk behind it recognized them and began apologizing profusely before they could say anything.

"We are deeply sorry for all the unpleasantness and inconvenience. We have moved you to a new room in light of the condition of your old room and the memories that must now be associated with it."

"But all of my things," she began.

He held up a hand. "We had your things moved as well. You should find everything in order. Here is the key."

She took the key he handed her and glanced around at the others.

"Thank heavens," Wendy said. "I couldn't have slept in that room tonight."

Susan thought of the broken window, shattered chair, and the mound of ash in the room. She was grateful to not have to spend the night with any of that, but her heart raced as she hoped that the box would still be hidden safely in her bag.

"We were in a car accident on the way here," Susan explained.

"Oh no!" the clerk said, his eyes widening in dismay.

"My aunt and uncle are with the car still. Could you please send help?"

"Are they injured?"

"I don't think so, but they need assistance."

She described the location and he promised to send the authorities there right away. For a moment she thought about heading back, but realized they would probably be a lot safer without her around. She flirted with sending Wendy back, but didn't want her walking back alone.

As they climbed the stairs she could feel Raphael's eyes on her. She tried to still her heart, afraid that he could hear it. When they exited the stairwell she walked quickly toward her new room, Wendy a step behind her.

She slid the key card into the slot and twisted the handle. The door swung open easily and she stepped inside. Wendy made a beeline for the nearest bed and sat down on it with a sigh.

"Raphael, I'll see you later."

He laughed, a slow, sexy laugh. "You don't want me to go yet; invite me in for a little while, just to make sure you're okay."

She gaped at him, but didn't know what to say. The look in his eyes told her he wasn't playing around, though, and she was afraid of what else he would say or do if she left him standing out there.

"Um, sure, come in," she said, in a small voice.

She closed and locked the door quickly and then turned to glare at him. He was standing in the middle of the room, an arrogant look on his face.

"What a night," Wendy sighed.

Without even turning his head to look at her Raphael said, "Sleep."

Wendy fell backward, her head landing on the pillow.

"Don't do that to her!" Susan exclaimed.

"You'd prefer to have this conversation with her listening?" Raphael asked, lifting one eyebrow.

She couldn't think of a thing to say in response. Instead she turned aside to her suitcase and rifled through it. To her relief she discovered the box nestled deep within.

"So, what is in that box that is so important to you?"

"Nothing," she said.

He made a hissing sound and then he was standing in front of her, grabbing her chin and forcing her to look into his eyes. "Don't lie to me."

"It's none of your business."

"As of right now anything that has to do with you most certainly is my business."

"Don't bury yourself in the role. You're not my boyfriend," she said.

He smiled. "Is that what you think I'm doing, playing the role of boyfriend?"

"Aren't you?"

He laughed low and deep and hard. "No, Susan of Bryas. If I was playing the role of your lover you would know it."

Raphael stared into Susan's defiant eyes. She was tired and hurt, but still had the strength of will to stand up to him, to defy him. That made her one in a million. He held her chin and continued to stare down at her. Her lips trembled with anger. Or was it fear?

He breathed in deeply. There were lingering traces of fear about her, but that wasn't what made her tremble. It had to be anger then.

She grabbed his hand and flung it away from her and he let her do it.

"What's in the box, Susan?" he asked, quieting his voice.

"I wouldn't tell you, not even if you were my—"

He slid his arms around her waist and pulled her close, sealing her lips with his own. She stiffened, grabbing his arms and trying to push away. And then, she stopped.

Her skin grew warmer, her body became more fluid, and she was kissing him back. It inflamed something deep inside and he kissed her harder, deeper, and she matched his intensity, sliding her arms up around his neck.

And this time there were no games, no mesmerism. This time she truly wanted him. He could feel it in the curve of her body, the subtly changing scent of her skin. She pressed closer to him until her desire became his desire. Until all he could feel was her. All that he wanted was her.

He picked her up in his arms and she didn't fight him. He kissed her mouth, her cheeks, her jaw. And then he made his way to her throat. As his lips touched the hot skin passion exploded in his brain. He had to have her. He crushed her tight and she gasped.

He bared his fangs and slid them down the soft skin, looking for the place where he would bite her. Sudden searing pain flashed through his jaw and with a roar he jerked his head back, dropping her onto her feet.

She landed with a thud and then toppled backward, falling onto the floor with a startled cry.

With his hand he felt a thin line of burned flesh tracing a path across cheek and chin, touching the corner of his mouth. Bewildered he looked down at her and then saw the chain that held her cross glinting around her throat.

The chain. The chain had burned him even though it

shouldn't have. He crashed to his knees in horror at what he had almost done, at what it had almost cost them both. She scrambled to a sitting position, eyes wide with terror, and her scent changed again.

In that moment he realized that she was more afraid of him than she ever had been before.

She was right to be afraid.

"What did you do to me?" Susan whispered, even though she knew in her heart that he had done nothing. This time it had been her kissing him, wanting him, wanting things she had never even dared to let herself think about before. Just like he had told her she would after that first kiss.

What was wrong with her? She was just so exhausted and hurt and afraid and so very tired of being all of those things. She had read somewhere once that the same chemicals in the brain that were linked to fear were also linked to desire.

Was that all it was, just a bunch of crazy hormones and enough exhaustion that I didn't try to fight them? That had to be it. There was no way she could have wanted to kiss him on her own.

He didn't kill the dog. Even when he should have.

She stared up at him and saw the line of scorched flesh on his face, and she didn't know what had caused it. He buried his head in his hands and it was the most human gesture she had seen him make.

"I'm sorry. I almost killed you," he said.

"But you didn't."

"No."

"Why?"

He looked at her. "The chain on your cross, it touched me, it burned me. It made me stop."

She touched the cross. Her grandmother could never have guessed it would save her life. But looking at Raphael she could see his pain, his fear. It wasn't the scorch mark on his face that hurt him or the cross that frightened him. *He doesn't want to kill me.* She shook her head slowly. "The burn got your attention, but I don't think that's what made you stop."

"I don't know what you mean."

"Why don't you want to kill me?"

"But I do."

"But you don't. A hundred times over you could have killed me. You said in the hospital that you were a monster, the most evil of the evil. So, why don't you kill me?"

"I need you."

The look he gave her was so vulnerable it took her breath away. She shook her head in wonder. For just a moment it was possible to see him as something other than the dark, frightening killer that he portrayed himself as. *The dark, frightening killer he is, forget that and you're dead*, she reminded herself.

She reached out and grabbed his hand. He nearly crushed it in his own.

"Why do you need me?" she asked.

"I just... I just do."

"Why me? I need something better here than a 'because' or a half-truth. I need to understand."

"There aren't many people who can handle the truths of my existence or the war that's coming with others of my kind. Most people don't truly understand the nature of good and evil."

"And you think I do?"

He nodded. "I've...met...members of your family before, going back to long before you were born. They have always shown great courage and the innate ability to understand good and evil in very real, very complex ways. So many people see the world as black and white. Increasingly many people see the world as shades of gray with no black and white. The truth is there is black and white and many, many shades of gray. The supernatural exists, right alongside the natural. Evil people can become good with enough time and good people can become evil with enough provocation."

"That's both encouraging and terrible."

"Exactly, but you don't have a problem accepting it as truth."

She shook her head. "Why would I?"

The ghost of a smile twisted his lips. "And the fact that you are puzzled by that is exactly what makes you special, exactly why I need you in this battle."

"I still don't understand how I can fight against vampires and possibly hope to bring something to the table there."

"I watched you in that cathedral the other day."

She shivered at the memory.

"You could sense my presence. That is a gift. You are gifted with discernment and can use that to feel evil, know where it is and how to reach it or avoid it. It's a skill you can learn to hone. Also, vampires are compelled to sleep during the day, including me. I need warriors, people who can kill vampires when they are at their most vulnerable. It's safe for humans to hunt during the day and I will do my best to protect you by night."

"So, you do need David as well."

Raphael shook his head. "He seems to have volunteered himself and I have decided to accept the help. The more people I bring in the more dangerous it gets for everyone. We can't risk exposing the secret to the world. And I can only protect so many."

"There's a lot you haven't told me."

"More than you know."

"I'm going to need you to trust me if you expect me to trust you."

He nodded. "It's a fair request." He was regaining his composure. She could watch it just as she was watching the skin on his cheek heal. Both were unnerving. Within moments it would be like his injury, his vulnerability, had never happened.

And what of our kiss? Will it be like that never happened, too? she wondered.

"I will help you," she said.

"Thank you."

"But I need to know more. Start by telling me why that vampire was different. You called him a Raider."

"The Raiders are four warriors who rode with Quantrill during the American Civil War committing atrocities, few of which have ever even been heard of. They were raised together; vicious and cruel in life, they were recruited by my enemy and now in death are his fiercest assassins. They never stop once set upon someone. They can and will track them to the ends of the earth. Now that I've killed one of them, the other three will know and will not be far behind."

Raphael stood and began to pace in front of Susan, reminding her of tigers she had seen at the zoo. There was a coiled strength about him, a sense that at any moment he could pounce and crush his prey.

She just hoped she wasn't that prey.

It seemed so unbelievable to her that he was there, in her room, an actual vampire. She scoured her memories trying to recall if her grandmother's stories had ever included vampires. Gypsies had figured prominently in many of them along with the occasional ghost and even a werewolf. But vampires? She couldn't remember any. And now she was being protected by one and hunted by others.

Raphael finally stopped pacing and stared at her, eyes narrowed. "Susan, it's not an accident that we met."

"You've been stalking me...since the church," she accused.

"Our involvement goes back a lot further than that," he said with a faint smile. "Two destinies crossing and uncrossing, never touching exactly, but so very close to each other. But that is a story for another time."

"You're not making any sense."

"No, I suppose I'm not. In a few years I'll be nine hundred years old, a vampire for most of that."

Curiosity stirred deep within her. "You said you were cursed, by who?"

"Some would say by God Himself. In my particular case His instrument was a nobleman, a vampire named Gabriel. He was one of the lords present in Damascus during the fighting. Dark stories swirled around him, frightening. He had the ear of the king himself, or so it seemed to others. I've never met anyone who scares me like he does, even to this day. He was the one who cursed me."

"Why?"

"Because I deserved it."

"You said you were evil, and I believe you. There are times when I can feel it, but I don't think you are evil now."

"Not anymore it would seem."

"Explain."

He nodded his head. "I told you earlier that vampirism was a curse bestowed upon an evil person by another vampire."

"Yes."

Raphael stared hard at Susan, trying to see only her and not the past that twisted and writhed like a living thing inside his mind. He could smell it, taste it; sometimes it seemed more real to him than the present. One could only repent for the past if one could remember it clearly and vampires were gifted with perfect clarity of remembrance so that their crimes, their victims, would live forever in their minds in a hell of their own making.

"I was a very evil man and the only way for the unrepentantly evil to find salvation is to be forced to live long enough with themselves to see the error of their ways. Vampirism is a curse bestowed upon so few, because so few are beyond the call of God in the span of an ordinary lifetime."

"I don't believe that," she whispered.

He shrugged. "Believe what you will, but it is how it was told to me. And I can attest that I wouldn't even accept the possibility of God for the first three hundred years. Age brings wisdom. Some acquire it more slowly than others."

"And now?" she asked.

He turned away. "I believe that I believe there is a God. I'm just not sure what He wants of humanity, let alone me."

"That's not a very good answer."

"And yet it has taken me nearly a millennia to come up with it. As I said, enlightenment takes time for some. So, I was cursed. And, eventually, I found one who was in need of cursing. I turned him, changed him into a vampire. But something was wrong. Instead of bringing temperance and penitence, age only made him worse."

Susan shook her head. "Even if what you say is true, what does all this have to do with me?"

"An excellent question."

Raphael took a deep breath as he struggled with how much to tell Susan so soon. The night was quickly fading, and it offered him an excuse. "I promise to answer the rest of your questions later, but right now I want to make you as safe as possible," he said.

"How are we going to do that?" she asked.

"Keep wearing that cross. Never take it off. Sleep with it."

"Okay."

"And you're going to want to get some garlic."

"That really works?"

"Yes."

"What does it do?"

He hesitated, hating going into detail. But he needed to trust her if he was going to use her and continue to put her life in danger. "It produces a sort of allergic reaction. It makes us nauseous and weak."

"How weak?"

"Used effectively it can incapacitate one of us."

"Why?"

"I don't have time to explain why right now," he growled. The truth was, all vampires wondered the same thing. There was a rumor, a legend, dating back to the very first vampire, but he still wasn't sure he believed it.

"What else?"

He took a deep breath. "We have to secure the hotel room."

"Don't worry, I won't be inviting anyone else I don't know inside, not even by accident."

"It's more than that. We don't actually need an invitation to come in."

Her eyes widened. "But you said—"

"I said it was polite. I didn't say it was required. We just like people to think it is."

"Then, vampires, those Raiders, could come crashing through that door right now!" Her eyes flew to Wendy, the fear for her cousin bright in her eyes.

"That's why we have to protect it, the window, too."

"How do we do that?"

"Are you familiar with the Biblical story of the first Passover when the Jews were trying to leave Egypt?"

"Yes. The angel of death came and took every first-born. The way to escape it was to sacrifice a lamb and smear its blood on the door frame to mark the house so the angel of death wouldn't enter."

"The blood of the lamb worked to repulse the angel of death. We can do something similar to stop vampires from entering. Think of it as a magic force field, God's gift of protection to humans."

"How come I've never heard of it in all the vampire legends?"

"Because we've worked hard to suppress the knowledge. Bram Stoker knew the truth when he was writing *Dracula*. One of my kind mesmerized him and forced him to forget."

"How does this help me, though? I'm fresh out of sacrificial lambs and I couldn't bring myself to kill one even if I wasn't."

"Fortunately, you don't have to. The blood sacrifice of the lamb works against the angel of death. Repelling my kind requires a different kind of blood sacrifice and it must be made by one who dwells inside the place where it was put."

"A hotel room isn't exactly a house or an apartment."

"So long as you sleep here, it doesn't matter if it is only temporary."

She took a deep breath and he could tell she was preparing herself mentally. "What kind of blood sacrifice are you talking about?"

He smiled. "Yours."

CHAPTER TEN

And the blood shall be to you for a token upon the houses where ye are: and when I see the blood, I will pass over you, and the plague shall not be upon you to destroy you, when I smite the land of Egypt.

—Exodus 12:13

Susan stared at Raphael in horror, convinced that she didn't want to know what he was saying. Finally she found her voice and asked, "Mine?"

He nodded. "You must spill a little of your own blood to ensure the safety of those inside this room."

He glanced over toward Wendy, but Susan continued to stare at him.

"How much?"

"Not much, a few drops will do. You can prick your finger and spread it on the outside of the door frame and window casing."

"That's it?"

He nodded and she felt herself sag in relief.

"Let's do the door first," he said, moving toward it.

She followed and he opened the door. There was no one in the hallway and he turned to her. "Do you have a needle, anything sharp?"

"No."

She saw a blur of motion, felt a tug followed by a sharp prick on the index finger of her left hand, and stared dumbfounded a moment later as blood bubbled to the surface from a small cut.

"What just happened?"

"I scratched you. It wasn't my first choice, but there you have it. Now press your finger against the outside of the frame."

"Where?"

"Anywhere, just make sure you smear some blood on it. Fortunately the wood will disguise it so you shouldn't have to worry about overzealous maids."

Dutifully, Susan pressed her bleeding fingertip against the wood to the right side of the door, sliding it down about half an inch. When she pulled it away the wood looked wet and shiny. She wondered for a brief moment if hers was the first blood that had graced it, but then forced herself to focus as she began to feel squeamish.

"So, I don't have to do both sides and the top?"

"No. Now it's getting late and it's time to do the window."

She stepped back inside and he closed the door behind her and vanished. She blinked in shock and then turned and saw him at the far end of the room, shoulders hunched, eyes glowing.

"Are you okay?"

"It has become very uncomfortable to be here. Once you finish the job it will be impossible."

"But, I have more questions."

He shook his head. "The night is almost over. They will have to wait for tomorrow night." He looked at her pointedly. "Will you still be here?"

She nodded slowly.

"I will come for you then. Wait in this room."

He opened the window and climbed out. "Seal this one off behind me," he said. "I will stay until I see that you have."

He dropped from sight. She hurried over and looked down to see him standing on the street.

She pressed her finger against the outside of the window casing and he took several steps back before giving her a thumbs-up sign. Then he turned and melted into the night.

She closed the window, making sure to latch it. The blood might ward off vampires, but it took locks to ward off humans. When the phone on the nightstand rang, it made her jump. She answered, and was relieved to hear Aunt Jane's voice. They were back at the hotel and wanted to see Wendy, but when Susan told her Wendy was sleeping, they decided to go to bed themselves and come by in the morning.

Susan showered and put on her nightgown, then slid under the covers of the new bed and tried to go to sleep.

From the next bed Wendy snored softly. Raphael still hadn't released her cousin from his sway. Until he did that, no matter how much Susan wanted to go home, she couldn't.

Home.

Where was it? Her little apartment back in California? Or a piece of land she had never seen in France? She thought of the key tucked safely away with the deed. What did it unlock? She was fairly convinced that it opened something inside the home in France. Otherwise why box them together? And why make her come all the way to Prague to get them?

Her thoughts returned to the lawyer, Pierre, and she shuddered. He had frightened her with what he said about Raphael. More than that, though, she had been unnerved by how very much he wanted to see the cross.

She reached up and touched it to reassure herself it was still there.

Why would he care?

Why did anyone care about her or anything she had?

As she lay there, unable to sleep, the sun rose, spilling its light inside the room. What she would have given for a little of its illumination in her heart and mind. Finally she gave up, rose, and got dressed. She needed to talk to someone and only one person came to mind.

To her relief she found her great-uncle Clarence downstairs having breakfast by himself. She sat down at the table and he raised an eyebrow. "Heard about what happened to you. You okay?"

"Yes, thank you," she said, wishing she could tell him what actually did happen to her. Sitting across from him she began to wonder if it had been such a good idea to seek him out in the first place.

The waitress came by and Susan ordered some food just to have some excuse to continue sitting there without having to tell him why she had sought him out. It didn't work. As soon as her food arrived he looked at her with shrewd eyes.

"So, what did you want to ask me?"

"You said that Grandmother came back here twice?"

He nodded. "Once in her twenties and again about three years ago."

"How come I didn't know?"

He smiled. "Constance liked to play her cards close to the vest. She had secrets even I don't know."

"But why?"

"When Constance wouldn't talk about things it was either to keep people from getting hurt or to keep them from interfering with something she felt she needed to do. My guess is that no one knew for one of those two reasons."

"Did she hint at why she came?"

"No. And believe me, I asked. In the end, though, I figured she had her own particular purposes."

She forced herself to eat a few bites of food. When she looked up again he was still staring at her.

"Now, are you going to ask me what you really came down here to ask?"

It almost made her smile because it was so like something her grandmother would have said. Apparently the two of them shared the ability to read people.

"Do you believe in the supernatural?"

"I'm a Christian. Believing in stuff I can't see or explain kind of goes with the territory."

"I'm not talking about God or the devil or angels, but other...things."

"Ask what you got to ask, honey."

"Do you believe in, say, ghosts or magic or vampires?" she tried to sound casual and knew she failed miserably.

"Are you asking me if I believe vampires exist?" he asked.

"Yes."

"I don't believe they exist."

She nodded her head slowly, disappointed. She looked at him and then he gave her the smallest of winks.

"Susan, I *know* they exist."

* * *

Raphael lay on his bed, struggling against the sleep that was forcing itself upon him. He needed to be stronger, better, if he was going to fight Armand and take back that which was rightfully his. That which had been entrusted to him.

DAMASCUS, 1148

"I understand that you are a rather efficient soldier," the king said.

Raphael longed to give a brief demonstration but had to content himself with responding, "What I do is for the glory of God and Your Majesty."

"You may have to kill a great many in order to carry out the task I have for you. Although, let us pray that is not the case."

"Yes. Pray," he said, trying hard to hide the pleasure the thought gave him.

The king signaled and a young man Raphael's age stepped forward. Unlike Raphael he was washed and dressed in clean clothes but he looked ill at ease in the company he was keeping. In his hand he held a small wooden box encrusted with a few jewels. It was lovely, but paled in comparison to the jewels that adorned the king's person.

"This is Jean, the new Marquis de Bryas, and he brought us a most excellent gift...for the pope."

Louis held out his hand and Jean gave him the box before retreating back to a corner of the tent. His discomfort was clear and it sparked Raphael's curiosity.

"You want me to take it to Rome?"

"No!" the king said, a little too forcefully. "To France. It must be kept safe until I can personally hand it to His Eminence."

"May I ask what I am to protect with my life?" Raphael asked.

The king gave him a thin smile and then opened the box. He stared inside, struggling to understand the significance of what he was seeing.

"I want you to depart at once. Make haste and let none take this from you," the king was saying.

PRAGUE, PRESENT DAY

But in that, as in many other things, he had failed. And with that failure foremost in his thoughts, Raphael succumbed to sleep.

Susan stared at her uncle in disbelief. He gave her a weary smile and drank the last of his coffee.

"You asked."

"How do you know that?"

He narrowed his eyes as though studying her. "Probably the same way you do. I met one once. It was when I was very young. Kept it to myself all these years, figured no one would believe me."

"Tell me about it," she begged.

He glanced at his watch. "Honey, I'd love to, but I've got to leave so I can catch my plane." He reached over and patted her hand. "Don't worry, we can talk all about it in a few days when you get home."

She stared at him disbelievingly. *What if I don't make it home?* she wanted to ask him. In a tired voice she squeaked, "I don't know what to do."

"Stay out of the way, that's the best thing you can do, in my experience," he said. "Seriously, honey, don't get mixed up with one. I know they're not exactly what people think they are, but they're dangerous just the same."

She bit her lip, wanting to tell him everything. Before she could say anything else, though, he looked at his watch again, threw a couple of bills on the table, and stood. He kissed the top of her head. "See you back in California. Be safe."

"Thanks," she murmured to his retreating back. She continued to sit for a long time, just staring and thinking. And the thing she wished the most was that she had asked her uncle the name of the vampire he'd met.

David woke up and the clock on the table next to his hospital bed declared it to be one in the afternoon. He winced as he tried to turn, not wanting to put more strain on his ribs than he had to.

"Do you need any help?" a woman's voice asked.

He turned his head slowly until he could see the speaker. It was Wendy. He blinked at her in surprise. "What are you doing here?" he asked.

She gave him a dazzling smile and tossed her blond hair. "Playing nurse."

"Why?" he asked.

She moved around the bed so he could see her clearly. She picked up his hand and stared intently into his eyes. "Don't laugh, this is going to sound a little crazy."

"That would be par for the course this week," he said, returning her smile.

"Okay, it's just that somehow, in some weird way, I feel like it was me you saved, not my cousin. I feel like you came to my rescue." She rolled her eyes. "I know that makes no sense."

She started to pull away but he squeezed her hand tight. "Actually, it makes perfect sense," he said.

Her smile widened even more and he forgot about the pain in his side. "So, nurse, what do you recommend?"

"I recommend that you have some of the delicious-looking Jell-O they brought you while you were asleep and that you tell Nurse Wendy all about yourself."

Without letting go of his hand she pulled a chair forward and sat down.

"Actually, I'd rather hear all about Nurse Wendy."

"Okay, what do you want to know?"

"Everything. What do you do?"

"For a living? Nothing yet. I'm graduating in two more quarters. I was about to switch to theater studies, but I'm thinking I might stick out political science after all."

"So, you're a senior," he said. She was younger than he thought, but still probably only about four years his junior. Four years was okay.

"Yup. UC Davis."

"That's a really good school."

She nodded enthusiastically. "What about you?"

"I'm a computer programmer for Suntech. I'm over here on a three-month assignment helping with a research and development project."

"Sounds exciting."

"Not really," he said, smirking slightly as he realized

he'd already had far more excitement than he'd anticipated having during his entire trip.

A doctor entered, interrupting. Wendy got up and
moved a discreet distance away, waiting while he and the
doctor spoke for a few minutes.

"You need to immobilize that broken rib as best you
can for about three weeks. Keep it wrapped up and try not
to overly exert yourself."

"Anything else?"

"No. You're free to go."

Relief flooded David. "Thank you, Doctor."

The man gave him a brief nod and then left.

Wendy stepped forward with a grin. "Looks like
you've been given your freedom. Can I escort you back
to the hotel?"

He smiled at her. "That would be fantastic."

"Good." She moved to the closet and grabbed
David's shirt, which was hanging there. She brought it
to him and gave him a coy smile. "Do you need help
putting it on?"

"If I say yes will you think less of me?" he asked, unable to stop himself from flirting back.

"Not even a little bit," she said, her smile slipping
slightly as it was replaced by a more thoughtful look.

"I should probably try to put it on myself, you know,
get used to working around the broken rib," he said, suddenly feeling nervous and foolish.

She nodded. "That's probably best."

It hurt, but he managed to struggle into his shirt and
he buttoned it quickly, staring at her. She had turned half
away as he was doing so and her cheeks were tinged with
pink. He hadn't thought she would embarrass so easily,

but he was glad to see it. Something told him that there was a lot more to Wendy than met the eye.

"So, you ready to get out of here?"

"Lead the way," he said, standing up gingerly from the bed.

Outside she hailed a cab and the two fell silent on the ride back to the hotel. He couldn't help but study her surreptitiously. It was strange. In many ways he had known her longer than she had known him. The fact that she had no memory of that first, all so brief, encounter was still unnerving to him.

When they arrived at the hotel he realized that their time together was bound to come to a quick end once they reached his room. They were strangers to each other and as much as she had enjoyed joking about being his nurse she wasn't going to stay to talk with him.

He was exhausted, mentally and physically, but he didn't know when he would see her again. For all he knew now that the funeral was over she was getting ready to hop a plane for home. The fear of not seeing her again cut through his pain and weariness.

"You know, I really must complain about the service in that hospital," he said as he got out of the cab.

"Why? Did they hurt you?" she asked, eyes widening.

"In a manner of speaking. They killed my appetite."

"Complaining about hospital food?" she asked.

He smiled. "Only thing worse than airplane food."

"There's a café around the corner that should be serving lunch."

"I thought you'd never ask."

She turned and began walking and he fell into step beside her. He wasn't really hungry. His stomach was still unsettled from some of the painkillers they had given him, but he refused to let her go without at least trying to get to know her better.

On an impulse he brushed her fingers with his. She didn't move away. Emboldened he caught her index finger with his and held it. They walked like that for several steps before slowly intertwining their fingers.

"So, political science. You want to rule the free world someday?"

"Why stop there?" she said with a laugh. "I mean, there's an entire universe out there just dying to be ruled."

"Empress of the universe. I like it."

"I'm glad someone does. Hey, then my family would have to respect me, right? I guess in the end it's better to rule than be ruled."

He smirked. "Better to reign in hell than serve in heaven."

"I wouldn't go that far," she said. "No, I just think that too many people let life happen to them, they don't study the past or anticipate the future. Half of them don't even understand the present."

"Sometimes I'm pretty sure I don't," he admitted.

"What's not to understand?" she asked, turning to look at him.

Why you're here with me, why you don't remember me, how vampires exist and what it is I should think or feel or do about it. He took a deep breath.

"What his story is," he said, nodding toward a man sitting on a bench across the street, clutching a bunch of flowers in his fist and wearing a bright red cowboy hat.

She laughed softly. "Let's see. He's met a woman, been corresponding with her, but they haven't shared pictures yet. She's agreed to meet him at last, somewhere public because she is cautious. He told her that he'd be wearing the hat because he was afraid of her not seeing him or mistaking someone else for him. He figured nobody would wear a hat that obnoxious here on the streets of Prague."

He stared at her, completely enchanted.

"What?" she asked after a minute.

"I never met someone else who does that, makes up stories for people they pass by. It's fantastic."

She smiled coyly. "I could make a pretty great story up for you, but I don't have to."

"And why is that?"

"Because you already have a great story."

He stopped abruptly. "What makes you think that?"

"You have to have a great story. Only people with great stories carry secrets as burdensome as yours."

David was stunned as he stared at Wendy. "How do you know I'm carrying a secret?"

"It's written all over your face. It's there every time I look at you. Don't feel bad. I'm not going to ask you about it."

They continued walking and a minute later reached the café. As Wendy perused the menu David looked at her instead. The waiter took her order after a few minutes and then turned to him. David pointed to something on the menu.

"What did you get?" she asked curiously after the waiter had left.

He shook his head. "I don't know," he confessed.

She laughed so hard he thought she was going to hurt herself. When the food finally came David was pleasantly surprised by his chicken in wild mushroom sauce.

"Okay, so you. Do you make a habit of going around and rescuing women?"

He nearly choked on his food before remembering that she had no memory of him trying to rescue her. She was only referring to her cousin. He quickly took a drink of water and fought to regain his composure.

"Sorry about that," he said at last. "To answer your question, yeah, I guess I kind of do. It's a bad habit."

"I've heard of worse," she said with a smile that lit up the room. "So, how does a guy in this day and age become a knight in shining armor?"

"I don't think of myself as a knight in shining armor."

"Then what would you call it?"

"Being a good man, a dutiful son, I don't know. My dad served in the army. He was killed when I was very young. I don't remember him really. But my mom always talked about him, set him up as this amazing hero like in the old-time myths. He was Hercules and Samson and Lancelot all rolled into one."

"Big shoes to fill."

"Yeah, I guess. Mom always called me her little miracle, the best gift Dad ever gave her. When I grew up I wanted to join the military like him, fight for my country, protect people."

"Why didn't you?"

"Because I knew it would break her heart if something happened to me, too. As much as I wanted to save the world it was more important to me to save her. So, I went to college, then got a job working for a computer company."

"I'd like to meet the woman who commands so much loyalty and devotion," Wendy said, her tone sincere.

"I wish you could. She died two years ago. Breast cancer. I couldn't save her from that."

Wendy reached across the table and took his hand. Looking at her he felt that he would endure any pain, suffer any trial, if she would keep holding his hand like that and smiling at him like an angel.

Raphael awoke and waited impatiently for the paralysis to pass. When it had he sat up with a groan. Paul was sitting, staring at him with an amused expression on his face.

"Woman trouble?"

"Don't joke," Raphael growled.

"Seriously, what are you doing?"

"We need warriors who can move in daylight."

"If that was your only concern, you'd have asked Gabriel for help."

Raphael's hair stood on end and he gritted his teeth. "I don't think I need him around."

"One of these days you're going to have to make peace with him."

"If we both live that long then someday I will."

But how do you make peace with someone who did that to you? To someone who saw you as a monster and called you what you were? And how do you make peace with someone who terrifies you still?

Raphael closed his eyes, shuddering as he always did when thoughts of his sire came.

OUTSIDE DAMASCUS, 1148

Raphael was headed to France, on his quest for the king. Night had fallen and he had made camp, as he had a thousand times before. But something seemed different. He thought about the gift that the king wanted him to carry that was for the pope. All of those people had believed in it, in what they thought it was and what it meant, and yet he couldn't see why.

"There is no God," Raphael said aloud.

"You know that's not true," a voice purred in his ear.

Raphael turned, his knife in his hand. There was no one there. Heart pounding he looked around. The nearest cover was fifty feet distant. No one could have moved so quickly that he would not have seen them.

The hair on the back of his neck stood on end and he found himself gasping for air as a man drowning. "Who's there?" he shouted.

The wind rustling the tops of the trees was all that answered him.

He had heard a voice. He knew he had. Yet no man stood before him.

God?

"Who's there?" he whispered.

There was no one. He couldn't have imagined it, though. The voice had been soft but filled with a raw power the likes of which he had never heard. Perhaps it was the ghost of some long dead holy man chastising him for his unbelief.

Whatever it had been Raphael wanted to saddle up and continue riding. There was no moon, though, and he didn't want to ride blindly through the forest.

He finished making camp, and the fire did a little to dispel the shadows gathering around him. Still, he felt uneasy and couldn't shake the feeling that something lurked just beyond the reach of his eyes. Whatever it was it seemed content to wait, though.

Before lying down to sleep he made sure that both sword and dagger were nearby and could be reached in the blink of an eye.

Just before dawn Raphael was awoken by the sound of his horse screaming in fear. He grabbed his weapons and leaped to his feet. The sound stopped as swiftly as it had begun but he ran to where he had left the animal.

The horse's silhouette was at last visible to him. The beast was still on its feet but its whole body had an oddly lax posture, as though he were asleep.

He looked all around but could discern nothing that should have frightened the animal so. It was a horse trained for war and tested on countless battlefields. Not easily would he startle.

He reached the horse and put a hand on its neck. There was some dampness on the creature. Sweat? Raphael pulled his hand away and as the first rays of the sun broke the horizon he saw that what he had thought was sweat was blood.

There were still several drops of it on the horse's neck as well. Raphael spun around again. What manner of creature could have done this? There was nothing there, just shadows that retreated before the rising sun. His fear from the night before returned threefold.

He quickly saddled the horse and gathered his things. The animal was placid and his steps were slightly sluggish as they set out into the forest.

They rode straight through the day, stopping only once to allow man and beast some water. When evening came he considered riding straight on but he could tell his mount was exhausted and he had no way of knowing how far he would have to travel before he could find a new one.

He made camp quickly. As the sun slipped below the

horizon he unsheathed his sword and stood watching the fading light.

There was a soft laugh and Raphael spun around.

A tall man was standing before him with dark hair and piercing eyes that seemed to shine with an unearthly light. He wore a long cloak but Raphael could discern nothing else of his dress.

"Good evening, Raphael."

"You have me at a disadvantage." Raphael raised his sword slowly but knew in his heart that it wouldn't protect him.

"I am Gabriel, Lord of Avignon."

"Why is milord here?" Raphael asked, lowering his weapon.

"I have been watching you closely for a while now."

Raphael shuddered and took several steps back. He had spent the last couple of years doing his best to be noticed but not by this man. There was something about him, some subtle menace that was beyond Raphael's ability to explain but he felt it nonetheless.

"Why have you been watching me?" he challenged.

"You have invited the attention yourself. Let's just say I was curious about what manner of man you are."

"And what manner of man am I?" Raphael asked.

"A monster." Gabriel smiled and Raphael wanted to run but couldn't.

PRAGUE, PRESENT DAY

"Raphael, what do you plan to do about Michael?" Paul asked, interrupting his train of thought.

"What?"

"While you've been dealing with your humans, I've been searching for any sign of him or Armand. The two have both hidden themselves well."

"They must have if you can't find them," Raphael said, struggling to put the dark memory behind him.

"I didn't say I couldn't."

"You found them?" Raphael asked, starting up.

"I found Michael. He's well guarded by humans and a few vampires. Not a surprise there."

"Unfortunately no."

"We're not ready to go up against him."

"But we'll need to be soon," Raphael said with a weary sigh. "Before he makes a move against us. If we know he's in the city odds are good that he knows we're here."

"Well, you, at any rate. You haven't learned to make yourself inconspicuous."

"I need to go to Susan," Raphael said. He had already wasted precious moments talking when he should have been hurrying to collect her and take her somewhere safer where the Raiders weren't looking for her.

"Why her?"

"She's special. I felt it when I was watching her pray in the church. There's a strength, a power about her. And she's related to Carissa of Bryas."

Paul stood swiftly, eyes glowing. "Does she have the cross necklace?"

He nodded.

Paul's excitement washed through the room and Raphael felt a small victory in having moved his grandsire to an obvious display of emotion. "Is it, does it—"

"I think so, but I'm not positive."

Paul sat down slowly, clearly struggling to regain composure. "Until you know for sure you can't let her out of your sight."

"I've been trying not to."

"Well, you've done a lousy job of it. You're here. She's not."

Paul was right. Raphael had left Susan too much on her own. It was going to get her killed.

"I have to go," he said, rising swiftly.

Without another word Raphael left. As he raced toward Susan's hotel he tried to calm himself. Maybe if he could set a trap for the other Raiders he could kill them before they got to her. Then the best thing for her would be to return home. She would be safer there.

Until Richelieu discovers what it is she has. Or until the war is lost and then no one will be safe.

When he was finally standing before her door he was relieved that he could hear her inside. The blood that she had placed hours before, though, kept him from approaching too close.

"Susan," he called.

After what seemed like an impossibly long time she opened the door. Her face was pale but resolute, as though she had struggled for hours with a decision finally reached.

"What is it?" he asked.

"We should talk inside."

"I can't come in, remember?"

She sighed. "How do I remove it?"

"Get a washcloth and clean it off."

She disappeared back into her room and returned moments later with the washcloth. She dutifully scrubbed until he could feel the blood on the door no more. Together they went into the room and he sat down, waiting to hear what she had to say.

"I haven't slept today. I have been thinking and praying."

"And?"

"I will help you with whatever it is you need me to do."

He felt himself sag with relief. Before he could speak, though, she held up a hand.

"But first I need answers."

She got up and retrieved the box that he had seen before. She opened it and showed him the deed and the key.

He stared at them in surprise. He hadn't been to Bryas in a very long time, and he hadn't known that her grandmother possessed the land.

"Congratulations. You will make a fine lady," he said.

"Thank you."

"What is the key for?"

She shook her head. "That's what I have to find out."

He handed her back the key and she tucked it and the deed safely in the box. His mind raced. Would she actually go to Bryas? Even he had to admit that she was being drawn there. It made sense in a way. The journey of her ancestors had begun at Bryas. Maybe it was time a woman of Bryas returned home.

She was determined to know more, to seek answers, and there would be no talking her out of it. He could tell that by the way she held herself. The only thing he could do to stop her would be to mesmerize her and he didn't want to do that. That freethinking and independent spirit was part of what he needed about her, what drew him to

her. Another word bubbled up from his subconscious but
he refused to grant it admittance.

There was only one thing he could do.

"In that case," he said, "I'll help you."

Susan was surprised and excited to hear Raphael say that.
It also filled her with a great deal of trepidation. Their relationship, whatever it was, so far had been volatile and
unpredictable. She could only imagine that prolonged,
sustained contact would make that worse.

She pulled her cross out from her shirt, needing to actually touch it and reassure herself that everything was
going to be okay. His eyes followed the movement, nar-
rowing to slits as he stared at the cross. He didn't say
anything, though.

"What about David?" Susan asked.

"There's someone I can have help him. It's not ideal,
but it will have to do."

"But I thought the war wouldn't wait."

Raphael sighed. "Susan, you *are* the war."

As David and Wendy continued to talk, their waiter po-
litely came around every once in a while to check on them
but made no motions to hurry them up. Finally, the man
came back with menus in his hands. "Would you care to
see our dinner menu?" he asked.

Wendy laughed, "Is it that late already?"

David turned and glanced outside and realized the sun
had set. He had not meant to stay out so late, had not
meant to keep her out so late.

"We really should be going," he told the waiter, struggling to keep the stress out of his voice.

The man nodded and left.

"David, what's wrong?" she asked, putting a hand on his arm.

"I'm getting really tired, it just sort of hit me all of a sudden," he said.

The truth was if that had been the only problem he would have kept himself glued to that chair and shared dinner with her, staying to talk until they kicked them out of the restaurant.

"I'm sorry. I've kept you out too long," she said, rising.

"Please, don't apologize. I can't remember ever having a better lunch or sharing it with better company."

He groaned to himself. It sounded like a line one of his uncles would use. He was too tired and nervous to be clever, though. As they got up he briefly considered calling a cab, but a glance outside revealed many people strolling. Better to get back to the hotel fast and it was close enough that they could probably walk there before a cab reached the restaurant.

Outside she entwined her fingers with his again as they walked. Where he had earlier thrilled at the contact he found himself worrying that if she was holding his hand he wouldn't have it free to defend them quickly if need be. *Relax and just enjoy being with her. You don't know how long she'll be in your life*, he told himself. But he couldn't.

He walked quickly, his side throbbing, and his heart rate increasing with each step. Next to him Wendy took long strides to keep up, but she didn't question or complain. They were within line of sight of the hotel when a figure stepped out of the shadow between two buildings right into their path.

David blinked for a moment and then shoved Wendy hard. "Run!"

She gasped and he heard her trip, but he couldn't turn to look at her. He didn't dare take his eyes off the man for a second. Shock rippled through him. The vampire baring his fangs in front of him was the one David had killed the night before in her hotel room.

CHAPTER ELEVEN

*And he said, What hast thou done? the voice of thy
brother's blood crieth unto me from the ground.*

—Genesis 4:10

D avid stared at the vampire, stunned. "I saw you turn
to ash," he whispered.

"Did I?" the creature snarled, its features twisted in
rage.

Behind him he could hear Wendy staggering to her feet
and he winced. He hadn't meant to shove her that hard.
So much for her running and getting away. No, the only
thing that stood between Wendy and a vampire was him.

And the other time that happened I lost, he reminded
himself.

"Yes," David said, forced to stand his ground instead
of backpedaling like he wanted to. That would put the
vampire closer to Wendy and he couldn't have that.

"Did you really think we died that easily?"

The creature lunged forward and David tried to twist
out of its grasp, kicking at its knees. He connected and the
vampire stumbled. David spun and saw that Wendy was
halfway down the street, running for all she was worth. He

moved to run after her and then tripped over one of her high heels. She must have abandoned them before beginning to run. Even as he crashed to the pavement he couldn't help but admire her quick thinking.

Fire exploded through his side as he hit the ground. He felt hands grab the back of his shirt and flip him over. He jabbed at the vampire's eyes with his thumbs, and clawed with his fingers. His fingernails sliced through skin, drawing blood.

They bleed as easily as we do. Then why can't we kill them?

The vampire bared its fangs and batted away David's hands. That was when he noticed that the creature's nose was flatter and its eyebrows much thicker and closer together than he remembered.

"You're not the same vampire!" he gasped. "You're not the one I killed yesterday."

"That would have been my brother," the creature snarled.

They can die by staking. Die and stay dead.

If only I had a stake.

He brought his knees up and kicked hard, throwing the vampire backward. The creature stood up slowly and began to laugh.

In that moment David knew he was going to die.

Then something flashed in front of him. He blinked and he saw a monk in brown robes. He tried to shout a warning, but it was too late. The vampire had turned his attention to the monk, spinning to grab him.

The monk, almost in slow motion, brought his hand up, holding a large, plain cross and pressed it to the vampire's chest. David could hear the sizzle of burning flesh.

The vampire screamed and jumped back, pressing both hands to the wound. The monk followed with lightning speed, grabbed the vampire's head with both his hands, and twisted the head off.

The body and the head fell into ash and the monk brushed his hands together to wipe it off.

David lay, mouth agape, as he watched the ash float from the monk's hands and land on the pavement.

"How did you do that?" David panted.

The monk turned to look at him. He was short, with pale skin, a large nose, and close-cropped black hair with a hint of curl in it. He crouched down next to him and extended a hand. "Years of practice and meditation. You may call me Paul."

David shook the hand and immediately noticed that the skin felt odd, neither hot nor cold, just…there. He glanced up and there was a glow fading from the man's eyes. David tried to jerk back as the implication hit him, but the monk held his hand firmly. Slowly he smiled, revealing wicked fangs over an inch in length.

"Sometimes, there are advantages to being a vampire. One of God's little jokes, I suppose," the man answered.

David's eyes dropped to the cross the monk was wearing on a rope around his neck. With his free hand the monk picked it up, holding it in his bare hand. "God does not burn us all, only those who struggle against Him."

"You're a vampire," David gasped.

"Yes, obviously."

"You're a monk."

"Yes, I would think even more obviously."

"How?"

The vampire stood, lifting David up with him easily.

"You and I will have many hours to discuss such things, but for now, we will have to decide what to tell your friend."

David turned in the direction the vampire nodded and saw Wendy standing there, a dazed look on her face. Her knee was skinned from where she had fallen.

David rushed over to her. "Wendy, are you okay?"

"I don't know. I was running. You told me to run. And then I was afraid you were going to die, and I couldn't let that happen. So, I came back, but then I realized I didn't know..."

"It's okay," he said, reaching for her hand.

The contact seemed to shake everything loose. "What was that?" she shrieked, jumping backward.

David bit back a howl of pain as she yanked his arm and liquid fire knifed through his side. He crumpled to his knees, tears stinging his eyes. The monk strode forward and David looked up just in time to see him pinch the artery in her throat. Seconds later she slumped in his arms and he let go of the artery.

"It's one of the most humane ways to render someone unconscious if you can accomplish it. I think we had better go to your room before anyone becomes too curious."

Pain wracking him at every step David led the way while Paul put Wendy's arm around his neck, lifted her almost imperceptibly off the ground, and walked beside him.

As they passed through the lobby David thought he caught the desk clerk shaking her head at them. He tried not to think about it as he hurried the other two to his room. He quickly opened the door and walked inside.

"Do I have to invite—" he began.

"No," Paul interrupted, "but thanks for the thought."

The vampire crossed the threshold in the blink of an eye and was depositing Wendy on the bed before David even realized he was inside. He quickly shut the door and hurried over to her. She looked so innocent and so peaceful.

"Is she going to be okay? You didn't hurt her did you?"

"She will wake up shortly and should suffer no ill effects. In fact, she'll be feeling much better than you will be. You need to rest and let yourself heal."

"Why didn't you just mesmerize her?" David asked as he sat down stiffly on the side of the bed.

"She's had too many minds impose their will on her; one of them hasn't released that hold yet. It wouldn't have been good for her. This was the safer way."

"The humane way," David said, using the vampire's earlier word.

"Yes," he said with a simple smile, one that somehow still hid his fangs from sight.

David remembered the sight of those fangs. "Your fangs are longer than on any I've seen before."

"That's because I'm older than any you've likely seen before. With humans the hair and nails continue to grow for several months after death. Ours continue to grow after our deaths for the rest of our days. But, our incisors grow as well. The age of the vampire is marked by the length of his fangs, a difference so subtle it's usually only noticeable to other vampires."

"To what purpose?"

"A warning against the young, a symbol of maturity and, hopefully, wisdom, in the old."

"Why don't you scare me like the others do?"

"Because just like all creatures you have instincts, deep, powerful instincts. And those instincts accurately tell you that I am no threat to you."

"How is that possible? You're a vampire. Don't all vampires kill people and drink their blood?"

Paul smiled again. "We will spend much time together, you and I, and I will answer your questions, but for now we should focus on the young lady. She is waking up."

"How do you know?" David asked, turning back toward Wendy.

"Changes in the rhythm of her breathing, a quickening in her pulse."

"You can hear those things?" David asked as Wendy's eyelids began to flutter.

"Of course. You could, too, if you trained yourself."

Wendy's eyelids flew open and she stared up at David. "What happened? How did I get here?" she asked.

"I carried you," Paul said.

She glanced over at him and without warning she began to scream. Paul covered her mouth with his hand.

"Shh, child, I mean you no harm."

Her eyes were wide and her whole body tensed and for a moment David thought she was going to start thrashing and hurt herself. The door to his room flew open and Raphael leaped across the threshold, Susan on his heels.

"It's not what you think!" David shouted.

Raphael stopped suddenly, though, his eyes on the other vampire. Slowly the tension left his body and he caught Susan around the shoulders. "It's fine," he told her.

David fought back the urge to laugh hysterically. The irony was not lost on him that this time it was Raphael coming to rescue Wendy from him.

Susan glared first at him, then at Paul. She sat down on the bed and Wendy crumpled into her arms. She held her cousin, rubbing her back and making quieting noises.

"Anyone care to tell me what's going on?" she asked at last.

"I'm not sure I know myself," David said. "Wendy came to visit me in the hospital. We went to lunch after I'd been released. On the way back here we were attacked and this…monk…saved us."

Susan regarded Paul. "How on earth are you a monk?" She turned to Raphael. "Do you know him?"

Raphael didn't like any of it. Some vampires shared their secrets with others, loved ones, friends. A few of his sire's servants from centuries before had known exactly what he was. What they both were. Raphael, though, had never chosen to draw a human in, to unmask himself and to burden them with the knowledge that he had already given to Susan. It went against every instinct he had. Knowledge was power and he was loath to give too much to any one person no matter who they were.

He glanced up and saw Paul glaring at him. The monk should understand; he guarded his secrets more fiercely than Raphael. Instead of finding understanding, though, he found only forcefulness in Paul's eyes.

"It's time they knew the truth…about everything," Paul said pointedly.

Raphael growled a warning low in his throat, which the other vampire chose to ignore. It was a hollow threat and he knew it. Age played just as much a role in power as fighting skills and years of practice did.

Paul turned to the humans. "You'll have to forgive

Raphael. He's suspicious by nature and keeps his own counsel. It has nothing to do with you in particular. He's always been that way and I imagine he's too old for us to hope that will be one of the ways in which he can change."

"Keep talking, old man," Raphael said, irritation rising inside of him. The truth had a way of coming back to bite a person as Raphael knew from bitter experience. Part of him just hoped he lived long enough to see Paul's truth bite him.

Wendy had slid as far away from both of them as possible. She sat with Susan's arms still around her, supporting her, keeping her calm. Both were clearly curious.

David was cautious but deeply interested in what Paul was saying. Raphael sighed.

"All right," he said, standing to walk over to the window. He stared out at the city. Paul enjoyed talking and he would let him. *Too much time spent as a monk and not a preacher. He's got all those bottled-up words.*

Behind him, Paul began: "As you have become aware, vampires exist. We have walked this earth as long as there have been humans. We are cursed creatures, doomed to lives of immortality, but much of what you think you know about us is wrong."

Wrong? Monster. Killer. Abomination. Drinker of human blood. All that's right enough.

"Vampirism is a curse passed from one to another and bestowed upon the wicked. In order to be so cursed, a person must be evil, truly evil and unlikely to repent in their lifetime. When a vampire is cursed, they go crazy and whatever their particular vice, they overindulge, unable to stop themselves. After several decades the things they once took pleasure in make them sick."

"I don't understand," Raphael heard Wendy say in a tiny voice.

"What is your favorite food?" Paul asked.

"Pizza."

"Okay, imagine that you could only eat pizza for the rest of your life."

"That would get really old after a while," Susan said.

"Yes," Paul said, humor in his voice. "Now, imagine that it's not just a meal but a compulsion. Imagine that you ate it continuously, without being able to stop yourself, even if you were full. You ate and ate until you threw up and then you kept eating and couldn't stop and couldn't do anything else, sleep, work, anything."

"That would be a nightmare," David muttered.

"It is a nightmare," Raphael said. "One from which you can never awake." *So much for letting Paul do all the talking.*

He turned to face the others. "When you become a vampire it's the nightmare you live. Whatever your vice, whatever your sin or addiction, you obsess on it mindlessly until you learn to hate it, until it makes you physically ill and spiritually ill."

Paul smiled at him. "And that is where the true miracle, the true transformation, happens. When your obsession drives you mad and turns to something you despise that is when you begin to change. You start to live your life a different way. You see the sins of your past clearly and learn to repent. And eventually, not only do you become a good person, but you find salvation. For most this process takes centuries."

"And have you found salvation?" Susan asked, her eyes large and shining and fixed on Paul. Paul had a way of speaking that wrapped the listener up and swept them away with him to wherever he wished them to go. It was a kind of charisma that was above and beyond any common mesmerism. He was wasted in a monastery. *He's hiding.*

David and Wendy were similarly caught up in what the older vampire had to say and their faces betrayed their eagerness to hear his answer to Susan's question.

Paul smiled. "Salvation was never so much my problem. However, I like to believe that God, and the vampire who was His instrument, have taken an evil man and made me good. I have put away the old life, so to speak, and become something new."

Raphael shook his head and Paul winked at him.

"And you?" Susan asked, turning her eyes on Raphael. He winced. He had been sure she wouldn't ask him.

"I have not found salvation."

"But, he has become a good man," Paul interjected. "Salvation, I feel, is not far away."

It was a discussion Raphael didn't intend to continue. Not then; not with them. "That is how things normally are with a vampire," he said. "You live long enough you become a good person. However, there have always been rumors that once in a great while it doesn't work."

"No salvation?" David asked.

"More than that. Instead of learning to understand the sins of their past these individuals just become worse and worse with time, more obsessive instead of less, until the monster they are is far worse than the monster they were."

"Is that where stories like *Dracula* come from?" Wendy asked in a small voice.

She was spunky, working hard to adjust to what the others had already known. For her the revelation of vampires was just a few minutes old. When he released her from his power he would restore her memories of what had happened to her. She deserved to understand how she had gotten pulled into this mess at the very least.

"Is that what we're dealing with now—a vampire who hasn't repented?" Susan asked, trying to meet his eyes.

"Yes. A while back I met a man who was in need of being cursed," Raphael admitted. "He had once been a good man who had become twisted and perverted by his own fears and obsessions. He had such great potential to be so much more, though. I cursed him. Now, he has become even more powerful and gathered an army about him. Instead of growing older and wiser he has just become stronger and more insane and now he's a danger not just to us but to the entire world. He's a fanatic who believes that there is only one way—his way. Cursing him was my greatest mistake."

"You could not have known that he would be so . . . broken as to be unable to be fixed," Paul said. "No one knows for sure what causes these rare mutations to occur."

"You called him Armand before. Who is this vampire?" David asked.

Raphael closed his eyes and as though from a distance he could hear Paul say, "They deserve to know."

FRANCE, 1642

"What are you?" the red-robed cardinal breathed.

"A thought, a nightmare, a demon, your damnation,"

Raphael said, breathing in the other's fear.

The cardinal was the same man he had met years ear-lier, but changed. Time had made him even more fanati-cal than Raphael remembered. He had heard the stories, the whispers, but the look in the other's eyes hurt him, like a physical pang. He had gone too far and he wasn't going to stop until someone stopped him.

"You're slaughtering innocent people," Raphael said.

"Casualties in the war to save France."

"Save it from whom?"

"Everyone."

Raphael began to breathe, his chest rising and falling powerfully. "And who will save you?"

"France."

"Not God? You're a cardinal."

"I love the church, but France is my calling, my pur-pose. France will save me from anything."

Raphael smiled. "Not from me."

He grabbed the cardinal and twisted his head to the side, exposing his throat. Raphael sank his fangs into the man's skin, blood flowed freely over his tongue and down his throat. He could taste the obsession, the insanity, the evil as he drank. And he knew he was right. Richelieu de-served to be cursed. Just as he had.

PRAGUE, PRESENT DAY

Raphael shook his head and forced his mind back to the present. Susan, Wendy, and David looked at him expectantly. Paul already knew who it was they were fighting and he was watching the others.

"Richelieu," Raphael told the assembled group at last. "The vampire we're talking about is Richelieu."

Wendy blinked and seemed to come out of her shock. "As in Paris, as in cardinal?"

"The same. When I met him he was obsessed with the safety of France and consolidating the power of the monarchy, crushing the power of the nobility."

"And now?" David asked.

"Now he wants the same thing, only on a global scale. He wants to rule the world, consolidate the power in one person for the safety of the world."

"Antichrist," David muttered.

"No, at least, not as far as I can tell," Paul said, his face and tone inscrutable.

Sometimes even Raphael couldn't tell whether the monk was joking or serious.

Raphael turned and looked at Susan, feeling her eyes upon him.

She was staring at him intently. "Where did this happen?"

"I met him in Avignon." Raphael paused and then admitted, "I cursed him in Bryas."

She turned pale and then slowly rose to her feet. "Then we really do have to go to Bryas," she whispered.

CHAPTER TWELVE

And the chief priests took the silver pieces, and said, It is not lawful for to put them into the treasury, because it is the price of blood.

—Matthew 27:6

A momentary silence greeted Susan's proclamation. Then, blinking, Wendy asked, "Where's Bryas?"

"It's in France. It's where our ancestors came from."

"Why do you have to go?" David asked, clearly confused. He glanced nervously at her. "This seems like really bad timing."

"There are so many secrets. I don't even know where they all begin let alone where they end. But, I believe I have a chance of finding out; that I hold...the key...to understanding everything that's happened and that will happen."

"Susan, what are you talking about?" Wendy asked.

You know what you have to do, a voice whispered in Raphael's mind.

"I have to go to France."

"And I'm going with her," Raphael said, turning to look at Paul.

The other vampire met his eyes, nodded briefly, clearly

not surprised. He shouldn't be. *After all, he was the one who gave me the lecture about leaving her alone.*

"So, where does that leave us?" David asked, indicating Wendy and himself.

"With me," Paul said swiftly. "There is much to do. If we are to defeat Richelieu we have to learn more of his plan and you have to train to fight his soldiers, both human and vampire. You can do that here with me."

Wendy shook her head. "Not me. I don't want to fight in a war. And besides, I'm going home soon with my parents. I have school and the rest of my life." She turned and looked at David and she turned beet red. "I'm sorry," she whispered.

He reached out and took her hand. "Don't be sorry. Be safe. I'd much rather have you home in California than here risking your life."

"You'll be my knight in shining armor?" she whispered softly.

Raphael couldn't help but feel that the rest of them were intruding on a private moment.

"I will," he said, clearing his throat slightly.

Raphael rolled his eyes. One lovesick, broken-ribbed warrior without instincts or tools was not what he had in mind. He glanced at Paul who was watching the entire scene unfold with obvious enjoyment. Raphael was glad that David was going to be Paul's problem. Training him was going to take the patience of a saint.

Susan took a deep breath as she ended her call with the airline and headed to her aunt and uncle's hotel room. Her heart was beating fast but with fear or excitement she couldn't tell.

She knocked on the hotel door and her aunt answered it, ushering her inside. Aside from a couple of bruises everyone seemed to have escaped the car accident pretty much unscathed.

"What's wrong?" her uncle Bob asked as he glanced up from the laptop on the small desk in the room.

"I just wanted to let you know I won't be going home when I originally planned. I changed my flight."

"Decided to leave early and come home with us?" he asked.

"Actually, I decided to go to France for a few days, see Paris."

From the way they looked at her she might as well have told them she was going to the moon.

"It's a man, isn't it?" Jane asked, the first to seemingly recover her voice.

"No, it's not a man. Why do you always assume it's a man when I do anything unusual?" Susan asked.

Jane sighed. "Whenever a sensible young woman like you does anything crazy, it's a man."

"Going to France is not crazy," Susan said, furious with herself that she was trying to justify it. It wasn't their decision, they had no say in whether she stayed or went. She owed them nothing. They hadn't even been the ones who raised her after her parents died. That had been her grandmother who more than once had been accused of doing crazy things herself. Susan was only doing the courtesy of telling them about her change in plans.

"It's a little bit crazy," Bob said. "Especially when you're still looking for a job."

"I'm just going for a couple of days. I mean, we're

in Europe. Who knows when I'm ever going to get the chance to see it again."

Jane was still staring intently at her. "Susan, dear, when are you going to find yourself a nice guy and just settle down?"

The nice guy speech, great. Of course I want a nice guy, but that's not the only requirement. He's got to be more than just nice. He's got to be interesting and passionate and fun. I want a guy who is so much more than they're dreaming. "I want to find a guy who loves me for everything I am," Susan said, trying not to get upset. "Someone who wants to be with me. Someone who would die for me."

Jane slapped her leg and turned to Bob with a look of triumph on her face. "There, I knew she was going to France because of a guy."

How on earth do you draw these conclusions? she wanted to ask.

"It's not safe for a young woman to travel alone. I've seen that Liam Neeson film," Bob said.

"I'm not eighteen, I'm twenty-three, and I know how to be careful. Besides, a friend will be going with me."

"What kind of friend?" he asked.

"A close friend."

"This close friend, is it a woman?" he asked.

She hesitated for a moment, biting her lip. "No."

"I told you it was a guy!" her aunt crowed.

"It's not that strange man from the hospital, is it?" her uncle asked disdainfully.

Susan crossed her arms over her chest and tried to keep her gaze defiant. "As a matter of fact, it is."

"Oh, honey, I don't like this at all," Jane said.

"Seriously? You give me grief when I'm not seeing someone and now that I have a boyfriend you're not happy, either?"

Did I just call him my boyfriend? she thought, her mind racing. *Well, why not, that's how he was introduced to them. As far as they're concerned he is my boyfriend.*

"Of course we want you to have a man," Jane said.

"Just not that one," Bob said.

"And what's wrong with that one?" Susan demanded.

"There's just something off about him," Jane said. "He seemed very . . . help me out here, Bob."

Evil? Dark? Old? Intense? Dead? Vampiric?

"Immature."

"Exactly! Immature. That's what he is. Maybe you need to find a guy a couple of years older."

Susan began to giggle. She couldn't help it. And then it burst forth as full-fledged laughter.

They stared at her and it just made her laugh harder. She couldn't help it.

"Honestly, Susan, he seemed very shallow," Jane said.

"Guys like him want only one thing from a young woman," her uncle added.

Yeah, but not the thing you're thinking of. It was just so absurd. Vampires were real. They were trying to kill her. And they thought Raphael was too young for her.

Finally, wiping her eyes, she turned to go.

"Susan, are you all right?" Jane called out.

Susan lifted a hand and waved.

She made it back to David's room where the others looked up at her startled, as though she had interrupted something.

"What's going on?" she asked.

"Why do you care? You're leaving," Paul said.

"I do care," she said, temper flaring. "I have to go to France. There are questions I need answers to before I can throw myself into this, whatever this is. But like it or not I am a part of what's going on."

"Susan, go home or go to France and then home, whatever. I just don't think you should be mixed up in all of this. Get out while you still can," David said.

She spun to face him. "You, too? What has he told you that he hasn't told me?"

"Nothing," Raphael said. "But David has committed himself to this struggle."

"What? When? How? I'm out of the room for twenty minutes and suddenly you're fighting in his war when three days ago you didn't even know vampires existed?"

"Three days ago I'm guessing you didn't either," David said quietly. "All that evil needs to succeed is for good people to stand by and do nothing. I don't want any part of this. If I had a choice I would turn and run as far and as fast as I can."

"Sensible," Raphael said.

"Then why don't you?"

"Because I don't have a choice. I feel like I was led here, to this place at this moment even though I didn't know why or for what. Suddenly everything is so clear. Raphael says he needs warriors to help him. I may not be a warrior, but I'll do everything in my power to stop this enemy. You're leaving, and that's for the best."

"I'm only leaving for a few days! And Raphael sounds like he needs an army, certainly more than one warrior." She half couldn't believe what she was saying, but what David had told her made sense. Had she not also been called? There were things she had to do first, but the war would be there when she returned.

"You're no good to us in France," David said.

"I will be back. Unless you're planning on fighting and winning this war within the next week then I need to know what's going on, what will be expected of me when I return."

"Dear Susan," Paul said, shaking his head, "if we haven't won the war in that time then don't bother returning, because the world will be ending and we will be dead."

"That's enough," Raphael said. He was uneasy. In a couple of hours he would be on a plane with Susan, leaving behind Prague, Richelieu, and that which had been stolen from him. It didn't feel right, but he couldn't let Susan go alone.

Am I afraid she won't want to come back?

It was possible. The overriding fear he had, though, was that something would happen to her and she would be unable to come back because she'd be dead.

Of course, he was also struggling with the realization that for the next several days, maybe weeks, he was going to be vulnerable to Susan. She would know where he was when he was asleep and would be in a position to harm or kill him easily.

He hadn't trusted any human with that knowledge, that power, for centuries. He just hoped he wasn't choosing poorly now.

Susan was grateful that things had calmed down. She had booked herself and Raphael on the first flight to France that she could. It gave them barely enough time, but she felt it was important to go before the others could talk her out of it. An hour later her good-bye with Wendy was much more poignant. The two embraced and there were tears shed on both sides.

"You take care of yourself," Wendy said.

"I will," Susan promised.

"And don't let any vampires bite you."

"You, either."

When she left the room she turned back once more to see Paul standing by the window and Wendy sitting on the bed crying, with David's arm around her.

Raphael didn't seem to be in a mood to talk during their flight and she was secretly relieved. Once they landed in Paris he rented a car and steered it out of the city.

Paris fell behind, a glittering jewel in the night, and Susan kept glancing behind to see it until it disappeared. She looked over at Raphael; his jaw was clenched and his hands were gripping the steering wheel tightly.

"Is anything wrong?" she asked.

"I don't like driving."

"Have you...been doing it long?"

"I drove a Model T when they were new. I didn't like it then, I don't like it now."

"But the convenience, the speed," she said.

He snorted in derision. "What convenience? You have to constantly fill them with gasoline, oil, air in the tires, and guard them against theft, injury, rust, and a host of other calamities. They constantly need repair and last only a few years."

"One could say many of the same things about horses,"

she said, finding humor as she compared. "Theft, injury, fuel, water, shoe them, keep them healthy and running and how many years can you get out of one at average?"

"Very funny," he said, glancing at her sideways. He didn't look amused, though.

"And cars are faster than horses," she said, turning back to face the road.

"But not faster than vampires."

She glanced at him, startled. "You can run as fast as a car?"

He shrugged. "I've never timed myself, or indulged in a race, but I should be able to hold my own and I am not confined to the roads. I can get where I need to go faster when I'm not so encumbered."

By me, she thought. Still, she hadn't asked him to come. He had done that all on his own.

They had barely made their flight and she had felt guilty leaving Wendy alone. Then again, David had been with her as well as Paul. There was something terrifying and oddly comforting about that vampire. Either way she had committed Wendy to God's care, knowing that she had to make the journey to Bryas, especially in light of what Raphael had told her.

Bryas was about a hundred miles outside of Paris, but would take several hours to drive to she had been told. She glanced up at the moon shining low in the sky, casting light down upon the road.

"Are we going to make it before dawn?" she asked.

"No, but there's a small inn we can stop at along the way and resume our travels tomorrow night. You'll like it, it's very old. Been in the same family for generations."

"That's one of the things that's so fascinating about

Europe, how old and established things are. I grew up in California where if it's more than eighty years old, it's ancient."

He laughed out loud. "Eighty years is young in my book, for a person or a building."

It was hard to reconcile his actual age with his physical appearance. She constantly had to remind herself that he wasn't in his early twenties like her.

"So, when do we reach this inn?"

"About an hour. Just relax."

"Said the vampire who hates driving."

She watched the countryside slip by under the silvery light and wondered what it had looked like when he was a young man. The same moon, the same fields, so much changed in the world and yet so much probably the same. She couldn't help but wonder what changes she would see in her own lifetime. *If I survive the next few days.*

She desperately wanted to ask him more about Richelieu, but he had shut down conversation on that topic back in Prague. She would just have to wait. It was hard to fathom that a man she had read about in books was the mastermind behind a modern plot to take over the world.

She glanced at Raphael. It seemed she was getting good at believing the unbelievable.

Sooner than she would have thought they arrived at the inn. Raphael parked in a small area for cars about a hundred feet from the building. It looked old and weathered, but proud and regal. A sign above the door was in shadow and she couldn't read the name.

They got out of the car and walked to the front of the inn. They climbed the steps and Susan's fingers tingled as they slid up the railing, feeling the history of the place.

At the top of the stairs Raphael pushed open the door. They found themselves in a small foyer of sorts. A staircase directly in front of her led to the upper floors. To the right, Susan could see a large, cheery room with tables and chairs and a roaring fireplace. A couple of lodgers were sitting in front of the fireplace, drinking and talking quietly. From the left a large, jovial-looking man appeared, wiping his hands on an apron around his waist.

He seemed to size them up and then began to speak to them in heavily accented English. "Welcome. It's late, I apologize. I didn't expect anyone else for the night."

Raphael wrapped an arm around Susan, startling her, but he held her tightly. "My wife and I decided to stop for the night and continue our travels later. We apologize for the inconvenience."

"No inconvenience. We have the perfect room for you on the third floor. Would you like something to eat first?"

Raphael turned and looked at her. "Do you need anything, honey?"

"I'm tired. I'd prefer just to go to sleep," she said, flushing.

"Very good. If you'd follow me," the man said, turning and leading the way up the stairs.

When they reached the third floor he opened a door and stepped back. Susan walked in with Raphael on her heels.

"Does it meet with your approval?"

"Yes, thank you," Raphael said.

The owner bowed and closed the door behind him.

Susan rounded on Raphael. "Why did you tell him we were married?"

"To save your reputation," he said, raising an eyebrow.

"What?"

"Back in Prague you were so angry when I allowed the one staff member to make assumptions about our activities that I thought it best to at least claim to be married."

"Why didn't you get us two rooms so we wouldn't have had to claim to be anything?"

"I'm not letting you out of my sight until our purpose is accomplished, Susan. Now, I suggest you stop complaining or tomorrow at breakfast I'll let it slip that we are actually lovers trying to avoid discovery by your real husband."

She quaked with rage as she stared at him. She wanted with everything she had in her to slap him, but knew it would be a futile gesture. "If you weren't dead, I'd kill you."

"It's a good thing that I am dead then. I've never been defeated in battle except by one and I would not give much for your chances."

His eyes glittered at her in the moonlight that filled the room. He looked wild and dangerous and there was something about him that seemed to make her soul quicken within her. Her breath caught in her throat and she turned away, not wanting him to realize how he was affecting her.

"What's wrong?" he whispered.

"I just feel bad."

"Why?"

"Only one bed. It looks like you're going to have to sleep on the floor." She wanted to sound tart and clever, but it just came out tired and matter-of-fact. She shook her head. Even when she wanted to flirt she wasn't very good at it. In nearly the same breath, though, she was upbraiding herself for that thought. He was a vampire, not flirting material. There was nothing he could offer her, not a home or a family or love. Not even a warm embrace and a beating heart.

"It's fine," he was saying, his voice also having changed and sounding more clipped and businesslike. "I've slept more often on floors than I have in beds. I'm used to it."

"Good," she said, vaguely disappointed that he hadn't challenged her decision.

She sat down on the edge of the bed and realized that she was far too uncomfortable to wear her nightgown in front of him. She cursed the decision to bring it instead of her sensible flannel pajamas with the cavorting cats. The flowy, white cotton garment had seemed much more appropriate given that she hoped to focus on the romance of her grandmother's birth city. Now she'd rather have the practicality of her grandmother's upbringing.

"You should get some sleep," Raphael noted.

"I will," she said, wrapping her arms around herself.

"When?" he asked suspiciously.

Unwilling to confess her embarrassment over the nightgown she answered, "When you do."

The words hung in the air between them as she realized what they implied. It was a good idea, but not what she'd meant by it.

His eyes glowed and he pounced, grabbing her by the upper arms and shaking her. "After all I've done for you, you still don't trust me? How can we fight together without trust?"

Her sudden fear gave way to anger. "Trust you? How could I? You're a monster, you said so yourself. You've told me every opportunity you could and then last night... last night you nearly killed me. And besides, what have you done for me? Wendy's still mesmerized, just by you not that other vampire. You've turned my world upside down. And because of you I've been attacked by a vampire and seen the inside of a Prague hospital. By my count, you owe me, not the other way around."

He was close to her, so close that she could have reached out and kissed him if she wanted to. She struggled to silence the pounding of her heart, focusing on the danger she was in and the anger she was justified to be experiencing.

"My life was just fine before I met you!" she wailed.

"Oh really?" he asked, his voice colder than she'd ever heard it.

"Really!"

He crushed her to him, bringing his lips down to hers, hands moving to her waist and encircling it.

"I was fine," she tried to protest, but she was a liar and they both knew it. Susan wanted the kiss to go on forever. That realization terrified her and she pushed him away. He moved willingly, looking at her with a question in his eyes.

"It frightens me, how I feel when I'm kissing you." She hadn't meant to admit it to him, but there it was.

He smiled and the sight of his fangs flashing frightened her even more. What was she thinking? He didn't have full control over his own urges.

She stared at the fangs. What if one of them should pierce her lip when they kissed? What would the taste of her blood do to him? She shivered and moved away from him in the room.

Another thought occurred to her. In all his years, surely she couldn't be the first woman to have to worry about such things. How many had there been before her? And how had it ended for them? Badly, she suspected. How could it be otherwise? If vampirism really was a curse it was unlikely that he would willingly curse anyone he had cared for in a romantic way. No, any woman he had loved could only have ended up dead. It was something she needed to keep in the front of her mind at all times lest the same thing happen to her.

"Have you ever been married?" she blurted out.

"You are a strange woman."

She blinked at him.

He sank down on the bed and stared up at her. "In all my years, I've never had a wife."

"And now you have a fake one," she joked.

"So it would appear."

"So, why am I strange?"

"There are a thousand questions I'm sure you have, and yet you don't ask me about being a vampire, the history I've seen, the war before us, Richelieu, my experiences at Bryas, any of the natural questions. No, you ask me instead if I've been married."

She smiled. "You've lived for centuries, yet you don't know women very well if you think that's an unnatural question for me to ask at this point in time."

He laughed. "I'm not sure any man really understands women, no matter how many centuries he's lived."

She started to laugh and ended by yawning.

"You haven't slept much lately," he noted.

"Who can sleep?" she asked.

"Vampires are forced to sleep. I think sometimes that is an advantage over humans. However, it is also one of our greatest weaknesses. The morning is coming. It is time for us to sleep."

"I'm not a vampire," she protested, yawning again.

"No, but while you're in my company, you will find it easier to keep my hours."

She nodded. It made sense.

"And don't worry," he told her, "I will sleep on the floor."

She moved to her suitcase and pulled out her night-gown. She glanced at him and debated whether or not to just sleep in her clothes. She was uncomfortable, though, and tired.

"Where's the bathroom?" she asked, looking around.

Raphael smiled. "A hundred years ago it was still outside. Today there's one down the hall."

"A shared bathroom?" she asked. She had heard that a lot of European hotels still had those, but she hadn't looked forward to experiencing it.

"It's a small inn, and the rooms have no space for private restrooms. Just be grateful you don't have to go behind the stable," he said with a smirk.

She lingered for an extra ten minutes in the restroom, not eager to return to her room.

She stared at herself in the mirror. "You can do this," she whispered, trying to screw up her courage.

"You can go to Bryas, find what you're meant to find, stop Richelieu from taking over the world. And most importantly, you can avoid kissing Raphael again."

She blushed at the very thought and she splashed cold water on her face.

When she finally returned to the room the curtain had been drawn over the window. She went and peeked outside and saw the light of dawn on the horizon. She turned and saw Raphael, on the floor, unmoving. She shut the curtains again and went and stood over him.

He wasn't breathing. She panicked for a moment and then tried to remember if she'd ever seen him breathing. She nudged his leg with her foot and he didn't move. For a moment she wondered if she could kill him while he slept.

She shook her head. She couldn't do that. Not to him. Not without reason.

But maybe I should. He is a vampire. Being near him does put me in danger. And if I can't stop myself from feeling the way I do, from wanting to kiss him... it's only a matter of time before he kills me.

She glanced around and saw on the wall a small decorative sword and shield. She wondered if the crest belonged to the owners of the inn or to a renowned visitor from olden times. She moved over as if drawn to them and touched the sword. It was made of wood. She pulled and it came easily off the wall. She twisted it around in her hands and then turned and stared at Raphael's sleeping form.

Is he really asleep? Or is he just waiting for me to fall asleep? The thought of being that vulnerable, that exposed, terrified her.

She walked forward until she stood over him. She put the tip of the sword against his chest and held her breath, waiting to see if he would wake up.

He didn't move.

Her blood began to race as she realized she had

the means to kill him in her hands: wood through the heart.

She could do it. She could shove the sword into his heart and kill him.

It's the right thing to do, he's a monster.

Her hand tightened around the hilt of the sword. She stood there for what seemed like an eternity and then she lifted it free with a gasp. She quickly moved across the room and replaced the sword. Then she hurried over to the bed and slid underneath the covers. She put her head down on the pillow and squeezed her eyes shut.

Raphael smiled to himself as he heard Susan slip into sleep. The pull of the sun was strong and in a few more moments he, too, would be asleep. At least now he knew that he could sleep in peace. If she was going to try to kill him, she would have done it when she had the sword pressed against him.

It had taken all his willpower not to move, but he had to know. And now he did. He could trust her, even with his life. It was a nice feeling.

As the sun claimed him and he slipped into unconsciousness he was, for once, at peace.

The sun struck the glass and it sparkled. Shafts of light crept slowly across the beige carpet, bringing illumination but no enlightenment. David sat in the chair at the desk and Wendy still sat on the bed, knees tucked under her chin, a position she kept returning to since Susan and Raphael had left.

Neither had moved much or spoken for hours. He had a thousand things he wanted to say to her, to ask, to explain, but he couldn't find the words and after a while he was too afraid to break the silence even if he could voice what he was thinking.

So, he sat and watched the sunlight as it marched across the room. It brought a strange sort of comfort because he knew that very sunlight would have chased the vampires into their lairs. He stirred at the thought, wondering what had happened to Paul.

The vampire had managed to slip away shortly after Raphael and Susan had left. Still, it was as though he could feel his presence in the room, as if he had never really left. David worried that he might have been mesmerized by the vampire and not realized it.

The light shone on the bed and edged toward Wendy. Finally it touched her foot and her toes wiggled slightly. He thought about her shoes, probably still lying on the street below unless someone had taken them. He should go see if he could find them. It would be the gentlemanly thing to do.

Her toes continued to wiggle and slowly she moved her knees out from under her chin and slid her legs into the shaft of light. She took a deep breath and he couldn't help but wonder if she was feeling the same relief at seeing the sunlight.

She turned and looked at him and her eyes were wide, fearful, but quickening with thought. He tried to force a smile.

"There are vampires," she whispered.

"Yes," he said, his voice gravelly.

"Susan has always…felt things. Not me. I've never felt things, never believed there was anything"—she shuddered—"in the dark."

He thought about his own life. Had he known? Had he felt things in the dark? He wasn't sure that he had. When he was a child, maybe, but as an adult?

"I'm sorry," he told her, because he couldn't think of anything else to say.

"The things they said, about Richelieu, about him wanting to take over the world, you're going to fight, aren't you?"

"Yes."

"Why?"

"Because I can, and because who else is there?"

"So you can be a soldier, save the world like your dad?"

"No, because I figure God put me here for a reason, in this city, this hotel, this time. It can't all be an accident. I believe I'm meant to help."

"I think Susan thinks the same thing," Wendy said quietly.

"And you?" he asked, hope stirring in him.

"No. I don't think God put me here to fight. I just want to go home."

She hadn't changed her mind. Disappointment and relief flooded him. "Then you should go home before anything else happens," he said, trying to hide how he felt.

"It's not about you," she said, standing suddenly and walking over to him.

Her blond hair swung loose around her shoulders, her dress was torn and wrinkled. Tears had streaked makeup all over her face. Yet somehow she was the most beautiful thing he had ever seen. She reached out and touched his cheek with her hand and looked him in the eyes.

He saw terror there, tinged with regret.

"I like you. A lot," she admitted. "More than I should. I just can't stay. I can't be part of this."

"I understand," he said. "For what it's worth I wish we had met under different circumstances. I think—"

She put a finger across his lips. "Don't think," she whispered. Then she leaned down and kissed him. When she pulled back her eyes were brimming with tears.

She walked out of the room, without turning to look back, and then she was gone.

He stood up and crossed over to the bed and lay down without even bothering to take off his shoes. He grabbed one of the pillows and instantly regretted it. It smelled like her. He closed his eyes and breathed in deeply, sure that whatever happened in the war, whether he lived or died, he would never see her again.

Whatever would have happened, could have happened, between them he would never know. He groaned deep in his soul. When he opened his eyes again it was nighttime and Paul was sitting at the table watching him, an amused expression on his face.

Susan woke late in the afternoon and flipped onto her side, fear filling her. There, on the floor several feet away, Raphael was where she had last seen him and she breathed a sigh of relief.

She got up and headed down the hall to the restroom where she washed up and changed into fresh clothes. When she returned to the room she thought about going downstairs to get something to eat, but decided to wait for Raphael to wake instead.

She studied him as he slept. There was a hardness to

his face, even when he was unconscious. Suddenly his eyes flew open and she jumped, startled.

He lay still, staring, for several seconds.

"Raphael, are you okay?" she asked.

He didn't answer and she stood up to get a closer look. Then his whole body seemed to spasm at once and he made a gasping sound as he turned his head toward her.

"Yes, fine, I'm awake now," he said, rising quickly. He went to the window and threw the curtains open. In the distance the sky still held the faintest blush of pink from the setting sun.

In the hall outside she could hear movement. The smell of dinner was beginning to waft upward from the dining room below as well.

"I'm hungry," she said.

He turned to her and for a moment he looked very old and sad. Then he seemed to shrug off the mood like one would shrug off a jacket. He dipped his head toward her. "Then let's get you some food and be on our way to your home."

She opened her mouth to tell him that her home was in California, land of the golden sun, but decided against it. After her own doubts she could hardly blame him. She knew what he meant. For him, she belonged to Bryas. Apparently her grandmother had thought so, as well. Excitement stirred in her. She hoped she would soon understand what both of them thought and felt when she stepped foot in the place herself. She nodded to him.

"Sounds like a plan."

She moved toward the door and, with an earsplitting boom, it suddenly exploded into shards.

Chapter Thirteen

He that eateth my flesh, and drinketh my blood,
dwelleth in me, and I in him.

—John 6:56

What are you doing here?" David demanded of Paul. The vampire shrugged. "I promised Raphael I would look after you, train you in his absence. There is much you have to learn if you are going to help us."

"So I've been told. What happened to Wendy?"

"She left for America with her family shortly before I arrived," Paul said.

David closed his eyes. He had still hoped... He shook his head. It didn't matter what he had hoped. The important thing was that she would be safe, even if he would never see her again.

"What do I need to do?"

"We need somewhere to train, somewhere we can stay that is not so public."

David sat up quickly and moved to grab the phone.

"What is it?"

"I was supposed to check out of the hotel today. I'm getting an apartment here in Prague and it was going to be ready for me today. I should have left here hours ago."

"Hello?" the clerk at the front desk answered.

"Yes, hi. I was supposed to check out earlier today, but I...overslept...and just realized what time it is."

"No need to worry, sir, the young lady already told us you would be staying an extra night. She paid for it."

"What young lady?"

"Miss Wendy. I believe the two of you know each other."

"Thank you," he said, and hung up.

"That was thoughtful of her," Paul said. "I have a suspicion that she cares for you."

"A lot of good that does now."

Paul smiled. "If there is one thing that I have learned in all my years, it's that we never actually know how anything will turn out. Not really, not with complete certainty. Friends I thought would live forever died young. Enemies have become friends. If she cares for you and you for her as much as I believe you do, don't be surprised if you find each other again. What is it they say about love finding a way?"

"We barely know each other," David protested. How could he explain the feelings he had for a woman he barely knew?

"Love is a funny thing. It can build slow and strong for some while for others all it takes is a single moment in time, the blink of an eye, and the miracle is there. Perhaps your souls have already reached an understanding with each other."

David nodded slowly. "Maybe after this is all over I can go to California and look for her."

Paul chuckled. "Maybe after this is all over her cousin will give you her phone number."

"You really think Susan is coming back here with Raphael?" David asked.

The smile disappeared from Paul's face. "I pray so, for all of our sakes."

As the wooden missiles flew around her Susan screamed and threw her arms up to protect her face. Behind her she heard Raphael roar in surprise and pain.

She could hear shouts from people outside and someone rushed by her, hitting her just hard enough to spin her around. Someone else grabbed her from behind, yanked her arms down and back, and lashed her wrists together with something that felt like rope.

She was pushed and she fell face-first onto the bed where she struggled to flip over, kicking the air in case anyone was coming near her. The smell of garlic filled the room, so pungent it made her eyes water. She heard the sound of a body crashing to the ground followed by vomiting.

"What is happening?" she shrieked as she twisted.

She slid off the bed and her knees hit the floor. She rolled as she fell and she landed on her side, staring into Raphael's eyes as he lay, body spasming, ropes of garlic draped over him.

"What is happening?" she whimpered.

He didn't answer, just continued to retch. The stench of rotted blood and garlic turned her stomach and she twisted her head away, struggling only to breathe through her mouth.

There were four men in the room, all of them shouting

in French. Were they vampires? Raiders? She shook her head. If the garlic was making Raphael ill, then it would be affecting them, too. No, these were humans who were attacking them. But why? Paul had hinted that Richelieu could have humans working for him as well as vampires. But how would they have found them? She forced herself to focus. For whatever reason the people trying to kill them weren't vampires, but humans. That was a very good thing.

Humans she could fight.

She kicked out with her feet and caught one of them in the side of the knee. He fell with a cry as she struggled to stand. The other three were far more intent on Raphael, clearly considering him the greater threat. That was their mistake. After having incapacitated him, they should have worried about her.

One of the guys turned to her and she kneed him and then smashed her forehead into his nose. Blood went flying and they both staggered under the blow.

"Kill the vampire, then deal with her," one of the men barked.

Susan twisted so that she could grab the garlic rope in her bound hands. Then she straightened and ran with it, heading out the door, feet skidding slightly on chunks of broken wood. She was at the bathroom when she heard a roar behind her and the sound of breaking wood and glass.

She turned and ran downstairs. She made it down the first flight then turned for the second. A couple of steps down her foot caught in the trailing rope and she went flying, landed on a stair on her shoulder and began rolling. She did a somersault and bounced twice before hitting the ground floor, screaming in pain.

She looked up and saw the owners of the inn standing there, mouths gaping.

"Help him, please! There are people trying to kill him," she wheezed.

They blinked at each other and then turned back to her. "Dear," the woman said in a heavy accent. "That's because he is a vampire."

"He's not evil!" Susan shouted at them.

From above sounds of battle raged on punctuated by the occasional scream.

"He's your guest! Doesn't that mean something? Aren't you supposed to protect him?"

"We will protect you, but not him," the man answered.

"Then untie me," she begged.

"Not until it is over," the woman said.

Sobbing, Susan tried to stand up, but quickly realized her knee was dislocated. She struggled to sit and she forced her leg to straighten and pushed the kneecap against the bottom stair until it began to move. She screamed in anguish and as it slid back into place she nearly collapsed. She forced herself to try to stand, though, using the stairs to help push herself up.

Once she made it she hopped toward the kitchen, unable to put any real weight on the leg. The man and woman parted before her. She crossed the threshold before losing her balance and falling, slamming onto the floor on her stomach.

She looked up and saw a butcher knife on the counter above her. She sat up and pushed up onto her good knee until she could reach it with her teeth. She grabbed it and dropped it onto the ground.

With her hands still behind her she grasped the knife

and tried to angle it so it cut into the ropes binding her wrists. The knife slipped and sliced her skin and she whimpered, but kept going, trying to rub it back and forth. She cut herself twice more and soon she was having problems keeping her grip on the knife because it was slick with her blood.

She felt a tiny give in the rope and she strained her muscles, trying to break it. It held, though, and she sawed away at it a little more. Finally it came loose and she pushed herself off the ground and hopped toward the stairs.

The man put a hand on her shoulder, seeking to stop her. "Don't go up there!"

She shook her wrist at him, sending blood splashing into his eyes. He screamed and jumped back. She grabbed the railings and half dragged herself up, listening to the sounds of battle continuing above her. As long as there was still fighting, Raphael had to be alive.

She made it to their floor and turned toward the room. Of the four men who had attacked them, only one remained. Another lay on the floor dead, and the broken window gave her a clue as to where the other two had gone.

The man who remained had Raphael on the floor and was steadying a stake against his chest. The vampire was covered in burn marks from the cross the man held in his hand and was bleeding profusely. His eyes had glazed over and she saw that there was garlic stuffed into his mouth.

"No!" she screamed, and flung herself forward. The man turned and swung at her, but she dropped to the floor beneath his arms. She plucked the garlic out of

Raphael's mouth and threw it out the window. With his swing not connecting to anything, the man lost his balance and staggered to regain it.

In the time that he did Raphael sat up, turned, and looked at him, eyes glowing, fangs protruding. "Run!"

The man paused, staring in fascination at the two of them, then turned and fled the room.

Raphael collapsed back onto the floor.

"We have to get out of here. The innkeepers know you're a vampire," Susan said.

"I can't believe this is how it's going to end," he groaned. "After all this time, a bad beginning and a worse ending."

"End? What do you mean end?" she demanded.

"They'll be coming back and I'm too weak to fight them off. Go, save yourself, Susan."

"But what about the war? What about Richelieu?"

"Those will have to become someone else's problem now. Paul, or others, will step up. Go!"

"But if I go, they'll kill you."

"And if you stay they'll kill both of us."

"I thought vampires were strong," she sobbed.

"I've lost too much blood, been too injured. I need to eat to regain my strength." His voice had dropped to a whisper. He looked so weak it terrified her. He was all that stood between her and the vampires hunting her. He couldn't die. She couldn't let him.

She looked down at her bleeding hands and wrists. Raphael needed blood to live. She was in a strange land with enemies she never knew she had. He was her protector, her friend, and...

She slid her left arm under his head, lifting it up into

her lap where she looked down into eyes that mirrored her own pain and fear. He looked vulnerable and her heart bled for him even as it began to pound with emotions too complex for her to handle.

Her cross dangled dangerously close to him and she took it off and stuffed it in her pocket.

"What are you doing?" he asked, voice weaker than it had been a moment before.

"I'm saving both our lives," she said, before pressing her bleeding wrist to his lips.

She felt his entire body tense. He moved to push her hand away, but he had almost no strength left. She pressed down tight, willing him to live, willing him to drink.

And then she felt his fangs slide into her and her blood began to flow into him. She gasped at the sensation. It hurt, but the agony paled in comparison to the sense of euphoria that swept her. He began to sit up and she pulled her wrist away and kissed him deeply, tasting her own blood on his lips.

He kissed her back, hard and passionate, arms wrapping around her and lifting her until she was the one lying in his arms. When his lips trailed down her chin and to her throat she whimpered low. When he bit her neck she felt her back arch, and she cried out as she grabbed his face and pulled it down harder, closer.

And when the darkness came to claim her she could feel him pull back from her and she felt so empty.

"God forgive me," he whispered. "What have I done?"

Raphael held Susan in his arms and for the first time in his life felt something he could only describe as grief. He had killed her. She had sacrificed herself for him and now everything was lost.

He bent to kiss her forehead, which had grown so very cold. Beneath his lips he felt something, the faintest of pulses, and hope surged through him. She wasn't dead. Her heart still beat, pushing what little blood she had left through her body.

He picked her up and carried her downstairs. The owners of the inn gasped and backed away at his approach. He snarled at them, making sure they got a good look at his blood-covered fangs.

"This is your fault and you are going to help me fix it," he said.

"We will never help a vampire!" the husband hissed.

The wife put a restraining hand on his arm. "But we will help her. What do you need us to do?"

"Do you know a doctor who lives nearby?"

They both nodded.

"Good. Call him and tell him to come immediately and bring what he needs to perform a blood transfusion."

The wife hurried to do as he asked as Raphael laid Susan gently down on a long table in the dining room.

"And you," he said, rounding on the husband. "You will bar the door and go upstairs and tell your remaining guests to stay in their rooms if they value their lives. If she dies, I will kill all of you and burn this place to the ground, salting the earth. Then I will hunt down the families of all those here and I will not stop until every last member of your bloodline is wiped out. Do you understand?"

The man nodded, ashen, and hurried to do as Raphael commanded. Sometimes you could get farther with terror and threats than the subtleties of mesmerism. Still, what

Raphael had promised to do he would if Susan died. He turned back and sat down in a chair at the table. He watched as her chest rose and fell in the most shallow of breaths. It seemed he willed each one into being. *Breathe. Breathe. Just once more. That's a good girl. Keep breathing. Breathe for me. Breathe for you. Breathe for us.*

The wife came back. "The doctor said he'll be here in fifteen minutes."

Fifteen minutes. Human life could be snuffed out in less than a second and he had to wait fifteen minutes. What if she didn't have fifteen minutes?

The woman turned to leave.

"Stay!" Raphael commanded.

He could smell the fear coming off her as she turned to look at him. She thought he was going to kill her and he didn't blame her. After all, he might.

"Do you believe in God?" he asked her.

"Yes," she said, lifting her chin proudly.

"Then, would you please...pray...for her? Her name is Susan and she does not deserve this."

The woman drew up a chair and sat down next to him. She took Susan's hand in her own and bent her head over her.

"Out loud, please," Raphael whispered. He might not be able to join in, but he desperately wanted, needed to hear the words.

The woman eyed him. "You could do this yourself," she noted.

"No, I really couldn't."

"Our Father, we offer up this child, Susan, to you. Hold her in Your arms but gently as we want her to remain with us. Speed her healing, give her body life and breath and the blood that it needs to continue on. Allow her to wake with no ill effects and praise Your name as the giver of all life. Amen."

He said the "amen" in his heart.

"You care for her."

It was a statement, not a question.

"I think I must. I don't know what it feels like."

"But you know that she mustn't die, for you would be diminished. She makes you better than yourself, makes you dream dreams you've never known."

"Yes," he whispered. It was true. When he held her, when he kissed her...for just a moment he was a man and not a monster.

"Then I shall pray for you both. If you can learn to feel this for another then you are not beyond salvation."

He turned to look at her. He knew his eyes were glowing still and that he was covered in blood. She didn't flinch, though. She just looked at him, the light of truth, of belief in her eyes.

"You remind me of a monk I know," he said. "How is it you are aware of my kind?"

She shrugged. "Our families have lived here a long time. This inn has held many secrets, seen much and revealed little. Vampires are not new to this area of France. Nor to us."

"And yet they are feared," he said.

"We've had reason to fear. We still do if I'm not mistaken."

"If she dies I will kill everyone here," he said, repeating his promise.

She inclined her head. "I believe you. But it is not because you are a vampire that you will do this."

"Then why will I do this?"

She patted Susan's hand. "Revenge. Because you love her."

He didn't say anything. It did little good to deny it. Let the woman think that. If she did then she might be more inclined to help Susan.

Susan. He looked down at her still form and hated himself for what he had done. She was his best hope for winning this war, though she did not yet understand why. He needed her. Surely that was all that it was.

But in his dead, cold heart he knew there was something more. The first kiss they had shared had been nothing more than an object lesson, his attempt to convince her that she needed to go with him to rescue her cousin. The others... he didn't know where they had come from. All he did know was that he had wanted them as much as she had.

The woman smiled at him. "You love her," she insisted.

As David stepped over the threshold of his new apartment he briefly considered painting his blood on the door to bar Paul's entrance. As much as it irked him, though, he needed the vampire's help.

"Come in if you must," he said.

"Your enthusiasm is so touching," Paul said as he followed him.

David looked around. The apartment had one bedroom and a large living room with a decent-size kitchen. It was twice the size of his apartment at home and only sparsely furnished.

"This room will be perfect for training once we move

the television," Paul noted, looking around the living room.

He pulled a small vial of clear liquid out of his robes and unscrewed the top. He then began to wet his fingers and sprinkle the liquid onto the walls of the room, moving quickly to cover the frame encasing the sliding glass doors that led out onto a small balcony.

"What is that?"

"Holy water. I'm blessing and consecrating your home," Paul said.

"No offense, but I'm Protestant not Catholic. I'm not into the whole blessing thing."

"Your belief and participation are unnecessary," Paul told him as he continued his journey around the room before disappearing into the bedroom.

"Will it keep out vampires?" David called after.

"No."

Paul returned a minute later. "And you should be careful. I mean, a vampire can be disguised as anyone."

David started laughing loudly. "Yeah, I kind of got that hint."

Paul looked at him with a puzzled expression, head cocked to one side.

David gestured indicating Paul's monk robe. Understanding lit Paul's face and a moment later David found himself slammed backward into the wall, a hand pinning him there, fangs an inch from his face.

"This is *not* a disguise. I have more faith than you could ever hope to attain. My devotion to God is real and absolute and I will have no one denigrate it or question it. *Ever.* Are we clear?"

"Clear," David stammered.

Paul released him and stepped back. His eyes were glowing but slowly they began to return to normal. David swallowed and moved guardedly away from the wall, keeping his own eyes riveted on the vampire.

"I am sorry. I did not mean to imply—"

"Forget it. Now, move that television. I have to go get a few things to help out with the training. When I return, we'll begin."

David blinked and the vampire was gone, only the suddenly open apartment door attesting to the means of his departure. With a sigh he closed the door and then moved the television into the bedroom.

When he had accomplished that he shoved the sofa and coffee table into the kitchen area of the apartment, freeing up the entire living room space for whatever it was Paul had planned.

He wondered how long Paul was going to take and after waiting a couple of minutes decided he might as well go about unpacking. Most of his things had been shipped over and the landlord had placed the boxes in the bedroom. With the exception of clothes David had brought very little. It was only a three-month assignment and he had felt no desire to risk losing valuables or mementos for such a relatively short length of time. Fortunately, he had another couple of days before work actually started. He shook his head, not wanting to think about how he was going to juggle a job and vampire hunting.

He examined the first box and found socks and T-shirts. He opened the top drawer of the dresser and began shoveling things in. Into the second drawer he dumped pajamas and shorts. The third drawer was where he planned to put his sweaters and cold weather gear, like his mittens. He bent over, pulled on the drawer and discovered that it was stuck.

He took a firm hold and yanked and heard a cracking sound. The wood of the drawer splintered in his hand, breaking into several jagged pieces.

A sliver drove itself under his thumbnail and he winced. He bit at it until he was able to suck it out. The immediate irritant removed, he looked at the shattered drawer.

"I'm not paying for that," he muttered. He'd have to call the landlord in the morning and see if he could get a new dresser.

He heard the front door open and close and he stiffened. He moved quickly to the doorway and was relieved to see that Paul was depositing a couple of duffel bags on the floor.

"Did you get what you needed?"

Paul straightened and lobbed a wooden stake at David. He caught it and stared at it, feeling the weight of it in his hand.

"Yes," Paul said, pulling a plastic bag filled with red liquid out of one of the bags.

David's stomach turned. "Is that blood?" he asked.

Paul nodded, ripped the top off the plastic bag, tilted back his head, and poured it down.

Bile rose in the back of David's throat and he wanted to turn away but found himself unable to. All he could do was stare in horrified fascination.

When Paul was finished he tossed the empty bag in the trash and wiped his hand across his mouth. "I missed breakfast," he said by way of explanation.

"Was that human?" David asked.

"No, gave that up centuries ago. Cow. Easier to get and it keeps me from smelling humans and instantly thinking dinner."

"Good to know."

Paul nodded and rummaged in one of the duffels for something.

"What do you have in there?"

"Your arsenal," Paul said, motioning him over.

David moved to stand over Paul's shoulder where he could peer inside. It made him intensely uncomfortable to be that close to the vampire, but there was no help for it. Paul squatted down and began pulling things out.

"Here is a cross," he said, handing David a wooden cross three inches in length.

"I'm familiar," David said, trying to keep the sarcasm out of his voice.

"The ends are tapered so in an emergency it can double as a stake."

"Good to know," David said, carefully setting the cross to the side.

Paul pulled a silver cross on a black leather cord out of the bag.

"What's that for?"

"To wear, around your neck. It will fit tight, but it will discourage a vampire from going for the throat, which is their natural instinct and their primary target."

David grimaced. "It's a necklace."

"It's a shield. Wear it and don't make me show you why you need to."

David nodded and started to put it to the side.

"No, now!" Paul snapped. "Put it on and don't take it off."

David looped the leather cord over his head and then tightened the ends so that the cross was sitting at the base of his throat. *Just pretend it's a tie*, he told himself. *A very thin tie. A string tie.*

"Ready?" Paul asked.

"For what?"

"To continue?"

"Yes. Go for it. Show me what else you've got."

Paul pulled out a bag of tiny, silver crosses, not that much bigger than confetti. David stared at them for a moment, wondering how on earth they could be much use.

Paul saw his questioning look and smiled. "They're for throwing. Keep a handful in your pocket and you can throw them at your enemy. Aim for the face. Vampires have incredible speed but they don't always use it because they rely on their strength and feel themselves impervious to most attacks. This will definitely surprise even the most seasoned vampire. If you're lucky it will burn them. At the very least it will slow them down and make them more cautious in their attack."

"That is really clever."

Paul shrugged. "I'd like to take credit for the idea, but a colleague came up with it. Problem is, most vampires can't or won't use this against each other. Good news is that no one will have ever had it used against them."

"Sneak attack."

"Precisely."

David took the bag and put it to the side as well.

Next Paul pulled out more vials of the holy water. "Holy water burns just like the crosses do. Throw it at someone, dump it in their drink, whatever you have to do."

"How effective are these things really?"

"What do you mean?"

"How many vampires are like you, immune to crosses and holy water?" David asked.

Paul shook his head. "A few, but none of the ones you will encounter will be that way."

"How do you know?"

"Because the vampires that Richelieu has created are without religion. Sometimes I wonder if they're even without souls."

"I don't understand."

Paul sat back and indicated that David should take a seat. After a moment's hesitation David joined him on the floor.

"We told you how Richelieu is broken, how for some reason the curse has not worked upon him."

"Yes."

"For a long time now he has been trying to raise an army, but he could not keep one because sooner or later they began to gain wisdom, turn from their evil ways. Then, about sixty years ago, something began to change."

"What?"

"It's been a subject of great speculation. He has seemingly found others as broken as he is. There are a great many theories abounding. Personally, I believe the modern age has brought with it a sense of moral ambiguity that has created people with no moral compass, no fundamental understanding of right and wrong."

"But all vampires started as evil people, from what you've said."

"True. But, in the past, even the most evil people had an understanding of right and wrong, good and evil. Even those who didn't know which side they were on at least recognized that there were sides."

"Relativism, moral equivalency. Are you saying that these things are creating broken people who can be turned into vampires who grow increasingly evil with the passing of time, instead of increasingly good?" David asked.

"Depravity feeds on depravity, and with no sense of right and wrong, there is nothing for them to hold on to."

"That's tragic."

Paul nodded. "Generations crying out for meaning in their life, for something to believe in beyond themselves, and afraid or unable to embrace faith. Tragedy is all around us."

"Regardless of why or how they are so broken, so lost, they must be stopped. Show me what else you have in your arsenal."

Paul indicated the stake that David had put down with the other items. "Through the heart."

"Raphael told me the easiest ways to do it."

"And later I will show you."

"It's only wood that works, though, right?"

"Yes. No metal or any other material piercing the heart will kill a vampire."

"Why do you think wood will?"

Paul gave him the ghost of a smile. "I believe, like so many things with our kind, it's the symbolism of it."

"What do you mean?"

"Vampires who do not trust God cannot touch a cross, the symbol of Christ's sacrifice of blood for salvation. That cross was made of wood and so I believe that wood can pierce the heart of a vampire and kill him. Had Christ been killed with a sword then maybe these stakes would be made of that material."

The religious symbolism appealed to David, but it didn't quite make sense. "But vampires, I'm guessing, were killed with wooden stakes long before the time of Jesus."

"And thousands of years before the crucifixion happened it was prophesied in what form the Messiah would die—on a tree. Just because vampires did not yet understand the symbolism doesn't mean that their Creator didn't."

"Wow. That's intense."

Paul shrugged. "It's only a theory and I have many of those."

David nodded. "So, what else?"

Paul pulled a short sword from the bag and David felt his eyes widen as he took it from him.

"Decapitation. I will show you how to accomplish it, as well."

Next he pulled forth a sealed bag. Inside was a single clove of garlic. Paul held the bag by its edge, gingerly, his nose wrinkled as he passed it to David.

"Garlic?"

"Yes."

"It repels vampires like the myths say?"

Paul chuckled. "Not exactly like the myths say. The smell incapacitates us, makes us ill, renders us nearly helpless."

"It's your kryptonite," David said.

Paul shook his head with a smile. "We say that kryptonite is Superman's garlic."

David smirked and added the bag of garlic to the pile. "Anything else?"

"One more thing," Paul said. He pulled a lighter out of the bag and handed it to David.

"Are you kidding?" David asked as he took it.

"No."

David flicked it and the light flamed on. Paul moved back slightly and David raised an eyebrow.

"Fire is lethal. Set a vampire's clothes on fire and he will drop you in a heartbeat in favor of extinguishing the flame. The sun does kill, as well, though how long a vampire can be in it varies, but generally no more than half an hour."

David nodded. "Then it's time to learn how to use these things. Hopefully, I won't need them all, but I want to know just in case."

"You have the heart of a warrior and the soul of a—"

"Poet?"

Paul shook his head. "Priest. Your faith is very strong."

David shrugged. "I guess you never really know how strong your faith is until it's put to the test."

"So, let's put it to the test."

"What do you mean?"

Paul smiled. And then he attacked.

CHAPTER FOURTEEN

For the life of the flesh is in the blood: and I have given it to you upon the altar to make an atonement for your souls: for it is the blood that maketh an atonement for the soul.

—Leviticus 17:11

The doctor took so long to arrive Raphael's fury had only grown and it took all his strength not to rip the man's throat out when he did come. The doctor was hurried into the dining room where Susan lay, her breathing still shallow and labored.

"What happened here?" the doctor asked as he approached. He glanced down at Susan, eyes taking in the wounds on her wrist and throat, and his face changed. "Oh, I see."

He glanced up at Raphael, eyes hard. "You did this?"

Raphael nodded. "Can you give her a transfusion, save her?"

"I can but try. Do you know what blood type she is?"

"No."

"I'm O negative," the innkeeper's wife volunteered.

"Then we should be okay. Let me set it up."

He opened his bag and took out his equipment and

then looked at Raphael. "I need you out of here. I can't work and worry about your bloodlust at the same time."

As much as he didn't want to go Raphael knew the doctor was right. He'd drunk a lot of human blood, the first in many years, and the cravings for more were already setting in. But he didn't want to leave her.

The woman put a hand on his arm. "She will be safe enough while you wait in the kitchen. And so will you."

He nodded and removed himself, pain squeezing his chest tight. He made it to the kitchen and was suddenly overwhelmed by the smell of blood. He glanced down and saw blood on the floor next to a butcher's knife. He took a deep breath. It was Susan's blood, he could tell by the smell. He felt a fever burning deep inside, a need for her blood.

Even if the doctor can save her, I'm not sure I can be near her again. What if I lose control? I can't risk killing her, but I can't leave her alone. She'll just be attacked again.

He buried his head in his hands. What was it the woman had said to him about praying?

A presence moved in the kitchen with him and he glanced up to see the innkeeper. The man was angry, but more than that, he was frightened. Raphael could sympathize and the realization moved him.

"Your wife will be fine," he said.

The man looked at him. "Even if yours is not?"

Raphael blinked at him as he realized that they still bought that part of the story. "Yes," he said, turning to glance into the other room. "Even if my . . . wife . . . is not."

The day before it had been a cover story, a sort of joke to tease her. Now, though, everything was different.

She had saved his life, willingly risking her own. She had given her blood of her own free will. No one had ever done that for him. And now her blood flowed through him, invigorating him, connecting him to her.

Wife.

He had never given serious thought to taking a wife. It had seemed like a useless gesture, binding one who was alive to one who was dead. And he wanted little to do with the vampires he knew who were women.

He pressed his fingers to his forehead. Such thoughts were insanity. Even if Susan survived she deserved a human mate. It was arrogance on his part to even assume that she would want him. They would fight the battles they needed and hopefully win. Then they would go their separate ways and within six months she would have relegated him to a story she wished she could tell her grandchildren one day if they would only believe her.

And could he even delude himself into thinking that he had real feelings, honest ones? Shared danger created a connection between people. That was all. He needed that to be true. Otherwise he was lost.

After what had seemed like an eternity the doctor appeared in the kitchen. Both Raphael and the innkeeper started toward him and he held up his left hand to fend them off.

"They will both be just fine."

The rush of relief Raphael felt was mirrored in the innkeeper's face. The innkeeper hurried past the doctor headed for the other room. Raphael started to follow when he noticed that the doctor was sweating profusely and there was a bulge in his right sleeve at the wrist.

Quick as thought, Raphael grabbed his hand and

yanked up his sleeve. The doctor had been hiding a stake. With a snarl Raphael ripped it away and tossed it across the room.

"Thinking like that is what caused this to begin with," he hissed, flashing his fangs. "I'm going to pretend that you weren't about to stab me in the back with that thing since you saved her. If you value your life, go now and speak of this to no one."

He turned without waiting to see the man nod. He should have mesmerized him. He was getting sloppy, too many people were aware of him, aware of his kind. But then, the doctor and the others had already known of his kind, it was just him that he should have erased from their memories.

When he entered the dining room he was relieved to see that the color was back in Susan's flesh and her breathing was deep and even.

The innkeeper's wife was lying on a table as well and looked considerably paler than she had a few minutes before. A large bandage on the inside of her elbow was testament to the sacrifice she had made. She and her husband had nearly gotten Raphael and Susan killed, and now she saved Susan. *Blood atones for blood.*

"The doctor said she shouldn't be moved for a couple of days."

"Normally I would agree, but under the circumstances I think it's best if we leave."

"You should stay, for her sake," the innkeeper said as he held his wife's hand.

"It is for her sake that we must go. She would not want any more bloodshed, ours or yours."

The wife nodded, clearly understanding him. The innkeeper disappeared up the stairs and returned with Susan's bag. Raphael slung it over his shoulder and then he picked Susan up in his arms and she groaned softly. The innkeeper scurried to open the front door for them and Raphael moved quickly through it, lest more attackers waited.

No attack came, though, and moments later he was placing her in the backseat of the car, trying to position her for maximum comfort and safety. Finished he slid into the driver's seat.

As soon as he hit the road he floored it, watching the inn retreat in his rearview mirror. With Susan in the back still unconscious and precious nighttime already wasted he accelerated far beyond what most would consider a safe speed.

They were nearly to Bryas when he heard Susan groan from the backseat. "Where am I?" she asked a moment later, her voice weak.

"We are almost at Bryas," he said, relieved to hear her voice.

"Why do I feel so awful?"

"We'll discuss it when you're a little more awake," he said.

She fell silent and he didn't know if she was thinking or had fallen asleep.

As he turned onto the winding road that would lead to the ancestral castle of Bryas she struggled to a sitting position in the back just as the castle came into view under the shimmering moon.

The castle was half in ruins, stones crumbling, a once proud structure falling prey to the ruinations of time and neglect. It had been so long since he had seen it that he was startled by its appearance and regretted that one more icon from his past should have been brought low while he himself carried on.

"Is this it?" Susan asked, her voice fearful and questioning.

"It is."

"I don't see what I'm going to find here."

He shook his head. "Maybe you'll be surprised. Perhaps we both will."

"Is it safe to go inside?"

"No way to tell without going in. Stay here while I scout ahead."

She touched his shoulder. "No, I'm going with you. I don't want to be left alone. And besides, I want to see this place."

"You're too weak to walk right now. You can see it after I've made sure it's safe."

"No!"

The fear in her voice was strong. Aside from being afraid of being left alone she was probably afraid that if he explored it he would deem it too unsafe for her to enter.

"I'll have to carry you."

"All right."

He got out of the car, opened the back door and gently helped her out. Her legs were wobbly, but she seemed in better shape than he would have expected. He put an arm around her back and another under her knees and lifted.

She clung to his neck with her arms. He could feel the warmth radiating from her body and he took it as an excellent sign. "Are you ready to meet your past?" he asked.

"It's now or never," she whispered.

She couldn't help but feel like a child as Raphael carried her in his arms into the abandoned castle. When they stepped across the threshold they were plunged into darkness.

"I wish we had flashlights, I can't see."

"I can, and trust me, you're better off this way, for now. There will be some lanterns at the very least that we can find and light. For now I think it's important to find a place where we can both rest."

She didn't protest. Even being carried seemed to be making her more tired. She felt a shift in his gait and then they were climbing a staircase. She clung harder to him, afraid that it would collapse beneath them and they would fall. Then a memory came to her and she began to giggle.

"What's so funny?" he asked.

"I remembered seeing an old Dracula movie when I was a kid. He carried her up the stairs in his castle and it was so very frightening and thrilling."

"Which one are you?" he asked, his voice husky. "Frightened or thrilled?"

"I—I don't know," she said, feeling a wave of conflicting emotions.

"That's okay because this is nothing like Dracula."

"And why not?"

He smiled at her. She felt it more than saw it. "This is your castle, not mine."

At the top of the staircase he took a series of quick turns and then at last stopped. She looked around. Moonlight was pouring through a slit of a window in the far wall. From it she could make out a few dark shapes in the room.

"Where are we?" she asked.

"One of the bedrooms. I'm going to put you down on a chair for a minute, okay?"

"Okay," she whispered.

He lowered her gently until she was sitting on a chair. Dust was thick on the arms of it and she wrinkled her nose in distaste and told herself not to sneeze.

"I'm going to be in the room next door for just a couple of minutes," he told her.

"Okay," she said again, feeling less than useless.

Then he was gone and she was alone in the dark. All the memories she had been holding at bay about what had happened to her came flooding to the surface.

Don't cry, you'll just make yourself weaker! She bit her lip to hold back the tears and winced in pain. Slowly she raised her hand to her neck and felt the two puncture marks right where she remembered him biting her.

Sudden sounds from the room next door captured her attention and she froze, terrified that more enemies had found them knowing she was too weak to defend herself. She relaxed a moment later as she heard the sound of something like a rug being shaken. Raphael must have noticed the dust and the dirt, as well.

He returned after what seemed a very long time and scooped her back up in his arms.

"I have a surprise for you," he said.

He carried her into the next room and her eyes opened wide. Lanterns were burning on two tables and a dresser in the room. The faint smell of lemons and mothballs filled the air and the bed had been freshly made.

"I found some pretty old cleaning supplies in the bathroom down the hall. I'm pleased to see they still worked," he said. "The linens were tucked away in a good, sturdy trunk and just needed to be shaken out."

"This is so thoughtful of you, I can't believe it," she said.

"Why? Just because I'm a monster doesn't mean I enjoy living in squalor. Besides, I can't take you to a hospital, the least I can do is make sure that it's clean." He set her gently down on the bed and pulled the covers up over her. "Now, you rest while I do some more exploring. I'll see you tomorrow night."

"Don't leave me," she said, panic flooding her.

"I won't. I'll be nearby if you need anything. A whisper from you and I'll be here. And when the sun rises I will return and sleep in here so that we may guard each other."

"Okay," she said.

"Sleep well, dear Susan of Bryas. You have earned it and you are home."

David lay panting and exhausted on the floor. He hurt in places he didn't know he had and he wasn't completely convinced he hadn't broken a second rib.

Paul had been merciless. For the last three hours he had attacked over and over again, criticizing every move David made and pushing him to be better, stronger, faster.

Now the monk was sitting, praying, his eyes closed and his body swaying gently to a chant he alone could hear.

The vampire monk made David nervous, and more than a little perplexed. He tried to keep his doubts to himself, though, not wanting to give the man a reason to go off his self-imposed diet of animal blood.

Exhausted, David felt himself drifting off to sleep. He was suddenly awakened, though, by a hand on his chest. He looked up at Paul.

The vampire looked calm and at peace. "You have done well, David. So well, in fact, that you are ready for your first test."

"Test? What do you mean?" David asked.

"The sun rises in one hour. Not far from here is a house where three vampires will be sleeping."

"You want me to find the house?"

Paul chuckled. "I have already found the house. I want you to kill them."

As fear flooded him David knew that he wasn't ready. "I can't!" David blurted out.

"Of course you can. What do you think we've been doing all night?" Paul asked, eyebrows arched.

"Teaching me how to fight, but that's different. I don't know how to kill a vampire when he's asleep."

Anger flashed ever so briefly across Paul's face to be replaced by a stern look as he ticked off on his fingers, "Staking. Fire. Decapitation."

"But you can't decapitate someone lying down, the angles are all wrong for what you showed me."

"Then pick one of the other two."

"But, it's easier to stake from the side or the back, not the front."

"Then set them on fire!" Paul said, the anger returning.

"I'm not an arsonist! I set a fire, a lot more than just vampires could get hurt."

Paul threw him into a wall. "A lot more people are going to get hurt if you don't. So you better tell me right now what your real problem is."

"It's not right, killing people when they're defenseless."

"Listen to me very closely. They are not people."

"But—"

"No! Not people. Not human. Creatures. Evil. And these are irredeemably so. They can kill you without thought, without remorse, in the blink of an eye, and believe me they will. And then they will kill everyone else. Do you want that burden on your conscience? Would you rather face one alive and die or destroy a thousand and live, saving the world in the process?"

Paul muttered something under his breath.

"What did you call me?" David asked.

"Cowboy. You Americans and your ideas about a fair fight. Well, I'm here to tell you that when you're fighting vampires, there is no such thing as a fair fight. There is surviving and dying and that's it. And if you forget that for even a moment, if you hesitate, then you are lost. And there is nothing I can or will do to bring you back from that. Now, either you face the truth or I might as well kill you now. At least by my hand the death would be swift, merciful. You won't even know I've touched you until you wake up and stare into the face of God."

"I don't believe you'd kill me," David said.

"Then you're a fool," Paul hissed. "I might wear these robes, and I might love almighty God, but I am not like you and killing you would be the simplest thing in the world. All it would require is for me to stop thinking for one moment. The only reason you and everyone else here isn't dead is because I control myself every moment, every move, every thought. If I didn't then the monster that I am would run free. You live because I will it."

The vampire left the room and David slid down to a sitting position on the floor. He reached for one of the stakes nearby and his hand was shaking so hard he couldn't pick it up.

He was still sitting there half an hour later when Paul returned. The monk tossed a pizza box on the counter and dropped another black duffel bag on the floor. David stood slowly and approached him warily.

As he neared he could smell the pepperoni and cheese and his stomach growled noisily. "I didn't order a pizza," he said.

"No, but I did. You need to eat, too, and humans seem to be obsessed with this food above all others."

"We also enjoy a good hamburger. I eat the cow's flesh, you drink the cow's blood ...," David said, trying to crack a smile.

"I don't care what you eat as long as you keep your strength up for the fight that lies before you," Paul said. "After you've eaten I'll show you how to stake a vampire who is lying down."

David scarfed down four slices of pizza and watched as the monk pulled a skeleton that looked like it belonged in a biology teacher's lab out of his bag. He put a shirt and pants on it and then laid it down on the floor, arranging it to look like it was sleeping.

"That's not real is it?" David asked as he got himself a glass of water.

"Of course it's real. It doesn't do us much good to have you practicing on plastic, does it?"

"That's disgusting."

"Imagine you're a student of medicine or anthropology, or something."

"If I could have imagined that I would have listened to my mother and become a doctor instead of going into computers."

"It would have been far more helpful if you had."

Paul handed David a stake and then picked up one of his own. "Ready?"

Not even remotely didn't seem like a wise answer. So David steeled himself and said, "Yes."

Five minutes later he deeply regretted that decision when he heard a rib crack beneath the stake that he was wielding. He winced and fought back the urge to grab at his own broken rib, which was throbbing in sympathy.

Finally Paul relented. "You need to get some sleep."

"Thank you," David said as he yawned. It was nearly dawn. "What do you want me to do when I wake up?"

Paul handed him a city map marked with a large, red *X* and a street address written next to it. He then gave him a key. "The three vampires sleep in the basement. Time your attack very carefully. I will not be able to be with you, but if things should go badly, I need time to wake up and rescue you."

"Can the vampires wake up while I'm trying to kill them, like in the Dracula story?"

Paul hesitated, casting his eyes downward for a moment.

"What aren't you telling me?"

"Vampires don't usually kill other vampires. It defeats the purpose. Besides, we're all asleep at roughly the same time. And I have never spoken with a human who has killed one while it slept."

"You don't know?" David asked incredulously. "Are you seriously telling me you don't know?"

"Yes, that is what I'm telling you. Which is why it is important that you do your work no more than five minutes before sunset in case it doesn't go well."

"A lot can happen in five minutes!"

"I know, that is one of the reasons I have been teaching you various methods of fighting. Closer than that, though, and you risk not finishing the job before the sun sets and the vampires wake."

"You've got to be kidding me."

"I wish I was, David. I wish I was."

When Susan awoke the room was light, but a makeshift curtain was obscuring the window and keeping the sun's rays from penetrating. She couldn't remember when she had slept so well. She glanced around the room. The stone walls were bare except for a couple of large tapestries hanging on them. The stone floor was covered in a few fur rugs.

There was an ancient-looking trunk at the foot of the bed. To her right there was a dresser and a full-length mirror. She slowly turned her head to the left and saw a sitting area with a writing table and a chair as well as a lounge. Stretched out on the lounge was Raphael, an arm flung casually over his eyes as though he had just lain down for a moment.

She watched for a couple of minutes and he didn't move. *It's like he's not real, only a statue when he's like this.* She sat up slowly, fighting the weakness in her limbs.

She threw back the covers and touched her feet to the floor. She wasn't sure if she could stand, but she had to try. Raphael had said something about a bathroom and she needed to find it, even if she had to crawl down the hall on her hands and knees.

She stood gingerly and her knees shook, threatening to collapse under her weight. She kept hold of the bed, moving down slowly to the foot. It took her over a minute and she gritted her teeth in pain as she did it. Once there she braced herself on the trunk and gauged the distance to the wall. It was at least three feet.

She stretched out her right hand and slid her right foot forward. *Moment of truth.* She let go of the trunk and stepped forward. Once, twice, and her hands touched the wall. She leaned her shoulder against it and began to slide down it toward the door.

Once there she looked both ways down the corridor, wondering in which direction she needed to go. She flipped a mental coin and started to the right. The second door she came to was the one she was looking for and she nearly cried in relief when she smelled a lemony scent and realized Raphael must have cleaned that room as well.

When she had finished and splashed some water on her face she prepared for the walk back to the room. It seemed to take longer and by the time she lay down on the bed she thought she might never move again.

She stared up at the ceiling. *God, why have You brought me here? What is it I'm supposed to find, learn?* It was something she hadn't even been adequately able to explain to herself yet, but she had felt compelled to come. It had been like if she didn't, something terrible would happen. *But why? What here is so important?*

She thought about the key in the box in her luggage. It clearly wasn't the key to the front door, or if it was, it wasn't nearly as necessary as one would expect or hope. She looked around the room again. Nothing there appeared to have a lock, at least not that she could see from her vantage point.

But then, that would be too easy, wouldn't it?

She closed her eyes and felt her body sink further into the mattress. She was so very tired and mysteries and keys and secrets would just have to wait a little longer.

Half an hour before sunset David stood outside the two-story building, duffel bag over his shoulder, hands slick with sweat, holding the key to the door, and wondered if he had completely lost his mind. He couldn't decide which made him crazier: believing that vampires existed or believing that he could fight them. In the bag he had every tool that Paul had given him and he was terrified that they wouldn't be enough.

He climbed the steps to the front door and inserted the key, half hoping it wouldn't fit. He had no idea where or how Paul had gotten it. It did fit and the lock twisted open easily. He tightened his grip on the bag, and opened the door.

He stepped inside and closed the door as quietly as he could even though he knew it wasn't necessary. He pulled a stake and the large cross out of the bag. The tiny crosses and the lighter were already in his pockets. He looked around, trying to remind himself to breathe.

The house was upscale with tasteful furnishings, vases, and art. It was hard to believe that it was a haven for creatures of darkness. He looked at the stairs and wondered if anyone else lived in the house. It would probably be better to find out sooner rather than later. He looked at his watch. He still had twenty minutes left before Paul wanted him to begin.

He took the stairs quickly, trying to remain quiet. If there were human occupants then it would matter how much noise he made, he rationalized. There were three bedrooms and a bathroom on the upper floor and they were all empty. They looked like they hadn't been much used in a while, either. He made his way back down to the first floor and checked those rooms as well.

That left only the stairway leading from the kitchen to the cellar. He took a deep breath. Better to be down there and ready when the time came, as much as he'd rather wait in the kitchen.

He eased open the door and made his way slowly downstairs until the light from above was too weak to illuminate his path. He shifted the cross to his right hand and pulled out the lighter. The tiny flame flickered over the railing and let him see the stair below him and nothing more.

I just have to have faith.

He moved down to that stair and then the next and then the one after. Finally he reached the bottom. The tiny flame illuminated a light switch on the wall and he paused as he debated what to do.

Paul had been adamant that nothing would wake the vampires except, perhaps, a stake in the chest. He couldn't hold the lighter and try to drive the stake at the same time.

He held his breath and flipped the switch. Overhead fluorescents hummed on, flooding the basement with light.

And the first things he saw were three beds with three

forms, lying asleep. He crept forward, approaching the one nearest the stairs so that if it awoke he was closer to escape.

The vampire was a man who looked to have been cursed while in his forties. His mouth was open and David could see his fangs, which relieved him. He had the right house; he was staring at vampires and not some helpless humans with strange subterranean leanings.

He looked at his watch. It was almost time. He set down his bag and made sure he could get at everything in it. He stuffed the lighter back in his pocket and placed the cross next to the bag. He grasped the stake in his hands and went through it in his mind, just like he had practiced the night before.

You can do this, David. You have to. Your foot is on the path and there is no turning back, not now, not here. You can do this. Dear God, help me do this.

He glanced at his watch. Two minutes to go.

He turned and looked at the others. Once he killed the first he would have to move quickly to kill the other two before sunset. He studied their clothes, judging where he would need to put the stake to strike. If he knew where ahead of time he could be faster than if he had to judge each one before striking.

I hope the time Paul gave me for sunset was accurate. Even a minute difference and it's over.

One minute to go.

Please, God, don't let them wake up while I'm doing this, he prayed.

Thirty seconds.

What do I do if they wake up? How do I strike? Which weapon do I use first?

Ten seconds.

He moved the tip of the stake so it was above the spot where he would strike. He had to be strong.

Five seconds.

Four.

Three.

Two.

One.

He plunged the stake downward and as it connected with flesh there was an earsplitting scream.

CHAPTER FIFTEEN

And David said unto him, Thy blood be upon thy head;
for thy mouth hath testified against thee, saying, I have
slain the Lord's anointed.

—II Samuel 1:16

Out of the corner of his eye David saw a flash of movement as he struggled to come to terms with the fact that the scream hadn't come from the vampire. Despite his best efforts the stake had struck bone and he frantically tried to push through it as he half turned.

Something slammed into him, bearing him to the ground. The air rushed out of his lungs and the momentary relief he felt that the creature landed on his good side faded as soon as he realized he was going to be killed.

By a human.

His eyes were wild, they looked like an animal's, and his hair was filthy and unkempt, falling into David's face and making him want to gag. "Get off of me!" David shouted even as he saw the flash of a silver dagger in the man's hand.

He reached up and grabbed the hand that held the dagger, struggling to keep it from descending. The man lunged forward and clacked his teeth together as though trying to bite him. David grabbed the man by the throat and tried to heave him off. The other was too strong and too heavy, though.

David tried to bring a leg up to help throw off his captor but hissed in pain instead as he jostled his broken rib.

He risked a glance at the vampires who appeared to still be sleeping. How many minutes were left to him? How many seconds?

He screamed and with everything he had he punched out and sent the man sprawling. Coughing and gasping for air David scrambled to his feet and picked up his fallen stake. He twisted, saw that the hole in the sleeping vampire's chest was healing, and aimed a half inch above it.

It slid in and a moment later the body collapsed into ash. The human slammed into him from behind, sending David face first into the pile of ash. He gasped, breathing it in, and he began to cough as the dust coated his mouth and tickled his throat. He twisted to the side and the man slid off his back, falling onto the floor, on top of David's duffel bag.

David slid off the other side, gasping in pain. He held the stake for a moment, poised over the second vampire. Its eyes flew open and David shouted in surprise and plunged the stake downward, striking bone.

The vampire stared at him, rage and terror filling its eyes. David shoved as hard as he could, sobbing with the effort. The vampire's head moved slightly, then its lips curled back. David could hear the sound of bone cracking.

The vampire's hands shot up and grabbed him by the

throat, shutting off his air. And then the bone gave way and he felt the stake slide in. The hands and then the rest of the body disintegrated before him.

He stood, gasping for air, and as the human slammed into him again the third vampire sat up with a roar. The human climbed onto his back and wrapped an arm around his throat, forcing him to his knees. He struggled to rip the man's arm away, but he was too strong. The vampire stood and stretched a hand out toward David. He touched his cheek with a long, pointed fingernail and laughed deep in his throat.

David gave up trying to free himself and instead plunged his hands into his pockets. He threw the tiny crosses at the vampire's face and was gratified that they hit their mark. The vampire screamed and clawed at his face. With his other hand David pulled out the lighter, flicked it on, and set fire to the creature's pants.

The man holding him gasped and David shoved the lighter back toward his face. With a yelp the man let go and David staggered to his feet and ran for the stairs.

Behind him he could hear shouting as the man attempted to help the vampire smother the flames. And then the shouting stopped and he knew they had returned their attention to him.

He put his foot on the first step and felt a hand close on his shirt. Above him, a figure loomed in the doorway. David's heart fell in despair. He was trapped.

The figure leaped downward, landing just behind David with a thump. There was a terrified cry and David spun around to see Paul crush the windpipe of the human before turning his attention to the vampire.

"You!" the vampire hissed.

Paul didn't say anything, just circled warily over to David's abandoned duffel bag.

"I've heard about you."

Paul still didn't say anything, but quickly grabbed a stake and the large wooden cross. The other vampire's eyes widened as he saw Paul holding the sacred symbol.

"It's true."

"What is?" Paul growled.

"Who they say you are. You used to be called—"

Paul lunged forward, swinging the cross first, and connecting with the vampire's mouth. "Better that the name of God be on your lips than mine," he hissed.

David blinked, stunned at the ferocity of the attack. And then, as David watched, Paul plunged the stake into the vampire's heart and moments later he was gone.

Paul turned slowly, surveying the scene. Three piles of ash and one dead human. He looked up at David.

"You did better than I hoped, especially given the surprise," Paul said, nudging the body with his toe. "I should have thought about it. I've heard of a few vampires training guard dogs to watch them while they sleep, but no one has kept servants in almost two hundred years. Then again, these vampires don't care about what is civilized, or even about who knows of their existence. It is dangerous and another reason why they need to be stopped."

"I thought you said vampires can't kill other vampires?"

"I said we usually don't. It's unnatural. It feels worse than it does for a human to kill a human. We're meant to let each other live to reach salvation. But, it can be done and in this case it must."

"I think I'm going to be sick," David said as the enormity of what had happened sunk in.

Paul rolled his eyes and put a hand on David's shoulder. "I'll give you absolution, if that will help."

David shook his head as he forced himself to stand his ground and not shrink away under Paul's touch.

"Let's get you cleaned up and get some food. Then we can rest and plan the next stage."

As they turned and walked up the stairs David took one last look at the basement and tried not to think what the next stage was going to look like.

When Susan woke again she was startled to find Raphael sitting on the bed staring at her. She jumped and he turned away.

"I didn't mean to frighten you," he said.

"What's wrong?"

"Nothing's wrong. I was just watching you sleep, making sure you were all right after...everything."

She sat up and realized that she felt stronger than she had earlier that day. "I'm okay."

"Are you hungry?"

"I could definitely go for some dinner. You?" she asked with a yawn, and then froze as she realized what she'd said.

"I've already eaten," he said quickly. "But I've prepared a nice dinner for you. I'll bring it up here."

He returned quickly with steak and mashed potatoes. "How long has it been since sunset?" she asked.

"Long enough."

She took a bite of the mashed potatoes and looked at him in surprise. "They have garlic in them," she said.

"I know," he said, wincing as if just hearing the word was painful.

"Why?"

"Garlic stays in the system for days. It is excreted through the pores during that time."

"You still haven't answered my question."

"It's so vampires won't be able to stand getting too close to you."

"Including you?" she asked.

"Especially me," he whispered.

"It wasn't your fault, what happened. You were weak, hurt, and I pushed and—"

"And things happened that should never have been allowed to happen."

She decided not to argue, but busied herself eating while he watched. After a while it became creepy. "Do you miss eating this kind of food?" she asked.

He smiled. "I don't remember."

"You don't remember if you miss it?"

"I don't remember what it tastes like. At first, I know I didn't miss it because all I wanted was blood. Then, after that began to pass I found I couldn't really remember the taste of food. Maybe that's normal, or maybe I just never paid much attention to it when I was alive. Guess I wasn't an epicurean."

She smiled. "Have you tried eating food since?"

"Once. About three hundred years ago. It didn't go so well."

She raised an eyebrow and stared at him for a moment, but decided she didn't need to know. She polished off her dinner and then seriously considered going back to sleep.

But then she thought about the key and she knew she

didn't have the luxury. "Time to explore this place," she said.

"Are you up for it?"

"I have to be," she said.

A few minutes later she was walking down the hall with him by her side. The key was in her pocket and she hoped she found the lock it fit quickly.

The bedrooms on the top floor were all very similar to hers. After a few minutes Raphael helped her down the stairs.

On the first floor they entered what looked like a sort of throne room or audience hall. Raphael lit the candles in the wall sconces around the room. As the light flickered on the walls she saw that they were lined with portraits. Raphael returned to her side and she walked slowly down the length of one wall. The first few were less than a century old with names and dates inscribed on small brass plaques beneath them. She stared at each face in fascination.

When they came to the end of the wall she walked slowly across the room and began to look at the ones over there. She stopped in front of one of the final portraits, that of a young woman with a sweet smile and gentle eyes. There was something about her that was striking. She stared more closely and then she realized that she looked a lot like Wendy, but with her own darker hair.

"Who is she?" Susan asked, not expecting an answer.

"Her name was Carissa and a great tragedy and darkness surrounded her in her time." Raphael spoke quietly, almost reverently. She turned to look at him and there was a strange light in his eyes.

"Was she my great-great-grandmother?"

"No. Carissa never had children. Her first cousin, Fleur, was your ancestress."

"How do you know this?" she breathed, amazed.

"I've been aware of your family since I was turned into a vampire in the generation before Carissa and Fleur."

And then Susan noticed something else about the portrait, something that sent her reeling and made the hair on the back of her neck stand on end. The young woman was wearing a beautiful silver cross, so shiny and new looking. Susan reached to touch her grandmother's cross. Raphael noted the gesture and smiled.

"It is the same cross. It belonged to her father, a knight who fought in the Second Crusade. And now it has found its way down through the centuries to you."

Hot tears stung her eyes. Was this the legacy of faith her grandmother had wished her to discover?

"Come," he said softly. "We have more to explore before the sun rises."

Reluctantly she went with him, her eyes still lingering on the face of the woman who had worn the cross so many centuries before. She wondered how many others had worn it as well.

They walked slowly through the rest of the ground floor, and while it was a fascinating tour, it didn't yield up any obvious opportunities to use the key.

"You're tired, it's time for you to go back to bed," Raphael noted at last.

As she turned to head back for the stairway she noticed a small door in a dark corner and pointed to it. "What's behind there?" she asked.

"The stairway into the dungeon."

"This place has a dungeon?" she asked, shuddering at the image her brain conjured.

"Oh, yes," he said grimly. "A rather unpleasant place."

"You went down there earlier?"

"*Much* earlier."

"How much earlier?" she asked suspiciously.

"Centuries earlier. I don't wish to repeat the visit."

She was burning with curiosity but there was something dark and unpleasant in his eyes that warned her against it. A conversation for another time. *If there is another time.*

She barely made it back up the stairs and was immensely grateful when she got back into bed. There were hours to go before the dawn but her eyelids were already closing.

"What are you going to do?" she asked.

"I'm going to go out for a little while, do some more exploration, find some more food...for both of us. I won't be gone long."

"Promise?"

"Yes. Take this, just in case. I carved a few earlier for you. You'll find them piled on the table."

She opened her eyes and saw that he was handing her a stake. Her hand felt heavy as she lifted it to take the weapon. She shoved hand and stake under her pillow. "Come back soon," she whispered as she fell asleep.

Raphael hesitated as he left Susan's side. He didn't want to leave her, but something didn't feel right. He hurried out of the castle and down the winding drive toward the main road. He stopped frequently to look and listen, even taste the air.

He shook his head, almost convinced that he was imagining things. He had been worried that someone might have followed them from the inn, but if that were the case, they would have attacked during daylight while he was helpless.

Still, there was something, just out of reach. The faint whiff of blood came to him and he stopped, twisting slowly until he could pinpoint the direction it was coming from. He headed toward the pasture where he had earlier found goats roaming free. He found the one he had killed, but the smell of blood had long since faded from the carcass.

The scent of another's blood was strong, though, and he moved forward until he spotted the other body lying in the grass. The goat had been freshly killed and Raphael bent to look at it. As he did he caught the whisper of footsteps and spun just in time to avoid being staked in the back.

The vampire who was attacking him tripped over the goat, sprawling for a moment in the grass. It was all Raphael needed. He scooped up the stake intended for him and struck. As the vampire turned to ash the body of the goat became visible again and Raphael stiffened. There were two sets of bite marks. He spun around. There was another vampire, and he was nowhere to be seen.

Raphael turned and sprinted back toward the castle. If the other vampire wasn't waiting for him, he was going after Susan. He had to reach her, save her.

He smelled the garlic before he smelled the humans. He twisted in midstride, turning to sprint the other way. They were coming for him and he should have known, should have anticipated. He had to escape and then circle back to find the other vampire and to save Susan from them all. He had only gone a dozen steps when a bola of garlic wrapped around his throat causing him to fall like a stone.

Fear ripped through him. His sire had been taken the same way when he was young. He struggled to remove the garlic but the crippling nausea washed over him and he could feel the strength draining from him. *I can't let it end like this!*

The humans were on him in a moment, a half dozen of them. They didn't smell the same as the ones who had come after them at the inn. They seized him and he tried to growl but just ended up coughing uncontrollably. One tied his hands and feet together and another shoved a gag into his mouth.

They're not killing me. Why aren't they killing me? They couldn't be the same group of people. Those had murder in their hearts, this was different. A burlap sack was placed over his head and he could feel and smell it as the garlic bola was used to tie it shut. He felt a needle prick his arm and everything went black.

Susan woke with a start. Something was wrong, she could feel it. There was a presence in her room, and it was growing closer. Evil was rolling off it in waves. It couldn't be Raphael. Dark and disturbing as his presence could be it was nothing like this. She was reminded of the feelings that she'd had in the nightclub where they had rescued Wendy.

It was much more like that. She kept her eyes tightly shut as her fingers took a firmer grasp of the stake underneath her pillow. *God, protect me, help me.*

She opened her eyes barely a slit, praying she would be able to see something without giving herself away. In the dim candlelight that filled the room a figure loomed over her. It was a woman and as she bent low Susan could smell blood on her breath.

The creature moved closer, seemingly unaware that her prey was awake. *Wait, just a little bit closer*, a voice seemed to whisper in Susan's mind.

She could feel the breath on her throat even as she sank the stake into the vampire's foul heart. The stake hit the woman's chest and blood began to spill out. The creature screamed inhumanly and fell upon her. It thrashed around for a moment, driving the stake further into its body until it dissolved into ash. Susan breathed heavily through her mouth, struggling to deny the stench. With an effort she sat up shaking. The dust covered her clothes and she could feel the grit on her skin.

Were there others coming? It had been a woman, and the Raiders were brothers. Was she connected to them in some way? Were they lurking nearby waiting to finish her? Surely if anyone had been within hearing distance they would have come when the creature screamed. But there was no one. Not even Raphael.

She staggered toward the bathroom as her stomach churned. Hastily she peeled off her clothes and stepped into the shower, shivering as the cold water hit her skin. Slowly she became aware of a burning sensation on the left side of her chest. She looked down and shuddered. Long fingernails had cut through her shirt and sliced open her skin. Her own blood was oozing out of the scratches, blood mixing with the water to run down into the bottom of the shower.

Raphael, where are you? she wondered. Would he be back soon as he had promised or had something happened to him?

She finally turned off the water and stood shivering in the cold air. She paused for a moment, listening to see if she heard anyone else, and then beat a hasty retreat to her room where she threw some clothes on over her wet skin and wished for a towel. She grabbed two of the stakes from the pile that Raphael had left on the table and settled herself in a chair to wait for his return. She fidgeted with them, trying not to remember what it had felt like when she sank one into the vampire. Even the memory left a bitter taste in her mouth. She distracted herself by turning her thoughts to Raphael and where he could be and when he would be getting back. *If* he was coming back.

I should go looking for him, she thought. *If he's in the castle he couldn't have gone far. But if he's in the castle surely he would have heard and come to see what was happening.* Maybe he was trapped or outside on the grounds. She worried that she wouldn't find him. She still wasn't sure how much strength she had. Her stomach knotted at the thought that he might be dead. She took several deep breaths, trying not to panic. If he was dead then searching for him was useless. On the other hand, if he was alive then he would be expecting to find her right where she was. If she went wandering off and found trouble, he wouldn't know where to find her.

Best to just stay where I am. After all, if he's alive he'll be back before sunrise.

She waited and the darkness and the silence stretched on endlessly. Shadows moved in the corners of her eyes and nameless fears assailed her, until she was terrified of everything and convinced that the end was upon her.

As the first rays of the rising sun reached into the room she began to sob with relief because she was alive and with grief because Raphael might be dead.

When she awoke stiff and sore with a cramp in her neck several hours later Susan realized that she had fallen asleep in her chair. She stood up shakily and crossed to the window. The sun was high overhead and her stomach growled painfully. Slowly she took stock of her situation. She was alone in an abandoned castle. She craned her head to look toward the front and saw the car where Raphael had parked it the night they arrived. So, alone, but not trapped.

A ways past the car she could see some fruit trees. She wouldn't starve.

Slowly she made her way downstairs, keeping a tight grip on the banister and taking the stairs carefully. By the time she got to the car she was out of breath but feeling more confident than she had felt in days. She found that the trees were pear trees and she couldn't help but smile as she plucked one and began to eat it. Pears had always been her grandmother's favorite.

She ate a second one, more slowly than the first, while she pondered what to do next. When she finished, she turned her attention back to the castle feeling like she was ready to continue on. Even if Raphael was gone, her purpose was not. There were still too many secrets, too many answers she needed to find. She had the key and she wanted to know what it unlocked so she could leave before nightfall, before more vampires came.

She walked back inside and returned to the second floor. After putting the key in her pocket she went slowly from room to room, moving tapestries on walls and pulling out drawers of chests searching for anything that would take the key.

There was nothing.

Refusing to get discouraged she turned her steps back to the staircase and made her way back downstairs where she turned in a slow circle, looking around. The rooms were large and she was growing more tired and didn't know where to start.

She pulled the key out of her pocket. "God, help me to find what this unlocks," she whispered.

She closed her eyes and tried to think, to focus, to concentrate. And then, she realized that was the wrong thing to do. She took a deep breath, cleared her mind, and tried to be open to what God had to tell her. A minute later she opened her eyes and headed straight for the door that led to the dungeon, the one place in the castle she hadn't been, the one place even a vampire didn't want to go.

She reached the door and stared at it. It was old and iron, heavy looking with sliding locks on the outside to ensure that whatever was inside would stay there. She reached out to touch the first lock and an involuntary shiver went through her.

She steeled herself and slid back the first bar, then the second, and finally the third, which moved with a loud clunk. She swung the door open and stared into the darkness beyond. The smell of damp and mildew and things she'd rather not think about assaulted her nostrils and she couldn't help but hesitate.

I don't want to go in there. What if I get lost and

can't find my way out? What if I get hurt? What if I get trapped?

She looked around and saw a heavy-looking chair nearby. She slid it across the floor and used it to block the door so it could not accidentally swing shut behind her.

She took a lantern and cast its light down the stairs. What she would have given for a real flashlight! She took a step forward and could feel the darkness swallowing her whole.

She put one hand on the wall as the stairs led downward. It was slimy and somewhat wet and she fought the urge to yank her hand away. She kept going, slow and steady, marveling at how much it reminded her of descending into the sewers of Prague. In Prague, though, she hadn't been alone and, though she had sensed great evil, she hadn't felt nearly the fear she did at that moment.

She reached the bottom of the stairs and two steps later discovered another door like the one above. Her hand shook as she slid the bolts to unlock the door and then swung it open, wishing she had something to hold it open as well.

"I can't go in there," she said to the darkness.

Susan paused and she lifted one hand and held it quivering in the air, trying to be still and just feel. There it was again. She had never before ignored the proddings of the Spirit, but never before had she sensed such fear, such hatred, such death in any place where she had walked. "God," she whimpered in a little girl voice. "Why do I have to go in there? I'm so afraid."

Still she knew that she had to go on. With the knowledge came strength and she crossed the threshold boldly. As she put her foot down she heard a scream. She looked down and stifled a cry. She was standing on the tail of a large sewer rat. It squealed again and she jumped back as it scurried away into the black.

Minutes later she was making her way down the dark tunnel by placing her hands so that one was on each wall. The lantern was looped around her right wrist but did very little to illuminate her path. Still, she refused to leave it behind. The stench continued to grow worse the farther she went.

Finally, she came upon the first cell; the door was open, the hinges rusted, a dirty blanket was on the ground. She stepped inside, feeling sick to her soul, and took a close look at everything, but there was nothing else to see.

There were six cells in total and the next four were just as barren. Then she stopped at the last one and the hair on the back of her neck stood on end.

It was large, easily large enough to hold a couple dozen people packed in together. In the center of it was a rudimentary table that had buckles and straps hanging off of it. Dark stains covered everything and she had a suspicion they were blood. A table in the corner held an assortment of strange-looking equipment including glass beakers and a complicated system of tubes.

Someone was tortured in here, she realized in horror, taking a step backward. And then a rush of understanding flooded her. *Raphael. Something happened to him here. That's why he wouldn't come back down here.*

She shuddered and continued backing slowly out of the cell. She turned and her eyes fell on a filthy cloth on the floor with a lump underneath it.

I can't touch that. I can't, I can't, I can't.

And yet, somehow, she knew she must. She forced herself to move over to it. She held her breath as she grasped it between two fingers and yanked it up off the floor and tossed it to the side as swiftly as she could. There, on the ground, dilapidated and decaying, forgotten by time, was a child's teddy bear.

She blinked at it, fighting back tears, trying hard not to imagine how it had come to be there. She started to turn away and then she realized she couldn't. She bent down and gingerly picked up the bear. It felt strange and stiff in her hand and though it was large it still seemed far heavier than it should have been. Beneath the fur she could feel something that felt like metal.

Puzzled, she turned it over and there, in the back, was a keyhole. Excitement rushed through her. This had to be what she was looking for. The key was in her pocket and she started to put the lantern down so she could reach for it.

But a whisper brushed across her mind and she clutched bear and lantern tighter. She shouldn't stay. She turned, and ran back down the hallway, slamming the door and locking it before bolting up the stairs and doing the same.

She slid to the ground, her back against the great iron door, and cried. There was something down there in the dark that she would not, could not face. As her tears dried she looked down at the bear. It had brown, tattered fur, and a comical smile stitched onto it.

Susan pulled the key out of her pocket and inserted it into the hole in the back of the bear. A creaking of tired metal greeted her as she twisted and then she pulled open a door in the bear's back. The bear was metal, covered with fur. A stuffed animal constructed around a small metal box.

She reached into the box and pulled out two thin sheets of paper. The first was very, very old and she opened it carefully. The handwriting was strong and flowing but the words looked to be in French. Frustration filled her as she regretted her decision to study Russian in college instead.

She turned her attention to the second paper. It was folded up with familiar handwriting on the front spelling out a single word: "Susan."

CHAPTER SIXTEEN

The righteous shall rejoice when he seeth the vengeance:
   he shall wash his feet in the blood of the wicked.

—Psalm 58:10

Susan stared at the paper with her name on it and felt excitement and sorrow tearing at her. The handwriting was her grandmother's. That meant she had found what her grandmother had wanted her to find, but there was an ache in her heart because somehow it made the loss much more real to her.

As the tears began to flow she realized just how much she was going to miss her and just how long and how hard she had needed to cry.

When the storm of emotion had finally passed, she opened the letter with shaking hands and began to read.

Dear Susan,
   I am so very proud of you. You have become the woman I knew you would. I hope I have raised you well and instilled in you all the lessons and faith that I could. But now I am sure you have questions and I will do my best to answer them.

I always told you that Prague was a beautiful, magical city. What I did not tell you was that there is a war coming and the city with all of its magic and beauty and horror will be at the heart of it. I know I told you a great many things about the place, and about keeping your mind open to things that others might ignore or dismiss out of hand. I did this for a reason and I hope I was able to finally tell you the truth I have known for so many years. In case you do not already know this, in case I or another have not told you already, it is important that you understand that vampires are real.

Susan stopped reading abruptly, her eyes refusing to move past that sentence. *Vampires are real.* Her grandmother had known then. It shouldn't have surprised her and yet somehow it did. But how had she known about the war? There was no date on the letter so Susan had no way of knowing how long ago her grandmother had written it and left it for her, though she suspected that it had been after her parents died. Her uncle had said that her grandmother last visited Prague three years before. Was it then that she had journeyed to France to leave the letter? She took a deep breath, trying to fortify herself against whatever was coming next in her grandmother's letter, since she suspected it would shake her world, and forced herself to keep reading.

I do not have time to explain all the hows and whys of that to you. All I have time for now is to tell you the really important things. A few of the vampires are good and can be trusted. The major-

ity you will encounter, though, are evil and must be destroyed. The coming war will pit those two sides against each other and without help from humans the good vampires will lose. And when that happens, the entire earth will be consumed as though by plague and there will be no hope left.

I am asking you, Susan, to join the fight on the side of good. I wish I could have fought instead of you, but that was not meant to be. I want you to seek out the vampire named Raphael. If he's still alive, he will be at the heart of this whirlwind. He has been chasing the vampire Richelieu for over a hundred years, and when the war comes, he will finally find him. Prague will be the place where the two will meet and confront one another. Only one of them will survive this encounter. Of the two, Raphael is the better, the closest to being a good vampire. I met him once when I was young, although I doubt he will remember me. When you find him, make sure to tell him that you are of Bryas. My name and yours will likely mean very little to him, but Bryas he will know.

The next thing that you should know is that the cross necklace I gave you is the key to everything and is the mightiest weapon you can wield in this battle. That might seem fantastic, but believe me it is the truth. I found this letter when I was very young and it took me years to track down the cross necklace described therein and that you see on the portraits of some of your ancestors. Read it carefully so that you can understand the great and terrible gift you carry with you, a secret that has been kept for millennia and is now entrusted to you. Guard this secret well, because, as you will see, it is one worth killing for.

Finally, the key chain I gave you on your six-teenth birthday can unlock this silver cross and reveal what is hidden inside. And here then is the great secret, known only to three before you. I knew it. The crusader whose letter this was knew it. And the vampire who spared his life knew it. And now it is time for you to know it. But I fear that even if you have read this far you will not believe me. So I leave you this letter written by Jean, Marquis de Bryas, so that you might read the truth of it from him. I love you more than you will ever know.

Grandma C.

Susan picked up the other letter and scanned it in frustration. Raphael would be able to read it, but she didn't know where he was or even if he was still alive. She had thought to leave before sunset in case more vampires came, but if she left and he was trying to make his way back to her he would not be able to find her.

She didn't want to entrust the translation of the letter to a stranger, especially if the contents were as important as they seemed. She fingered her cross necklace, trying to fathom what secret it could possibly hold.

Wendy!

Wendy had taken French. If she could fax her a copy of the letter then she could translate it for her. And she could also have her mail her key ring, which she had left on the hook at home. She had taken only her house key with her.

Susan took the letters upstairs to her bedroom and re-trieved her cell from her bag.

With dismay she realized the battery was dead. She would have to leave to contact Wendy.

And that would mean admitting Raphael was dead.

Tears slid down her cheeks. She had to give him a little more time. There was too much to do and the thought of fighting her way through it all without him scared her. If he was trapped somewhere, delayed, and unable to come to her once the sun rose then he would be coming tonight. She had to give him a little more time to find his way back. She owed him that.

By the time the sun was setting Susan had barricaded herself in her room in the castle with the supply of stakes Raphael had made for her and as many lanterns as she had been able to gather from around the castle. She had fashioned a couple of makeshift crosses out of pieces of wood and fabric and placed them everywhere she could. She had also painted the outside of the window and the door with drops of her blood as Raphael had shown her.

She was prepared to wait for Raphael to return. If he didn't, then she was sure he had to be dead.

And if he was then all her hope died with him.

Raphael woke up shuddering and coughing. The smell of garlic coated everything and the burlap sack over his head kept him from seeing anything around him. He knew he'd been drugged but he could also tell that the sun had just set, meaning he'd been unconscious for almost twenty-four hours. Twenty-four hours. In the old days that would mean he couldn't have traveled very far, certainly not more than an hour's run for him. In the modern world, though, a day might as well be a lifetime. He could be anywhere.

The overwhelming smell of the garlic kept him from being able to smell anything else around him. He had no clue where he was or who might be watching him. He tried to struggle to his knees, failed twice, and kept trying until he made it. Then he heard the rush of many footsteps, multiple people entering the room he was in. The sound of their steps seemed to indicate marble floors, which matched the hardness he felt against his knees. That ruled out the Bryas castle, which had stone floors, or the inn, which had wooden ones.

He had even fewer clues, he realized, about who had taken him and why. Someone moved around behind him and he tensed, even though he knew there was nothing he would be able to do to defend himself.

The hood came off and with it the garlic. Raphael coughed hard and then looked up. Rage ripped through him as he realized that a hundred years of searching had come to a sudden end, and it was not by his doing. Richelieu was sitting on a gilded throne staring serenely down at him.

"You," Raphael hissed, pulling in vain at the bonds that bound him and wishing for nothing more than to rip the other vampire's throat out and take back that which he had stolen from him.

Richelieu nonchalantly studied his fingertips. "That's an unimaginative way to greet your son."

"You're not my son!"

"No? But, you're my sire, my creator, the one who gave me this life. If you can call it that. So what are you, who are you, other than my father? And if you are my father then I most certainly am your son. So, how have you been, Father?"

Raphael glared up at him, unwilling to dignify it with a response. The garlic was still close by, closer to him than to Richelieu, keeping him weak. But, it also kept Richelieu from attacking him. For the moment, even though Raphael was the one bound, they were at a stalemate.

Richelieu stared down at him. "I hear you've been looking to get me a stepmother. Very thoughtful of you. Frankly, though, I'd rather have a puppy."

Once upon a time Raphael would have bandied words with him, but those days had passed and he just wanted to control his temper and not let the other bait him. The one thing his own sire had managed to teach him, before he had been taken and imprisoned, was that an angry vampire was a sloppy vampire. A sloppy vampire was a dead vampire. Raphael had had a temper long before he was a vampire, more so than Richelieu, and he refused to let his creation, his failure, use his weaknesses against him. Not this time.

Richelieu looked lazily into Raphael's eyes. Where Raphael should have been able to see a soul, he saw only a void and it chilled him. Richelieu arched an eyebrow. "Fine, no puppy. That's okay, though, because there'll be no stepmother, either. I'm sure you've already realized that the young lady is quite...dead."

Raphael closed his eyes. It was what he had feared. The people who had taken him had been human, which left one vampire at Bryas. The odds that Susan, particularly in her weakened state, could have survived an attack were too low to offer any hope. Grief swept over him. All that effort to keep her alive and he had failed.

He could feel the rage within him, threatening to overcome years of discipline. He could feel his conscious mind beginning to slip away, giving way to the emotions that flooded him. The one thought he clung to, though, was that Richelieu had some purpose for bringing him here instead of killing him, some reason why he wanted to drive him to the edge. And if hanging on to what shred of reason he had left to him would thwart Richelieu then he had to hold on for all he was worth.

He opened his eyes and realized he was breathing deeply. Except for a gasp upon waking, vampires only breathed when preparing to attack. That fact would not be lost on Richelieu. With immense focus he managed to stop breathing and slowly, very slowly, he smiled. He could tell it caught the other off guard and that made the effort worth it.

"It's for the best. I'm not really the marrying kind. Of course, you understand that, being a man of the cloth."

Irritation flickered across Richelieu's face. Richelieu's relationship with God, which had always taken a backseat to his devotion to France, had become increasingly complicated since Raphael had cursed him so many years before.

Raphael moved his eyes off the vampire and set them on a small table next to Richelieu's throne. On it stood a jewel-encrusted box that he recognized. The very box that Richelieu had stolen from him. The one he would give anything to get back. He steeled himself. Nothing he could do would bring back Susan, but he could save the world in her name. And to do that, he needed the box.

More specifically, he needed what was inside it.

* * *

David paced his apartment like a caged animal. The sun had been down for nearly an hour and Paul hadn't put in an appearance. David had slept only fitfully throughout the day, his nightmares haunted by images from the basement where he'd killed the vampires, most especially the eyes of the human who had been enslaved.

When the vampire did put in an appearance he looked worried. He walked into the room and didn't even seem to see David standing, hands clenched at his sides.

"What is it?" David demanded.

Paul looked up. "There is a rumor I've been trying to track down. They say that a vampire was taken, hooded and shackled, into one of the palaces in the old castle."

"Who was it? Was it Richelieu?"

"No, but he was being taken to see Richelieu."

"Then who?"

Paul shook his head. "There is much talk, as there always is among vampires as well as humans, but no truth. Some say it is the first vampire. Others that it is some great leader."

"Who do you think it is?"

Paul hesitated.

"Who?" David repeated.

"I believe they have captured Raphael."

David took a step forward. "And Susan?"

Paul shook his head. "There was no talk of a woman."

David felt sick deep in his soul. And he thanked God that Wendy had gone home. He didn't know how he could do what he had to do and worry about her at the same time.

He had tried not to spend too much time thinking about

her, or the way she made him feel. It scared him even more than the vampires he was fighting. It was like a piece of his soul had touched hers and now they were connected. He didn't know how it had happened. He wasn't even completely sure when it had happened. All he did know was that he needed her. He needed her to be safe. He needed her to be alive and happy. He needed her to live her life to its fullest and laugh and feel joy. He needed her to be out there so that when he was afraid of the vampires he could think of her.

I'm doing this for her. Because of what they did to her and what they could do to her again, he realized.

And what he had done earlier that day had been just the tip of the iceberg. Wendy wouldn't be truly safe until every evil vampire was destroyed.

He thought of Susan and said a prayer for her, hoping that somehow she was still alive. Because without her he was the only one to fight. Because if she was dead it would devastate Wendy.

He set his jaw and looked Paul in the eye.

"It sounds like it's time we took the fight to them."

Paul returned his stare. "You're not ready."

"Then make me ready. We now know that vampires don't wake when being staked. We need to worry about their human keepers, though. I won't kill people."

Paul smiled, his teeth flashing. "You kill the vampires and leave the humans to me."

"So, what do you plan on doing with your army?" Raphael asked. "You don't have enough vampires behind you to take the whole world by force."

"Who needs to take it by force? For decades I've been

quietly moving my people into positions of power in every government. All they are waiting for is the sign."

The sign. A feeling of cold dread washed over Raphael. He had met a few cult leaders in his day and they used phrases like that. Things never ended well. They always ended bloody and innocent people got hurt along the way.

"What sign?" Raphael asked, wishing more than anything he could stand up, walk out of the palace, and keep going, washing his hands of the entire thing.

Richelieu chuckled. "Let's just say, it's going to be spectacular. And the world will recognize it for what it is."

"What's the sign?"

Richelieu made a tsking sound. "Even you will know it when it happens. Until then, be patient."

"Taking over the world...that's a cliché."

"It's necessary," the other vampire said, eyes blazing. "Things are falling apart. The dangers are far greater than they were when I was human. The only way to save humanity is to take it in hand, guide and lead it and show it the way. Consolidation of power. It was the answer then; it's the answer now."

"I would have expected to be having this conversation with you in Versailles," Raphael said.

Richelieu wrinkled his nose distastefully. "The French people have lost their heart, their passion for war and world change. I am disappointed in them, too disappointed to allow them to share in my triumph."

"And Prague?"

"Why not? It's a beacon, a center of growth, which respects the past. The art and the culture here are flourishing."

"And the mysticism of this place has nothing to do with it," Raphael said sarcastically.

"I confess that doesn't hurt. Nor does our personal history here. You remember it, of course?"

How could he have forgotten it? The last time he had been in Prague had been the last time he had willingly killed a human. As he relived the memory, the more recent taste of Susan's blood superimposed itself and he shivered, craving blood like he hadn't in over a century.

"So, tonight you're boring me, what's your plan for tomorrow night?" Raphael asked, struggling to focus on something other than the irresistible craving.

"You know me, I need to unwind before big events."

"Theater or art exhibit?" Raphael asked, remembering too many events Richelieu had unwound before.

"Theater, if you must know. Pity you can't join me."

"Yes, pity," Raphael growled.

"But, you're going to be otherwise engaged. As much as I'd like to kill you, the whole patricide thing is a little distasteful. Besides, I've promised you to someone else. A gift, you might say."

"I can't wait," Raphael said as another needle slid into his arm. He felt himself collapsing back onto the floor as he lost consciousness.

When Raphael awoke he was in a white room, strapped to a table. The smell of antiseptic hung heavy in the air and cold dread settled in the pit of his stomach.

A vampire approached and stood over him for a moment.

"This seems very familiar," Michael mused.

"Because we've been here before," Raphael hissed.

"That's right. How could I possibly forget the vampire that escaped me?"

But looking in his eyes Raphael could tell he hadn't forgotten. Michael remembered just as well as he did.

"No matter. It won't happen a second time. You might have noticed that there are no rats here to save you."

"I see one."

Michael tsked at him as he tightened the straps on Raphael's arms. They should have been easy to break, but he felt overwhelmingly weak and sick to his stomach. "What have you done to me?" he asked.

"That would be the science you older ones seem to so despise. I have discovered that the touch of garlic affects us just as the smell does. So, your restraints are cured with extract from it. It's fascinating, really."

"And can your science tell you why garlic, of all things, brings us to our knees?" Raphael wheezed even as his skin began to absorb more of the poison.

"No," Michael said, failing to hide his irritation. "But it's only a matter of time."

Time. It was something of which Raphael was quickly running out. Michael would not repeat the mistakes of their past.

Michael lifted a surgical instrument from a tray next to the table. He dipped it in a dish of clear liquid. "You'll notice that I'm infusing this blade with the garlic extract as well. Fortunately for me, this particular liquid is odorless, so it only harms those it comes into physical contact with."

"Lucky you," Raphael muttered.

The blade descended and began to slice into him. The one thing he had sworn to himself was that he would never be back here, trapped on a table under Michael's knife. *No, that's not true, I also swore I would protect Susan.*

And Susan was dead, unless Richelieu was lying. Maybe she had been spared. Maybe God had intervened and saved her. The pain seared through him, tearing at his mind. And finally he screamed out to God, the universe, whoever might be listening. "You must help Susan!" He only hoped someone heard him, because he knew no one was going to be able to help him.

CHAPTER SEVENTEEN

The revenger of blood himself shall slay the murderer:
when he meeteth him, he shall slay him.

—Numbers 35:19

As soon as the first light of dawn touched the sky Susan took down the barricades and walked quickly through the rest of the castle, hoping for a sign of Raphael.

There was nothing. Finally, she had checked every room but the dungeon. She put her hand on the door and then pulled it away. She didn't want to go back down there. She took a deep breath and went in, sweeping everything with light from two lanterns. On her way back up the stairs she was running and she slammed the door shut and bolted it behind her, panting and heart racing.

When she was sure that he was not there she went back to her room and gathered up her belongings. She took them down to the car before turning back to take a last look at the castle.

It loomed, dark and menacing still in the early morning light. She didn't know if she would ever return, but she hoped that she would. There was a part of her that felt she belonged here, despite the gloom and the dark and the decay. There was something about it that called to her, spoke to her.

But now she had to go. There was much work to be done. She only wished Raphael could have survived to see it through.

At the thought of him a strangled sob escaped her. She was sure he was dead. Had he lived he would have made it back to her. She got into the car and headed for Paris, where she would get a flight back to Prague.

David stood in the middle of the room and surveyed the damage he had done. Six piles of ash were scattered around. He slowly climbed the stairs out of the basement and glanced at the crumpled figure of a man in the corner. Paul had found the vampire's servant and knocked him out before he went to seek refuge from the rising sun. He had promised that as soon as he could he would work to free the man's mind, along with all those who had been mesmerized and pressed into servitude to dark masters.

It was the second house he had hit that morning. Paul had managed to identify a few others, but without his help to remove the human keepers from the picture David couldn't continue.

Frustrated he stood, wishing there was more he could do. In his heart he could feel that they didn't have much time. It was as though a giant clock was counting down and where there had been days he now felt they had only hours. Maybe less.

And Paul still hadn't been able to find out anything

more about where the vampire they thought might be Raphael had been taken. Most of the night he had spent searching, questioning.

David made his way slowly back to his apartment. He started his new job in two days and the pressure that this was placing on him was nearly overwhelming. He didn't know how he would manage to juggle it and fight the war at the same time.

Once at home he paced the floor for an hour before forcing himself to try and get some sleep. He was worse than a vampire. Not only was he awake at night, fearful of being attacked, but he had to stay awake in the morning to execute his own attacks. That left very little time to sleep and it was all during the day.

When David lay down and closed his eyes he could see Wendy in his mind. With thoughts of her uppermost, he fell asleep.

At the airport, waiting in the terminal for her flight, Susan did a quick time calculation. It was late at night in California, but she went ahead and used a payphone to call Wendy's cell. It went straight to voice mail. She left a brief message and then tried her home.

On the second ring her aunt Jane picked up.

"Hi, it's Susan. Sorry if I woke you."

"Oh, Susan. Have you heard from Wendy?"

"No. Why?"

"Well, yesterday I went to the store and when I got back to the house I found that she had left. Her note said she was on her way back to Europe to be with you. It was very cryptic and we haven't heard from her since."

Susan's blood ran cold. "What does the note say exactly?"

"Hold on."

She heard some papers rustling and then her aunt returned. "'I must help Susan.' That's it."

Susan tried to keep her voice calm so as not to alarm her aunt. "I'll call you when she gets here."

Where is she going? Prague? Here? Does she even remember where in France I was going?

"I would appreciate it. I've got some words for her. I mean, I know she's taken to sudden flights of fancy, but this is too much even for her."

Especially given how much she wanted to leave.

"Aunt Jane, I need you to do something for me."

"What?" her aunt asked, voice laced with suspicion.

"I really, really need my keys."

"Your keys. Your house keys?"

"Yes. Actually, what I really need is the key chain, the silver one with the fleur-de-lis. I left it on the hook at Grandma's when we left for the airport."

"Seriously?"

"Yes. It's very, very important. I'll explain why later. I need you to ship it as fast as you can to me."

"Where do I send it?" her aunt asked.

Susan hesitated, glancing out at the darkened sky. "Prague," she said at last.

"Where in Prague?"

Susan retrieved the business card that the attorney had given her and gave Aunt Jane the address on it.

"I don't understand why you need it so badly."

"I just do. Please, hurry."

"I'll send it to you first thing in the morning."

"Okay, thank you."

"You're welcome." Aunt Jane hesitated then asked, "And you trust this Pierre?"

Susan paused and Aunt Jane was quick to pick up on it. "You don't, do you?"

"I don't have any reason not to trust him," Susan said. She sighed. How could she explain how she felt without having to explain how she had met him, the property, the key, and what she had found? She didn't entirely trust him, but he had given her the deed and the key. She couldn't be sure that a package sent to her at the hotel wouldn't be intercepted. "It's complicated, but I don't see that I have any other choice."

There was a pause so long that Susan thought she'd lost the connection.

"I'll make sure it gets to you."

"Thank you."

After they said good-bye Susan sat down in the waiting area and leaned her head against the back of the chair. Why was Wendy coming back? She had been so adamant about getting away from the war. If she had left a note saying she needed to see David again Susan would be less surprised, but then again, Wendy might not have wanted to admit that to her parents.

Where was she going? Susan hoped they would meet each other in Prague.

Why does everything have to be so complicated? she wondered. She fingered the cross around her neck. If Wendy was truly on her way to Europe, then Susan hoped she could at least translate the letter and one mystery would be solved.

Which only left about a dozen more.

*   *   *

David woke before sunset. After fixing himself some dinner and watching the sun set outside his window, he sat down to wait for Paul to put in an appearance. What seemed like an eternity passed and he chafed under it. He wished he had a way to contact Paul, but the monk carried no phone. He wondered where it was Paul went to sleep, how far away it was. It seemed a little unfair that Paul knew more about him than David knew about the vampire.

His phone rang and he jumped, startled. "Hello?" he said as he answered it.

"Mr. Trent?" a heavily accented female voice inquired.

"Yes, this is David Trent," he said.

"I'm calling from the Grand Hotel Praha. You were our guest recently."

"Yes, is everything okay?" he asked, wondering if he had left something behind.

"I just wanted to let you know that a young woman named Wendy was here a few minutes ago looking for you."

David lurched to his feet. "What? Is she still there?"

"No. She was very insistent, though, that she needed to speak to you about finding her cousin."

"When did she leave? Did she say where she was going? Leave a number?" David asked breathlessly.

"I'm sorry, sir. She didn't say where she was going or leave a number. She left about five minutes ago. A gentleman arrived who seemed to know her and she left with him."

His blood turned to ice. "This man, can you describe him?" he asked.

"Of course. He was very tall, black hair, and…"

"And what?"

"He had these dark, burning eyes," the woman said, sounding slightly shaken by the memory.

The phone fell from his fingers and he headed for the door, head spinning. Wendy was back here in Prague, looking for him and Susan. And he was sure she'd been taken by a vampire.

As he reached the door it flew open and Paul stood there. "I found where they're holding him. We have to go now. Grab your gear."

David tried to push past him. "I have to save Wendy first. She's back and a vampire just snatched her at the hotel."

Paul grabbed his shoulders and pushed him back into the apartment.

David reached in his pocket for a stake. "Don't try to stop me," he growled as he yanked it free.

"Do you even know which vampire grabbed her?"

"No, just that he was tall, dark hair, burning eyes."

A flash of something, recognition maybe, crossed Paul's face. Then the vampire pushed him back even further. "There's nothing you can do for her at this moment. But you can help me save Raphael. Then I will help you find Wendy. I promise you that."

"But she's in trouble! He could be doing anything to her right now," he argued, pushing forward, raising the stake menacingly.

"Yes, I understand, but there's nothing you can do to help her, not without more to go on."

"The desk clerk saw him, surely you could get a better description out of her if you pushed."

"It's possible, but not likely. We have to do this my way if we are to have a chance at getting either of them back," Paul said, his voice dropping lower.

"Don't try to mesmerize me!"

"Don't be an idiot. Come with me now before you force me to hurt you."

"I'll hurt you first," David threatened.

Paul moved in a blur of motion and David found himself on the ground, his stake halfway across the room and Paul's foot on his throat. "You need to get your head straight. I can't free Raphael by myself and you can't find Wendy without my help and possibly his. So you can leave now on a fool's errand and know that everyone you've sought to help will likely die because of it or you can come with me now and have a fighting chance of saving them both. Which will it be?"

He couldn't breathe and his broken rib was burning like liquid fire. But Paul's words penetrated the fog of his fear. He nodded and the vampire helped him up.

"Now, this is going to be unlike what you've done so far. Think of those as practice and this is the real thing. The vampires will be awake, and, if they're smart, ready for trouble."

David retrieved his duffel bag with all of his weapons. "Yeah, but they don't know just how much trouble we can be," he said.

Paul gave him a ghost of a smile. "Good boy. Follow me and try to keep up. With God's help we'll all live to see the dawn."

The sun had set by the time the plane landed. Susan stared out the window at the dark outside and had to will herself to stand up and leave the plane. She knew there were vampires, how many she could only guess at, in the city. Some of them were hunting for her. Suddenly coming back seemed like a colossal mistake. A smart person would have gone somewhere completely different. Japan maybe, land of the rising sun. Or Australia.

She pulled her carry-on out from underneath the seat in front of her. She'd been too paranoid to entrust it to an overhead bin even though it left her feet and legs unnaturally cramped.

She joined the line of passengers shuffling to get off the plane. Minutes later she was fishing her single piece of checked luggage off the carousel. She headed outside for where she knew the taxi stand was. Every few steps she glanced around, fear mounting, as she wondered where the other Raiders were. Had they gone to France or had they been waiting here for her return?

As people walked past her she jumped, fearing the worst. Finally, she reached the door leading outside and a man passing through held it open for her.

"Thank you," she murmured.

He gave her a strange little smile and she expected him to say something in return. Instead he slammed the door into her, knocking her off balance, and then a moment later grabbed her carry-on bag and began to run.

"Stop!" she shrieked at the top of her lungs before plunging after him. He leaped into a waiting black car, which sped off before he could even get the door closed. It veered around another vehicle and was lost to sight.

And just like that the letter from her ancestor, Jean the Marquis de Bryas, was gone.

Keeping up with Paul was even harder than David had expected. He didn't know why the vampire insisted they go the entire way on foot instead of taking a taxi. He did know that by the time they reached their destination he was completely winded and had to sit on a bus bench half a block away while Paul scouted ahead.

He did his best not to jump at every shadow. That's what his life had seemingly become, though, one filled with shadows. He thought of Wendy, a bright light if ever there was one, and then had to stop because fear for her was tearing him up inside. He needed to be able to focus, to concentrate.

When Paul returned he looked worried.

"What is it?" David asked.

"There are more than there were before."

"Where are we?"

"The building was rented by a vampire named Michael. He and Raphael have history, you might say. Michael is a scientist and he has been running terrible, brutal experiments on his own kind since he was cursed. He has Raphael in an inner room, torturing him. To get to it we have to make it through a dozen others, some human servants, most vampires. Michael has developed his own little following. I'm surprised Richelieu allows it."

"A dozen?" David asked. "How are we going to fight our way through so many?"

"A lot of luck and even more faith. I do not know how much longer they will keep Raphael alive, but we must try and wait until closer to dawn. Both he and I can stay awake longer than most. We'll need the edge."

"So, what? We just wait?"

"And pray. Join me now in prayer before battle."

David quickly bowed his head and listened as the vampire monk prayed for them.

CHAPTER EIGHTEEN

And I will take away his blood out of his mouth, and his abominations from between his teeth: but he that remaineth, even he, shall be for our God.

—Zechariah 9:7

Susan couldn't stop her frustrated tears as she talked to the police about her stolen bag. She gave them a description of the man to the best of her recollection, along with a detailed description of the carry-on and its contents.

"We will do everything we can to find your bag, madam," one of the officers assured her.

"What is your success rate for recovery?" she asked.

A second officer shrugged. "It is hard to say. We do not have many incidents of luggage theft."

Then why did it have to happen to me? she wondered in despair.

She hailed a taxi and directed it toward the Grand Hotel Praha. It was a risky move. The vampires knew she had been there before and might look for her return. But then, so might Wendy.

A few minutes later the driver dropped her off and she headed to the door leading to the lobby. Before she reached it, though, a man stepped in front of her, blocking her path.

He was tall, well over six feet, swathed in black. A cloak hung from his shoulders and on him it seemed the most natural thing he could ever wear. His ebony hair was pushed back from his face and his dark eyes smoldered with an inner fire.

He's dangerous, she realized, as shivers raced up her spine.

As if from thin air he produced a single red rose and handed it to her. All of his body except his gloved fingers was completely still, like a statue.

She glanced down at the flower. *Is it poisoned?* she wondered, her thoughts scattering in fear.

"I would not harm a lady of Bryas," he said, though she didn't see his lips move. His voice seemed to rumble like thunder but with the almost hypnotic quality of a cat's purr.

"Who are you?" she breathed.

"I am Gabriel of Avignon. But you may call me... uncle."

"Uncle? But why, who—" she stopped short. "Gabriel? Raphael's sire is named Gabriel," she breathed.

He nodded and his eyes began to glow. Her knees buckled and he caught her by the elbow and held her up.

"You have endured much and now I will take you somewhere that you may rest."

"I'm fine by myself. I have somewhere I need to go."

"I cannot permit that. The hour is late, the night is dark, and death stalks these streets in many guises. Mine is only one of them but it is one of the few that means you no harm."

He terrified her. Unconsciously, she grabbed her cross, squeezing it. He observed the gesture and his eyes ceased to glow. He put a gloved hand over hers and closed his eyes for a moment, as though in prayer.

"What are you doing?"

"A long time ago, my lady wore this."

"Your lady?" she asked, breath catching in her throat. She squeezed the necklace harder, pushing it sharply into the skin of her chest.

And in her mind she heard, *You're bleeding.*

She gasped and looked down at the thin line of red where the cross had cut her.

"It was you in the cathedral who was whispering in my mind!"

He inclined his head.

"But how? Why? Raphael didn't know you were there, did he?"

"No one knows where I am unless I let it be known. As for Raphael, I have watched him a long time and he has not known it."

She reached out and touched his arm. "Where is he? Something happened to him."

"He was captured by Richelieu's men and is even now being tortured by Michael, who will kill him soon."

"You have to save him," she cried, balling her hand into a fist and pounding it against his chest.

"That task is the burden of others who must rise to meet the challenge or risk allowing mankind to slide into darkness."

"Raphael is a warrior."

"Yes."

"And what are you?" she whispered.

"I am a hunter. And no prey has ever escaped me."

She blinked. *Am I prey?*

"We must go," he said, turning swiftly.

And, as though compelled, she went with him.

Raphael lay on the table, fighting to stay conscious, to push past the pain and the illness. Michael had moved away from him and he moved his head slightly so that he could see him standing near the door talking with one of his assistants.

The assistant was whispering something to Michael. Raphael steadied himself, pushing his focus outward, wanting to know what they were discussing.

"Richelieu...bait...girlfriend back..."

Hope flickered through him. Could they possibly be talking about Susan? Was she truly alive?

Michael turned and gave him an irritated glance. "We will have to wait a little while longer for the end, you and I," he said.

"I've got nothing better to do," Raphael rasped, his burned vocal cords scraping together.

There was frustration and impatience in the way Michael rolled his shoulders, turned, and stalked out the door, his assistant on his heels. The door swung shut behind them and Raphael frantically wiggled his right foot, striving to free it from the restraints. There was the tiniest bit of slack and he strained with all he had, shaking with the effort.

He tried bending his foot so that he could slide it through the restraint, but couldn't twist it enough. He braced himself and then he broke his ankle and was able to pull his leg free. He pulled his leg up and across his chest until he could touch the inside of his calf with his left hand. Then he gouged into it with his fingernails, grinding his teeth as he pulled apart his own flesh and dug into the leg until his fingers touched something concealed next to the bone. It was metal and his fingers grasped it tight.

He yanked the five-inch-long rat-tail file free. He had buried it there centuries before where no outside observer could see it, so that he would never be helpless again. As he twisted it and began sawing through his wrist restraints he reflected grimly that he was again being saved by a rat.

He had one wrist free and was working to undo the restraint on his other wrist when Michael came through the door with a roar.

David stood next to Paul, heart racing as they stared at the door that separated them from the worst odds they had faced. On the other side he could hear voices and bile rose in the back of his throat.

"Give no quarter, no mercy," Paul had told him before they had gotten to the door. David clutched a stake in his right hand and a cross in his left. He had packed and unpacked his pockets half a dozen times with the rest of his weapons, trying to determine what order he'd need them all in. He'd finally given up, leaving them as they were, because he realized he had no idea truly what to expect from the fight that lay ahead of them. *Other than blood.*

He took a deep breath and then nodded. Paul kicked in the door and together they charged through it. They found themselves in a large room that looked like a laboratory. A door on the far side was closed; beyond it would be Raphael, if Paul's intelligence was correct.

Around the room a dozen people looked up in surprise. Before anyone moved David sank his stake into the chest of the person on his right, praying it was a vampire and not one of the human servants. The man fell to his knees without a sound and David's heart skipped a beat. The body crashed backward and then, to his relief, fell to ashes.

The room suddenly exploded around him in a cacophony of sound and movement. Paul charged across the room, staking one vampire and killing a human in his rush for the door. If they didn't free Raphael fast, he would be dead long before they reached him.

A vampire charged at David and he was forced to take his eyes off Paul and face his attacker. He swung the cross up and the vampire ducked easily beneath his arm. David reversed the direction of his swing and brought the pointed end of the cross into the vampire's back. The creature grabbed David's throat with a hand tipped with long fingernails and began to squeeze. David kept his hold on the cross and drove the pointed end further, deeper, until he penetrated the vampire's heart. He covered his mouth as he gasped in air to avoid breathing in the ash.

He turned and saw what looked like a small army all charging him at once. *I'm dead*, he realized. Then he sensed something behind him. He twisted, reaching for another stake. Something struck the side of his head and everything went black.

Michael was kneeling on top of Raphael's chest, hands wrapped around his throat. Raphael's free hand flailed and found one of the surgical instruments and he stabbed Michael in the neck with it. The vampire's blood dripped down on him and he drank greedily. It would not heal him as living, human blood would, but it helped.

After a moment Raphael brought up his free leg and kneed Michael before throwing him off. The vampire hit the ground but was up in a flash. The door opened and a familiar figure raced through.

Sounds of battle raged from the other room, but Raphael focused his eyes on Paul. The monk seized Michael before the other had realized he was there. As the two began to fight, Raphael freed himself and fell off the table. He staggered to his feet and moved to help Paul.

"I've got him," Paul grunted as he pinned Michael's arms.

"You're not killing him without me," Raphael growled.

Together they picked up the other vampire and slammed him down onto the table.

"Who's out there?" Raphael asked, unable to ignore the shouts and screams from the other room.

"David."

"David? He's going to get slaughtered!"

"Hopefully not. He's shown great skill and courage. You should be proud."

"Still, let's get this done fast," Raphael said, lashing Michael down to the table. The minute the garlic infused straps touched his skin the scientist weakened. "You want to take some notes about how you feel?" Raphael growled.

And then, he could feel it. Sunrise. Sleep pulled at the corners of his mind. He turned and looked at Paul. The vampire gave him a tight smile and moved swiftly to the curtained windows.

"How many experiments have you run with sunlight?" Raphael asked.

"Many!" Michael hissed.

"Ah, but how many on yourself?"

One look at Michael's face revealed the truth. Raphael made a tsking sound. "I thought all great scientists sooner or later experimented on themselves. Bet you wish now you had."

Raphael nodded to Paul and the monk flung back the coverings. Light streamed through the glass, striking Michael and Raphael. As the other vampire screamed Raphael picked up the bowl that contained the liquid garlic extract and poured it down Michael's throat.

He choked and then his screams turned into a high-pitched keening. Raphael stepped back and watched as the vampire began to burn simultaneously from the inside and the outside. For one moment his skin, organs, bones, everything was completely translucent before exploding in a cloud of ash.

Paul closed the curtains and they turned back toward the door. Everything outside had gone quiet and the hair on the back of Raphael's neck stood on end. He took a step forward and then fell back as an imposing figure filled the doorway.

He gasped and sunk to one knee in an uncontrolled act of submission. It was his sire, Gabriel. Over his shoulder was the body of a man. Gabriel dropped the body to the floor and Raphael recognized David's still form.

"Don't worry," Gabriel said, addressing Paul. "I smelled you all over him and knew he was fighting with you. I just knocked him out to get him out of the way."

"And the others?" Raphael asked.

"Dead," Gabriel said, swiveling his head and focusing

the intensity of his eyes onto him. It took all of Raphael's willpower not to shrink back under that gaze. Instead he forced himself to meet his sire's stare.

"Raphael," Gabriel said, acknowledging his presence.

Raphael stood slowly, hands clenched at his sides, fear churning in his stomach as it always did in the other's presence.

"I told you, he's worth knowing," Paul said with a little chuckle. Raphael shot a surprised glance at the priest as he caught something in his voice and realized that even he was a little intimidated by Gabriel. That hadn't always been the case. What had changed?

Raphael shook himself. He still had work to do and people to look after. "I have to go find someone."

"If you're looking for Susan and her cousin you needn't bother. I have already...intercepted...them."

Susan paced the floor uncontrollably as she stared out at the rising sun. Gabriel had brought her to this home in the countryside beyond the city. When they had arrived she had been overwhelmed with relief and gratitude to find Wendy already there, safe and asleep.

Now Susan waited for Gabriel to return. She didn't know where he had gone, but she hoped he would bring Raphael back with him.

The sun had been up for more than twenty minutes when she heard a car outside. There was a covered portico that attached the drive to the front door, which she flew to open. There was a flash of movement near the car and instinctively she stepped back. A rush of wind passed her, the door slammed shut and she whirled to see Gabriel and Paul depositing two bodies on the floor. She took a step closer and screamed when she realized they were Raphael and David.

Gabriel jerked and turned to look at her. Wendy sat up abruptly on the living room couch.

"Do not worry," Paul said, "they are both just sleeping."

"We all should sleep while we may," Gabriel said, moving to draw the curtains around the room. "We're safe enough here."

Susan dropped to her knees next to Raphael and touched his cheek. So cold and still. She looked at his chest before remembering that she wouldn't see it rising and falling. David, on the other hand, was breathing deeply. Wendy knelt next to him.

Susan met her cousin's eyes over the two still forms and saw her own relief mirrored there. "I found you," Wendy said, marveling slightly, and seeming dazed.

"Why did you come?"

"This voice in my head. It told me that I had to help you. I knew that it was true and so I came."

Susan blinked, wondering whose voice Wendy could have heard. Whoever's it was, she was grateful, even though it meant her cousin was in danger by being there. She reached across and grabbed her hand and squeezed it.

Nearby Paul and Gabriel lay down and within moments were motionless.

Susan smiled. She and Wendy were the only two awake in the room. And given what they now knew of vampires and the supernatural, it felt like they were the only two awake in the whole world.

"What do we do now?" Wendy asked.

"Now," Gabriel said, startling them both, "we rest. Tonight we form a plan."

Susan nodded and so did Wendy. Day had come and with it the safety of knowing no vampires were after them. It was time to rest because night would bring new terrors. She thought of her stolen letter and wondered if she would ever see it again. Her grandmother had said that the vampire who spared Jean's life knew the secret of her cross necklace. She touched it and wondered if any of the three vampires in the room possibly knew the vampire she was referencing. Maybe she could find him and maybe he would tell her the truth.

And the truth will set us free.

EPILOGUE

Pierre de Chauvere sat at his desk, an overnight bag on the floor next to him. In his hands he held an antique letter and read the flowing French words eagerly. The man who had brought the bag with the letter to him had already left with a small fortune in cash in his pockets. Pierre had known there was a secret. He had believed that when Susan went to France she would discover it.

The letter told of Jean's experiences in service to his king during the crusade. It was a letter written to his daughter, Carissa, in the event that he died without having told her the truth. The lawyer knew that the letter had never reached its intended recipient but had been found by Susan's grandmother a few years earlier.

And finally, the letter came to the crucial part. And when the secret of the cross necklace was revealed, the paper fell from his fingers onto his desk.

All that time the necklace had been in his hands and he had never known. He screamed in fury even as tears of despair rolled down his cheeks. And he vowed that he would have the necklace again.

DISCUSSION QUESTIONS

1. Raphael has struggled for centuries with the concept of salvation while for Susan it is a simple thing that has been part of her life since she was a child. Why do you think the road to salvation is harder and longer for some people than others?

2. Have you ever felt a strong spiritual connection to a certain place as Susan does in the cathedral? Why do you think you had that connection? Is there someplace you would like to visit that has spiritual significance to you? What has stopped you from going?

3. Have you ever known someone like Susan's grandmother, who felt called by God to do things for people or reach out to them in ways that didn't seem to make sense to others? How did you feel about that person? Would you be like him or her if you could?

4. Do you know someone like David who is willing to risk his or her life to help others? Missionaries, po-

     lice officers, and firemen all understand that this risk is part of their job. Is there anyone you would risk your life to help? Why or why not?

5. After Jesus' resurrection some believed the truth from hearing others speak it. Thomas had to see Jesus for himself to believe. Is believing without seeing easy or hard for you? Why do you think this is?

6. What do you think about when you think of blood?

7. Read Deuteronomy 12:23 and Leviticus 7:27 to understand the prohibition against eating blood. What does the Old Testament have to say about blood?

8. Read John 6:53–61 and Mark 14:23–24. Why was what Jesus said so revolutionary and disturbing to some of His followers?

9. In the book Raphael insists that Susan is special, that he needs her to win the war. Do you believe that one person can make a difference in the world? Do you know anyone personally who has?

10. What are you doing to make a difference in your family, neighborhood, or world? What's holding you back? What can you do to overcome this challenge?

Turn this page for a preview of

KISS OF DEATH

by Debbie Viguié

Available from FaithWords wherever books are sold
and in mass market paperback in September 2013.

And look for the eBook exclusive short story
Kiss of Life.

FRANCE, 1198 A.D.

The crumbling stones of the prison reeked of death. The stench of unwashed humanity and decay had long been in the nostrils of the warden of the lowest level of the ancient dungeon. Cut into the earth centuries before by nobles, the prison had once been a castle, proud and strong. It was still strong, but no longer proud. Generations of the vilest criminals that France had known had lived and died inside its walls. Murderers, rapists, thieves, and witches as well as religious and political dissidents had all met their end within the tiny, dank cells which the warden now walked past.

The warden stopped next to Marcelle, his protégé who would be taking his place. The young man gravely nodded as they went over, once more, his duties.

"Every day you feed the prisoners," the warden said, as they paced slowly past each cell. "Someone doesn't eat for a couple of days, send men in to remove the body."

They walked a few moments in silence. Finally the young man asked. "Who is down here?"

The old man shook his head slowly. "I know all my prisoners, though I don't know who they were outside these walls nor what they did to be sent here. Men, women, gentlefolk and common, a few months in here and you can't tell them apart by conventional means anymore. But you learn to note differences."

He stopped before one cell. "This one won't eat anything that might be from a pig."

"Jewish?" the young man asked interestedly.

"Near as I can tell. And this one," he said, pointing to another cell, "sings after dinner."

"Good voice?"

"The finest I've ever heard."

"What about this one?" Marcelle asked as they stopped before the last cell. The massive door was ancient and battered, the wood bearing stains that might have been water or blood.

The old man paused for such a long time the younger one began to think he had not heard him. When the warden finally spoke it was slowly and in a hushed voice. "I do not know."

The young man felt as though a chill wind had just brushed against his spine. In the dim light he stared hard at the old man, waiting for him to continue, fearing that he would.

"There is – something – in there. I don't know what, but it's been there the whole time I've been warden, these last twenty years. The man who was warden before me said it had been here as long as he could remember."

"What is it?"

"I don't know," the old man repeated. "I only know that no food is ever slid beneath the door, but every so often a prisoner is put in there. I've seen dozens put in there, *and not a single one ever taken out alive.*"

He said the last in a whisper so quiet and fierce that it imparted a sense of danger and fear to the younger man. "Not ever?"

"Not ever," he said emphatically. "Never enter this cell, no matter the cause, if you value your life."

Marcelle stared hard at the door, trying to quiet the sudden sense of unease which had overtaken him. There should be nothing in this dungeon to cause him fear. He was, after all, about to be made the floor warden, in charge of the prisoners and guards for the entire level. It was a position of great responsibility and he had trained long for it.

Yet, suddenly he found himself wishing that he had never stepped foot inside the prison, even if he was a keeper and not a prisoner. Something about the giant door made him feel like running. He took a deep breath, though, and stood his ground. With a trembling hand he crossed himself, for he knew in his heart that he would be the one to discover what was on the other side.

Inside the cell *he* waited, listening to the murmurs from outside. He could smell the younger man's fear. The new warden was right to be afraid. He listened as the voices faded, the footsteps retreated until he was again alone with his thoughts and his thirst. He had spent far too long within the prison walls, but soon all that would change.

He dropped his head back against the stone wall, not feeling its cold. He didn't feel anything actually, anything but the hunger. It gnawed at him, a deep ache inside that he could not control. With the passing of each day it would grow until the pain was unbearable.

In the distance he heard a man begin to sing. Dinner was over, for all but him. Deep in his throat he growled.

> *See, I have set before thee this day life and good, and death and evil;*

> Deuteronomy 30:15

Death. It's all about death, Wendy thought in despair. She sat on a faded red velvet couch in a house somewhere on the outskirts of the city with her arms wrapped around her knees and stared at her cousin, Susan Lambert, willing her to wake up.

Susan lay on the floor, curled up, her chest gently rising and falling. *Proof that she's alive*, Wendy thought. A few feet away David Trent was also asleep. His face was bruised and even in sleep he kept wincing as though he was in pain. A soft whimper escaped every few breaths and it broke her heart.

And then there were the other three, the three who weren't breathing. The three who were dead.

Or not.

It took all of her willpower not to feel like she was going completely crazy.

Vampires.

She shuddered. Wendy had hoped that when she went home to California she would be able to forget that vampires existed, write it off as some sort of bad nightmare.

Her eyes shifted again to David and lingered on his face. *Even if it meant I had to write him off, too.*

She and Susan had come to Prague the week before for their grandmother's funeral. Their grandmother had lived in Prague as a little girl and had chosen to be buried there. Wendy remembered hours spent sitting and listening to her grandmother talk about the city she loved, about its magic.

She'd said nothing about its vampires. But within a few hours of arriving in the city both she and Susan had drawn the attention of the monsters who walked at night. And when they were attacked David was the stranger who helped save them.

Maybe that's why she felt inexplicably drawn to him. He was a hero. He had saved both their lives. When the good vampires had asked him to stand and fight a coming war against evil with them he had agreed. So had Susan. It still seemed incomprehensible to her that there was such a thing as good vampires. She had wanted no part of it and had fled back home where it was safe.

And now I'm back.

She wasn't sure exactly why. All she knew was that one minute she'd been home, breathing easier, and the next she'd been on a plane back to Prague, compelled by something to return and help her cousin.

Looking around the room she realized her grandmother was wrong. It wasn't a city of magic. It was a city of death. Last night, from what she had understood, David nearly became its next victim.

He had been unconscious when the vampires carried him in. He hadn't woken since then. Wendy thought they should have taken him to a hospital. But the vampires told her he'd be fine. So she watched over him, worried he might never wake.

He was handsome, with actual color in his skin he looked so different from the vampires surrounding him. He was also kind and considerate and very funny.

Wendy took a deep breath.

She wanted to wake her cousin and David and run with them while they still could. They could all go to California and escape this madness. But she already knew they wouldn't go. They felt called to stay and fight.

Whereas she had just been called.

She rubbed her head. The voice inside it that had insisted that she had to return and help her cousin had been so overpowering, so strong, that she had been helpless to resist. She had felt like she was moving through some sort of dream state until she had actually made it back to Prague and been reunited with her cousin. It was the vampire Gabriel who had found her and brought her here to this house last night.

She glanced again from the clock to the heavy curtains covering the windows. Now, night was coming and with it evil would walk again. She stood and moved over to one of the windows. She wrapped her hand around the rich velvet drapes and was about to pull them to the side so she could at least see out.

Suddenly a hand clamped tight around hers.

She screamed, spun around, and found herself confronted by a pair of smoldering eyes. Gabriel was staring at her.

Behind him she could see both David and Susan jump up, startled awake by her scream. Slowly Gabriel held up his other hand toward them, without looking away from her. They seemed to freeze.

What power does this man have to compel us all to do as he wills? she wondered. *Did he compel me to come back to Prague?*

He did have power, she could feel it. It was nearly tangible—thick and dark and far more menacing than anything she had ever felt before.

His jet black hair was pushed back and he was dressed in dark clothes, though the cloak he had worn earlier was on the floor where he had been sleeping.

"The sun hasn't gone down yet," she heard herself squeak. It seemed a stupid thing to say, but weren't the vampires supposed to be asleep while the sun was up?

"The sun does not have as much power over me as some," he said. "They must sleep, but I may wake as I will."

He let go of her hand and she in turn let go of the curtain, arm dropping to her side. He didn't move away, though. Instead he just kept staring at her and she could feel her heart beginning to pound in her chest.

Something flickered a moment across his face, but she couldn't read the emotion behind it. Her chest tightened more with fear.

"You look like Carissa," he said.

Carissa. Who is Carissa? She looked at Susan and saw understanding in her cousin's eyes. She would have to ask her who Gabriel was talking about. But later when the vampire wasn't around. Before she could say anything, he turned away. As if released from invisible chains both Susan and David hurried forward.

David was blinking at her in disbelief, eyes wide. "What are you doing here?" he asked.

"I came back to help," she said.

He reached out and hugged her tight and she clung to him, trying not to cry in fear and relief. From the way he held on to her he must have thought he would never see her again either.

A sob escaped her. The world was so much more screwed up than she could ever have imagined.

She glanced at Gabriel, still troubled by his presence.

"What happened last night?" Susan asked, staring at Raphael who still lay unmoving on the floor.

He looked dead, but that was probably fitting. There hadn't been time for answers last night before the sun rose and the vampires were forced to sleep.

"If he was gone he'd be ashes," Gabriel said, answering the question Susan must also have been thinking and not the one she'd asked. It clearly did little to calm her fears.

Gabriel left the room and Wendy watched her cousin let out her breath. After a few moments, she moved to sit on the couch where she could stare at Raphael's face as he slept.

Susan reached up and closed her hand around the cross that hung around her neck. *The one grandma gave her.*

Suddenly Raphael's eyes flew open and Susan jerked back. He stared, unmoving for seconds. Wendy had been told that vampires awoke at sundown but they did not all have instant control over their bodies. Wendy saw movement out of the corner of her eye and she turned to see the third vampire in their midst, the monk named Paul, rising to his feet.

She turned her eyes back to Raphael and Susan and a few moments later his entire body seemed to spasm and then he sat up.

Susan dropped to her knees next to him and threw her arms around him. "I thought you were dead," she whispered.

He returned her embrace. "I thought the same of you," he admitted.

"What happened?"

"Captured. Then Richelieu set his pet scientist on me. He's running experiments in hell now," Raphael said.

Susan visibly shuddered. "And Richelieu?" she asked.

"I saw him when his minions captured me and brought me to him. I think I know where he is," Raphael said.

Then he wasn't dead as Wendy had hoped. *Not dead like he should be*, she thought, her stomach twisting in knots. Richelieu, the king of the evil vampires, like something out of a book. The absurdity of the thought suddenly hit her. He was actually in several books, fiction and nonfiction. The one-time cardinal of France had been reviled for centuries.

And no one even knows that he's a vampire or just how evil he really is.

"We're all listening," Gabriel said next to her.

She jumped, not realizing he'd been so close, but forced herself to stand her ground.

"I think he's using one of the old palace complexes inside Prague Castle."

"It would appeal to his ego," Paul said.

"And his sense of purpose," Raphael said with a nod.

"Describe the place." Gabriel stared hard at Raphael.

Wendy glanced uneasily at David as Raphael described the room he had seen Richelieu in. David was still showing obvious signs of injury and favoring the ribs he had broken a few days before. It was too soon, not even twelve hours since they'd returned from the last battle. Maybe they could sit this one out.

"Not a chance, we need everyone we can get," Paul interrupted.

Wendy glanced over at him, startled. He gave her a grim smile. Susan had told her that she suspected that the monk could read minds.

"I know the palace you're describing," Gabriel said. "We will only have a small window of opportunity in which to strike if we are to maintain the element of surprise."

"He probably won't even hear about the attack on Michael and his lab for a few hours if we're lucky," Paul said.

Wendy knew that vampires could move swiftly but as she tried to follow the threads of the conversation she felt like they were also speaking abnormally quickly. She glanced at David, who seemed to be struggling more than she was to follow what they were saying. His hand was pressed to his side and he was breathing heavily.

What he needed were some of the painkillers the doctors in the hospital had given him. Wendy had searched his bag while he slept and couldn't find them.

He reached down and slipped his hand around

Wendy's. She gave hers willingly, hoping it would give some measure of comfort.

Everyone had a sense of urgency about them and Wendy didn't want to interrupt to ask for clarification. David looked longingly toward the couch and she wondered if anyone would care or even notice if he laid down and went back to sleep.

He squeezed Wendy's hand and she squeezed it back. He turned and smiled at her. She offered a small smile in return. They both turned back to watch the drama. She noticed that Paul and Raphael were doing most of the talking but both of them kept deferring to Gabriel though he spoke rarely.

They're afraid of him, she realized with a flash of insight. It was there in their body language, the way they stood, the distance that separated them, everything.

Susan was rubbing her cross necklace between her fingers obsessively. She was just afraid.

Wendy turned her attention to the conversation, focusing hard on what was being said.

"We know where he is and with any luck he'll have no idea yet that you rescued me and that Michael is dead. It's the perfect time to strike," Raphael said.

"Bearding the lion in his den is always dangerous, especially when we are so few and they are so many," Paul said. "It would be better to wait, figure out what he's planning to do, and confront him when he's exposed. Either that or find a way to lure him out. We could use Raphael's escape to our advantage there, too. Richelieu hates him and could be coaxed out of hiding if it gave him a chance to kill him."

Of the two arguments she liked Paul's best. It sounded safer to her, wiser.

"We don't know what he's planning. We haven't time to wait and find out because then it could be too late. We'll have no more warriors if we wait than we do now, and we'll have lost the element of surprise. I'm telling you the advantage is all on our side. It won't be for long because once he realizes we know where he is he'll vanish again," Raphael argued.

She wished David or Susan would speak up, give their opinions. After all, it was their fight too. But both of them remained silent.

"We got lucky with the attack on the lab. We can't count on being that lucky again," Paul said quietly.

"What lab?" Wendy whispered to David.

All three vampires turned to stare at her and she took a step back.

"A scientist, a vampire named Michael, who I had a run in with during the Renaissance, was working with Richelieu. I was given to him to experiment on," Raphael said. "David, Paul, and Gabriel rescued me from there last night and we killed Michael."

"What kind of experiments?" she asked.

Part of her brain screamed at her to be quiet, to stop drawing the attention of the vampires, but she was there and she had a right to know what was happening.

"Experiments with blood. Poisoning it, draining it. He's spent his life trying to figure out the physiology of vampires and how they exist."

"Better he had focused on the spirituality," Paul murmured.

Gabriel held up a hand and the others turned to him.

"Paul, you've argued as a strategist. Raphael, you have argued as a warrior. I understand both your points of view. But, I am a hunter and I trust my instincts. An animal feels most secure in its lair, which means it is the best place to kill him. That only works, though, if the creature you're hunting has no reason to believe you're coming."

"Which brings us back to the fundamental question," Paul said.

"Which is?" Susan asked, breaking her silence.

"Did Richelieu hear about Raphael's escape before the sun rose this morning?" Gabriel answered.

They all stood and stared at each other. Finally David cleared his throat. "There's no way to know for sure, but odds are while we've been standing here talking about it he has."

Gabriel nodded. "He might be expecting us, but we can't afford to lose him again. We're going after him tonight."

"You know what they say, there's no time like the present," Paul said with a knowing look to Gabriel.

Raphael didn't trust Gabriel, even if they did agree. But then, how could he? His relationship with his sire had always been violent and tenuous at best. The fact that Paul was treating him more carefully than he once would have also gave him pause. Even as they scrambled to get the weapons they would need to lay siege to Richelieu's palace he wondered if he could trust the vampire who would be fighting beside him.

"He's one of the good guys," Paul murmured at one point in the preparations, for his ears alone.

"But does he know I am?" Raphael whispered back.

Paul had simply clapped him on the back and gotten back to work.

It was bad timing. Half of them were injured. David was walking around with his mind seemingly more damaged than his body. Susan was worried for Wendy's safety almost to the exclusion of everything and *everyone* else.

And his body was not completely healed from the experiments Michael had performed on him. He needed to eat more and truth be told, rest for another day probably, before he'd be up for the battle ahead. Without both he couldn't fight, or even think, at the top of his game. But this might be their only chance to finish this war before it really ramped up.

Susan and Wendy began to rebandage David's ribs and patch up his other injuries. He wished they'd do it farther away where the smells and the sounds wouldn't be quite so distracting.

He smelled blood and he turned around with a hiss, struggling with the hunger that was threatening to overcome him. They had pulled off a bandage that was stuck on with dried blood and the wound started bleeding again. It was just a couple of drops but it was enough to set him off in this state.

And suddenly Gabriel was standing in front of him, fangs silently bared, eyes gleaming.

Raphael hunched his shoulders, panic flashing through him.

"It's good. He lost a lot of blood and hasn't had a chance to drink anything," Paul interjected quickly.

Gabriel continued to stare at him, as though daring him to move. Raphael caught the packet of blood that Paul threw at him and forced himself to meet Gabriel's eyes.

His sire didn't trust him either.

He broke eye contact, ripped open the packet and

downed it, belatedly wishing he had at least turned his back so Susan wouldn't see. When he was done drinking she was staring at him, eyes dilated wide.

He grimaced. He wasn't exactly putting on a good face for this little reunion for either of them. He closed his eyes. It had been centuries since he had seen Gabriel and those last few days had been anything but good.

VISIT US ONLINE AT

WWW.HACHETTEBOOKGROUP.COM

FEATURES:

OPENBOOK BROWSE AND
SEARCH EXCERPTS
•
AUDIOBOOK EXCERPTS AND PODCASTS
•
AUTHOR ARTICLES AND INTERVIEWS
•
BESTSELLER AND PUBLISHING
GROUP NEWS
•
SIGN UP FOR E-NEWSLETTERS
•
AUTHOR APPEARANCES AND TOUR
INFORMATION
•
SOCIAL MEDIA FEEDS AND WIDGETS
•
DOWNLOAD FREE APPS

Bookmark Hachette Book Group
@ www.HachetteBookGroup.com